GANGSTER MOLL

BOOK 2

BETHANY-KRIS
ERIN ASHLEY TANNER

Published by Bethany-Kris and Erin Ashley Tanner

eISBN 13: 978-1-988197-23-4
Print ISBN 13: 978-1-988197-24-1

Cover Art © Jay Aheer
Editor: Nina S. Gooden

DEDICATION

To all the wise guys and girls. You keep life interesting for
the rest of us.

CONTENTS

CHAPTER ONE..7

CHAPTER TWO..15

CHAPTER THREE...26

CHAPTER FOUR...42

CHAPTER FIVE...62

CHAPTER SIX..76

CHAPTER SEVEN...90

CHAPTER EIGHT..101

CHAPTER NINE..117

CHAPTER TEN..129

CHAPTER ELEVEN..147

CHAPTER TWELVE...159

CHAPTER THIRTEEN..174

CHAPTER FOURTEEN..189

CHAPTER FIFTEEN..209

CHAPTER SIXTEEN...216

CHAPTER SEVENTEEN..232

CHAPTER EIGHTEEN..238

CHAPTER NINETEEN..247

CHAPTER ONE

"Wake your lazy asses up," a male voice said.

Melina opened one eye and stared at the peeling gray ceiling above her head. A large piece of paint clung desperately to the ceiling. She was sure if she breathed too hard, the old paint would hit her in the face.

Death by lead poisoning.

Melina was sure that was what the pigs who ran the jail were hoping for. Too bad for them; she had other plans.

"Melina, are you awake?"

She opened both eyes, yawned, and stretched before she eased herself from the top bunk and down to the hard concrete floor. Melina did her best to ignore the guards walking up and down the block outside her cell.

"Does this answer your question?" she said to her roommate.

"Damn, girl. You don't have to be so hostile. You should be happy."

Folding her arms, Melina stared at the brown-skinned woman sitting on the bottom bunk. With black hair done up in thick rope twists that hung midway down her back and a permanent warm smile, Erika's morning cheer grated her nerves. It had from the moment they'd been assigned as cellmates.

"And why is that, Miss Sunshine?" Melina asked.

"Because tomorrow, you're getting out of this dump."

Melina opened her mouth and then promptly closed it.

Erika was right. Tomorrow she would be a free woman.

"How could you have forgotten about something as important as that?" Erika asked as she stood and moved to brush her teeth.

Melina shrugged nonchalantly. "I guess because I stopped counting the days a long while ago."

At least that was what she was saying out loud. Privately, the truth was a whole different matter. Five and a half months may not have been much time to Erika or some of the other women here, but to Melina it seemed a lifetime had been taken away.

A lifetime of burning kisses.

A lifetime of passionate lovemaking.

A lifetime of Mac.

Mac.

The boyfriend she hadn't seen or heard from since her sentencing.

Melina swallowed the hot bitterness that threatened to well up in her. It wasn't his fault. She knew enough about Cosa Nostra to understand why Mac had stayed away.

As a newly minted Capo of the Pivetti crime family, it wouldn't look good for Mac to be putting money on her commissary account, much less coming to see her on visitation days.

It didn't matter that they were in love.

It didn't matter that Melina would rather slit her own wrists than betray the man she loved.

She wasn't Mac's wife and to Cosa Nostra, that made her a liability.

Honestly, Melina was more than surprised that there hadn't been a warning delivered for her to keep quiet or another less than subtle threat. No doubt, she owed the fact that she was still breathing to Mac sticking his neck out for her.

It surely wasn't because Luca Pivetti felt like being merciful.

The man didn't like her and the feeling was mutual.

"Good thing I'm keeping up with it for you, then," Erika said.

She came close and placed her hand on Melina's shoulder.

"I guess so. I don't know how you do it."

"Do what?" Erika asked.

"Stay so upbeat."

"What good is being depressed or upset going to do? I did the crime and I have to do the time. Besides, maybe my good behavior will get me out of here earlier. You never know."

Facing three and a half years for marijuana possession with intent to sell, Erika's glass-half-full mentality truly worked Melina's nerves sometimes, but her cellmate was making some valid points. After all, Erika's stellar behavior had kept her from being sentenced to one of the harsher women's facilities and had gotten six months knocked off her initial sentence. There was even talk that the rest of her sentence could possibly be commuted down to strict probation. Perhaps if Melina had employed the same mentality, she'd have had some time shaved off her own sentence.

In what universe?

Melina wasn't like Erika. She had a rap as a prostitute connected to Cosa Nostra and for that reason alone, she'd been made an example of. What the hypocrites who'd imprisoned her hadn't realized was that she came from strong stock. Nothing was going to break her.

Not this incarceration.

Not even being separated from Mac.

"I guess you've got a point," Melina finally said.

"But you're not buying it."

"Let's just say life has rarely worked out for me the way that I've wanted it to. You learn the easiest way to survive is not to have expectations."

"Seems like a sad way to live," Erika said.

"It is."

Melina moved around Erika in the tiny cell to brush her teeth before the guards would come to escort them to the cafeteria for breakfast. If you could call it that. The food was terrible.

"You miss him, don't you?"

Melina stopped brushing and spit. "I don't know who you're talking about."

"Sure you don't. I've heard you call out his name in your sleep."

"And whose name would that be?" Melina said before she continued brushing.

"Mac," Erika said.

Melina rinsed her mouth out quickly with the bitter-tasting water while she tried to gather her thoughts. What could she say to her cellmate? A lie would be easier, so much easier than acknowledging the emptiness that had threatened to consume her during her imprisonment. For someone who'd vowed never to fall in love, she'd fallen and fallen hard. It was hard to remember the exact moment that Mac had wormed his way into her heart.

Maybe it was when he'd posted her bail.

Maybe it was when he'd defended her honor against Tip and Vin.

Or maybe it was when he'd gone down on his knees and given her a glimpse of heaven.

Melina didn't know and she didn't care. All she knew was that she missed him and wanted to be back in his arms more than anything.

That is, if he still wanted her.

"So what if I did say that name?"

"After all the time we've shared in this cell, don't you know by now that you can trust me?"

Melina raised a brow. "I trust no one."

"Fine, you don't have to trust me, but maybe talking about him will make you feel a bit better. Just think about it, okay?"

The heavy doors slowly slid open and Erika turned away, waiting to receive the go-ahead from the guard that they could exit the cell. When they were finally allowed to leave the small space, Melina considered what Erika had offered. Was it time that she let someone in? Perhaps a good talk was all she needed to center herself in preparation for whatever came next.

"I couldn't stand him from the moment we met," Melina confessed.

"Why not?"

Melina sat down next to Erika on a table in the recreation yard. In front of them, the other women of the facility played basketball, lifted weights and huddled together in clustered groups. During her stint in lockup, Melina had learned to keep her eyes and ears open and respect everyone's turf. That didn't mean that she wouldn't defend herself, when and if the need arose.

"Because he was so ... so arrogant, I thought."

"Well, obviously things changed, so what happened?"

Melina smiled. "I learned what I thought was arrogance was simply confidence and that we had a lot more in common than I thought we did."

Erika pulled her twists into an easy bun on the top of her head. "Like what? Go on."

"For starters, we're both survivors. Somehow or another, no matter how hard life knocks us down, we always find some way to get back up. There's an energy between us that I've never experienced before. It's scary sometimes," Melina confessed.

"Now that last part sounds romantic to me."

"I didn't really think of it like that, but I guess it is."

Erika rolled her eyes. "Call a spade a spade, honey. No one will think less of you because you're a closet romantic."

Melina shuddered. "I am not, I repeat, I am not one of those sappy women in the romance novels, so don't even think it."

"Whatever. So when did you go from detesting his entire existence to actually caring about him?"

"I saw him at a club and I was dancing with another guy. A normal guy would have brushed it off. Not Mac. The next thing I know, he had the other guy on the floor and me over his shoulder."

"And you went for that alpha male shit?" Erika asked as she raised an eyebrow.

"Hardly. I tried to beat the crap out of him, and then the next thing I knew, we were all over each other."

Erika opened her mouth to say something, but was cut off when two women started yelling at one another on the basketball court. Their voices were so loud, they drowned out practically all the other noise on the rec yard. A moment later, whistles were blown and the two women were separated and led away, no doubt back to their cells or worse, to confinement.

"Both of them are dumb for getting worked up over a stupid pick-up game," Erika finally said.

"Yep. No telling how that little stunt is going to come back and bite them in the ass." Melina tugged a fly away strand of hair back behind her ear.

"Anyway, now back to your Mac. Please tell me the two of you had some dirty club sex afterwards."

"Sorry to disappoint, but no."

"You know you missed a prime opportunity right?"

"Little Miss Good Girl is telling me I should have banged him at a club. I must have fallen down Alice's rabbit hole."

Erika thumped her lightly on the arm. "Hey. I'm not that goodie-goodie. I am in here, aren't I?"

"Your point? You're only here because the man you loved and trusted left you holding the bag. There's no way you'd be mixed up in drugs otherwise. It's not you," Melina said.

"And what about you?" Erika asked quietly.

"What about me?"

"Did Mac leave you holding the bag?"

Melina rose to her feet, nostrils flaring. "I can't believe you'd even ask me something like that."

Erika raised her hand in a defensive motion. "I didn't mean anything by it. I was just asking."

"I'm done talking about him."

Without giving her cellmate a chance to respond, Melina walked away. Stuffing her hands in the threadbare pockets of her blue pants, she blew a breath. She'd overreacted. Like a damn jackass. If anyone didn't have ulterior motives, it was Erika, but the younger woman had touched on a raw spot.

Melina was the one holding the bag.

There was no way she or Mac could've known Dulcea's place would be raided the day she'd been arrested. But still, intentionally or not, she was the one left holding the bag. To do otherwise would've forced her to sacrifice the one person in her life who'd slowly come to mean everything to her.

But was it fair that she'd been stuck in this Godforsaken place while Mac was free to live his life as if she didn't even exist? Tears burned in her eyes, but Melina blinked them away.

Cosa Nostra was everything.

Cosa Nostra came first.

But where did that leave her?

In less than twenty-four hours, she would be a free woman with convictions tied to her name.

A free woman who had nowhere to go and no one to depend on, if the man who loved her didn't keep his word.

Melina had never been one for praying much, but as she walked the length of the rec yard, she sent up a silent prayer that her fears were for nothing. That for once in her life, she'd found someone she could truly depend on, no matter where the chips fell.

You're worrying for nothing. Mac wouldn't abandon you.

She wanted to believe that. As the days went by, she'd held onto that belief. But here, now, right at the finish line, her conviction was faltering. Absence could make the heart grow fonder … or forgetful. Though she'd thought of Mac every single day, there was no guarantee that he'd done the same. Time and power always had a way of changing someone. Reflexively, Melina reached toward her neck, but her fingers only touched bare skin. Her necklace was gone, just like its prior owner, but she'd get both of them back tomorrow. That was her last thought as she was roughly forced to the ground and chaos erupted around her.

CHAPTER TWO

Mac Maccari wasn't a three-piece suit kind of man. He much preferred the comfort of wearing dark-wash jeans, a T-shirt, and combat boots while handling his daily business. It was a comfort thing, and a heat thing.

Glaring up at the bright sun in the sky as he crossed the street as quickly as he could, Mac swore he was melting under his suit. It was an unusually warm summer for New York. It was almost always muggy during the season, but this year Mother Nature decided to kick that shit up a notch.

Mac was less than impressed.

It probably didn't help that the majority of his day was spent running to and from different locations as he handled his crew and what the men were doing at any given time.

But ... it was what it was.

And he was damn good at his job.

Mac supposed that if he wasn't good at being a Capo, he'd already be dead. At least, for the time being, he had that going for him.

The heat wave, however, could go to hell.

Tugging his jacket off, Mac slipped into the business at the very end of the block, tossing the coat over his arm as a cool blast of air from the air conditioner smacked him straight in the face. He soaked in the cold air as he glanced around the place, taking in the woman behind the counter, who was animatedly talking on the phone and snapping a large wad of gum in her mouth at the same time.

She didn't even look like she noticed him standing there, for fuck's sake.

Mac didn't mind.

He wasn't here to see her, anyway.

Pulling his phone out of his pocket, Mac searched for the message he'd been left earlier in the day. *Infinite Insurance, ask for Ronnie*, it read. A few other details had been included, but Mac figured those weren't important until he found Ronnie.

Mac had come to find out, over his last few months as a newly appointed Capo for the Pivetti crime family, that Luca Pivetti had little to no patience for people who owed him something. It didn't matter what it was—money, action, or a word. If a person owed him, he expected them to pay accordingly.

Maybe even a little more, simply because he was kind enough to do business with them.

As the boss, it was Luca's due.

Mac didn't question why his boss hadn't simply sent an enforcer over to the place to handle his shit—that wasn't his place. He just did what the boss wanted done.

Bypassing the receptionist without so much as a "Hello", Mac strolled to the back of the insurance banker's business, finding a hallway with several offices. All had glass windows for walls, letting him see the men and women inside, sitting behind desks with either phones to their ears, or clients inside their offices.

Thankfully, plaques were attached to each door, names boldly inscribed on each one.

Mac found the *Ronnie* he was looking for mid-way down the hallway. The heavier-set gentleman was alone inside his office, from what Mac could see through the window, and didn't seem to be tied up with a phone call as he was busy sorting papers.

That was going to suck when he had to clean up the mess later.

Mac couldn't find much remorse for what he was about to do.

Business was business, after all.

Cosa Nostra business was even tougher.

It simply couldn't wait.

Mac didn't bother to knock on the office door, but rather, turned the knob and walked right in, depositing his jacket on one of the two chairs meant for clients.

The insurance banker—Ronnie—glanced up, startled, at Mac's sudden appearance. If Mac had to guess by the wrinkled dress shirt, the messy hair, and the tired gaze, Ronnie had some shit on his mind.

He was about to get more.

"You can't just barge in here," the man started to say. "Clients make appointments."

Mac reached over and twisted the blinds closed on the windows and glass walls—no one could see in now. He locked the door, ensuring no one would walk in during the … meeting.

Turning back to face the man he'd been sent to see, Mac offered a wide-eyed Ronnie a smile. Cold as it was, Mac figured the guy would take this better if he were a little loosened up before the actual warning came about.

Ronnie started to stand from his desk, confusion writing heavily over his features. "Who in the hell are you?"

"I'm not important," Mac said, rolling up the cuffs of his dress shirt.

Blood was a bitch to get out.

Maybe he'd avoid the few splatters that might occur, if it were possible.

But probably not.

"But Luca," Mac continued, shrugging like it didn't make a difference. "Now the boss and his money are a whole other story."

For the first time since Mac entered Ronnie's office, he saw the first trickle of genuine fear light up the man's eyes.

"I-I have his—"

"They all say that," Mac interrupted, knowing what the man was going to say.

Bullshit excuses.

Another stall tactic.

"Fact is," Mac said, keeping an eye on Ronnie in case he grabbed for something to attack with, "… you're two weeks late, according to the boss. And he was nice enough to fund your little project because, apparently, you go way back. Now you're ducking and dodging Luca like it's what you do for a living."

Mac chuckled, waving his hand around at the office.

"Clearly, you work in another business, and you're not very good at the ducking and dodging game," Mac finished with another smooth, cold smile.

"Let me call Luca," the man said quickly. "Please, we're friends. He'll understand, I'm sure."

Mac sighed.

Luca didn't care who a person was—friend, family, or enemy.

If someone owed him something, they owed him.

"Just let me make this easy," Mac said. "You've only got to bleed, after all. Nobody says you're going to fucking die from it. Now, if you make it hard on me, that's going to be a problem, and it'll probably hurt a lot more. Do us both a favor here, and let me get this over with."

Ronnie opened his mouth to say something, his gaze darting to the windows, the door, and then to Mac.

Mac knew that look. It was the look of a man trying to find his way out.

Well, he had news for the guy.

"Make a single sound, and I will cut your tongue out," Mac said quietly. "There is nowhere to run, and very few people left in the building. So unless you want your associates to know how you've been doing underground business with a mafia boss, I suggest you let me do what I came here to do."

Simple, right?

Mac knew it would be—it always was.

Flexing his split, sore knuckles, Mac strolled toward his Challenger, pulling his phone out of his pocket as he slipped inside the car. He hit the number two key on the touchscreen, watching the number light up to call the contact attached to the speed dial.

On the fourth ring, the boss picked up.

"Give me good news," Luca said.

"Your job should pay out by tomorrow evening, to the account you wanted," Mac replied.

That was code for: Ronnie is going to pay you the money he owes by the time you want.

Mac had gotten better at talking in vague sentences, or rather, in a sort of code that his boss would understand.

"And?" Luca asked.

"And, what?"

"Is it all well?"

Mac chuckled. "It probably needs to be looked over."

"Good, good."

The pleased tone of Luca's voice made Mac roll his eyes as he started the Challenger up and pulled out onto the quiet road. Luca had some kind of crazy about him— he liked to make people understand their wrongs in owing him anything.

Which meant, he liked for people in his debt to hurt a whole hell of a lot.

"It's good, boss," Mac assured.

"*Perfetto*. Now, onto other business."

Mac navigated the streets of downtown Brooklyn, wondering what other business there was that needed attending to. Nothing immediate came to mind.

"What's that?" he asked when Luca stayed quiet.

"My wife."

Mac's brow furrowed.

What did Neeya Pivetti have anything to do with Mac's job as a Capo?

"Go on," Mac said, keeping his tone level for respect's sake.

"She's been chatting my ear off for the last week—she knows what's coming up tomorrow, and she won't shut up about it. It would please her greatly if she could see Melina shortly after she was released, hmm?"

A dull pain settled in Mac's chest.

He tried not to talk about Melina to those around him. It wasn't like he had much to say. Sure, he kept up with what updates he could get from her lawyer, but his position as a new Capo, and Luca's demands, kept Mac far away from where Melina had been housed to serve her nearly six-month sentence.

It fucking killed him.

Every single day.

He woke up alone—so cold.

His thoughts almost always revolved around Melina in one way or another. He found himself considering how she was fairing, what she might be doing, and if she was missing him, too. But it was more than all of that.

Mac was constantly wondering about Melina's opinions on things in his daily life, like picking out a new vehicle, or settling into a new apartment in a better part of town.

He took that all as a sign of what he already knew—he intended to have a life with Melina. He wanted a future with her.

But she wasn't here.

He was still waiting on her.

Mac knew none of that was really his girl's fault—what happened couldn't be helped.

That didn't necessarily make him feel better about it all.

It could drive him damn near insane if he let it. So instead, he focused on anything and everything else that he could.

Work.

The gym.

His men.

Making money.

Territory.

Keeping the boss happy.

Every day, his cycle repeated.

But in the back of his head, Mac was counting down the days until Melina's sentence was served and he could keep his word like he'd promised.

Wherever she was, he'd be waiting.

The countdown was finally coming to an end, however. Tomorrow, his doll was getting out. Mac would be there—no question.

"Well?" Luca demanded.

"I will make time for Neeya to see Melina," Mac assured.

As soon as he could—after he'd had his fill.

It'd been too long.

Far, far too long.

"Remember, she still isn't your wife, Mac. Try to keep her quiet for a little while."

Mac scowled. He didn't need the damn reminder.

"I am still working on the wife thing," Mac said, not bothering to hide the annoyance in his tone. "I will ask when I am ready."

Or when Melina was, anyway.

Luca laughed. "How well do you think that will go over?"

With Melina?

Mac couldn't even begin to guess.

"Beautiful day," Cynthia said, patting her son's arm as they strolled together through the quiet park.

"It is."

Up ahead, Mac kept an eye on his sister, who had her Husky puppy on a leash. Victoria had showed up at his place with the dog, claiming she found him in a pet store, looking lonely and sad.

Mac figured his sister was one of those kinds of people who were emotional spenders. Those people liked to spend their money—even if it was their last dollar—on things that brought emotional reactions out of them.

His only problem with the dog was that on more than one occasion, Victoria dropped it off on him, leaving him to care for it.

Taz was a good dog—for a puppy.

Victoria, on the other hand, was a bit spoiled.

Mac blamed himself for that, because he couldn't tell his sister no.

"So," his mother drawled, bringing his attention down to her soft smile.

"Yes, Ma?"

"I like this," she said, patting a hand on the breast of his suit. "You look very … gentlemanly."

Mac laughed, and kissed his mother's hand before dropping it just as fast. "Is that so?"

"Grown up."

"I'm twenty-seven, Ma. I grew up a long time ago."

Cynthia grinned in that way of hers, sly and knowing, but it quickly faded. Her tone turned more serious when she said, "As much as I disagree with … things …"

The mafia, he knew.

Mac chose not to openly say it, given where they were, and the fact his mother despised his career choices.

"As much as I disagree with it all," Cynthia repeated, "I am happy that you've found your place, James."

"Mac, Ma."

"James to me, my boy."

Mac would always be James to his mother.

"And I just want you to be safe," Cynthia added after a moment.

Mac wanted to soothe whatever worries his mother had, but it was an impossible task. For one, because he was her son and she would worry about him regardless of what he was doing. He could be a damn surgeon, and she would still fret herself right into a panic over his welfare. And for two, because Mac couldn't promise he would always be safe in his job.

He was a made man.

A Mafioso.

And that put a giant target on his back every single day of his life.

"I'm good, Ma," he said quietly.

It was the best he could give her.

Cynthia seemed satisfied, at least for the moment. "I should thank you for dragging your sister over to visit me today. She's always so busy."

Something like that.

Mac didn't bother to explain to his mother that Victoria had found herself a boyfriend, because frankly, he was still trying not to kill that *boyfriend*, as it was.

"She didn't put up a fuss," Mac chose to say.

"Tell me …"

"What?"

Cynthia stopped walking, letting Victoria go on ahead for quite a ways before she let the hold she had on Mac's arm go, and turned to face him on the pathway.

"You know that you never have to lie to me, James, right?"

Mac smiled. "I know, Ma."

"Good. Tell me, what time are you going to get Melina from jail tomorrow?"

He might as well have turned into a statue.

Cynthia didn't bat an eye.

Mac had made every effort he could to hide where Melina had gone from his mother. Given Cynthia hadn't met her more than once, and that hadn't ended particularly well, due to an unexpected visit from Mac's cocksucker of a father, he didn't want his mother building bad opinions of the woman he loved.

Because he did love Melina.

Entirely.

Mac wanted his mother to love her, too.

So, he hid what happened, and made excuses.

"How did you know?" Mac asked.

Cynthia shrugged. "Picked up a paper one day and it happened to have an article in there, second page, with your face plastered across it. Hers, too."

Mac cringed. "The sentencing?"

"It was a *very* sweet picture, James."

He sighed, and scrubbed a hand down his face. Melina's sentencing had been the one day Mac had been given permission from his boss to see her before she was carted off. Luca told him that he was to keep his head down, not draw attention to himself, and steer clear of any reporters.

Mac fucked that up in a big way by kissing Melina, getting their picture taken by the press, and then having it printed two days later with quite the headline.

Suspected Mobster Kisses Convicted Girlfriend Goodbye

At least they hadn't called Melina a hooker in the headline.

Mac gave them that.

It was also the only reason why he hadn't burned the fucking newspaper's headquarters down to the goddamn ground.

He'd taken hell from Luca, which included a threat to skin Mac alive if he ever disobeyed his boss again.

Mac decided not to test Luca on that one.

"Well?" his mother asked, bringing him out of his thoughts.

"Around noon," Mac said.

Cynthia nodded once. "Great. I will have a supper ready. I want to see her."

"Ma—"

"This is not a discussion, James."

Well, that was that. Mac supposed he could hold off on getting his girl alone and in private for at least an extra hour or two.

Maybe.

CHAPTER THREE

Melina looked up at the wall again and silently cursed. She'd lost count of the number of times she'd done that today. It was stupid, she knew. There hadn't been a clock in her cell since she'd been imprisoned, and one was not about to magically appear because she wanted to count down the time until her sentence was finished.

"Shouldn't be long now," Erika said. She shuffled a pack of playing cards in her hands as she gave Melina a wide smile.

"Maybe. Maybe I still have a while," Melina said, more nonchalantly than she felt.

Erika rolled her eyes. "Would it kill you to have some optimism for once in your life?"

"Yes." And then Melina laughed.

"Ah, she does have a sense of humor. Too bad you're just now deciding to share it."

"Sometimes it's best to leave some things to the imagination," Melina said.

Sliding down from her top bunk, she stood and stretched, stealing a glance toward the steel-barred doors.

"Everything is going to be fine, you know," Erika said quietly.

"Miss Eternal Optimism rears her head again. What do you know that I don't, Erika?"

Putting down the deck of cards, Erika motioned for

Melina to take a seat next to her on the small concrete slab in the center of their cell. Reluctantly, Melina did as the younger woman asked. Flipping a long twist over her shoulder, Erika pinned Melina with a deep stare.

"You are a great person, Melina. Yes, you've had some bumps and bruises along the way. Yes, life may have given you a shitty deal, but you are a survivor. Your time here was just another little bump along the way to something much better."

Melina shook her head. "I wish I could have just an ounce of the faith you have. It would last me until I the day I took my last breath."

Erika smiled and reached for her hand. "Good thing, then, that I have enough for the both of us. Give yourself permission to be happy. From everything you've shared with me, it's overdue for you."

"And what about you?" Melina countered.

"I am going to be just fine. One day my time will come, too, and when it does, you better believe I will be skipping out of here with a happy song in my heart."

Melina smiled. "I have no doubt you will."

Erika opened her mouth to say something but before she could, the doors to the cell slid open.

"Morgan, it's time. You've got two minutes to get your shit."

Melina rose and glared at the guard, before she faced Erika again. She could see tears in the woman's eyes.

"Hey, none of that. No waterworks," Melina said softly.

"Oh, shut up and give me a hug."

Erika stood up and hugged her tight. The last thing Melina wanted was one of the asshole guards to see her being vulnerable.

But right then she just didn't care.

Melina hugged Erika tightly. "You take care of yourself. Who knows? Maybe we'll run into each other again someday."

Erika leaned back and wiped tears from her face. "I'll be looking forward to that day."

"Morgan, let's go or you can stay here on a permanent basis. Your choice."

Melina stepped away from Erika and walked over to the guard. "I'm ready."

Officer Ramsey stepped back to allow Melina to exit the cell, but not before ensuring that his arm "accidently" brushed against her breast.

"Pig," she whispered under her breath.

"You got something to say, Morgan? Trust me, I have no problems putting your ass back in your cage," Ramsey said.

"Melina," Erika said, a warning in her tone.

Melina knew that the guard was trying to provoke her.

The last thing he or his higher ups wanted was to release her back into society.

Especially because they'd failed to break her.

No doubt Ramsey would love another attempt to correct his failure, but she wasn't going to give it to him.

She had too much to lose.

"No, sir," she said.

Ramsey slammed the door shut. "I didn't think so."

Melina gritted her teeth but forced a smile to her face.

"Take care, Melina," Erika said.

"You, too."

And with a short wave, Melina was leaving her concrete prison behind. Raising her head high, she thrust back her shoulders and stood tall. She had no idea what she would be facing now, but anything had to be better than the hell she was leaving behind.

"All right, Morgan, you're free to go."

The heavy gray door swung open, and Melina was nearly blinded by the sunlight that shone directly in her path. It took a few moments for her eyes to adjust to the light as she stepped into the lobby. Blinking, she looked around and then she saw him. Arms folded, leaning casually against the far wall wearing a perfectly tailored black suit, Mac was a sight to behold. He wasn't looking in her direction, which gave her time to study him.

His hair was freshly cut and his face clean shaven. Melina licked her lips. She wasn't used to seeing him in a suit. No doubt it was all part of the new Mac—the Capo. Taking a deep breath, she moved toward him, unable to quiet the fluttering of tension and nervousness in her belly.

Would the new Mac still want his Gun Moll?

Or had their time passed?

"Mac," she said softly.

He turned toward her and in one single, fluid motion he was off the wall and moving toward her. And as he stopped in front of her, he reached out and tipped her chin up toward him with one finger.

"Doll," he said.

Nothing could disguise the reverence in his voice.

Melina tried to contain her trembling as his hazel eyes bored into hers.

There was so much that she wanted to say, but words wouldn't come.

She was frozen and suddenly afraid.

Afraid of a future that she had no control over.

"Love you, doll."

His lips curved into a crooked smile and then Mac was kissing her. His lips met hers in a hot, demanding kiss that set her soul on fire. Melina could taste the desire on his lips, the love, and just there hiding beneath it all, his own hint of uncertainty.

She pushed him away, knowing someone was watching.

Mac raised a brow. "Is something wrong?"

"Could we get out of here?"

It was as if a haze had cleared from his eyes as he looked around them, before focusing his attention firmly back on her. "Of course."

He offered his hand and she took it. Together, they left the jail lobby and walked out into the sunlight. Mac gripped her hand tight as they walked down the sidewalk and toward the parking lot. Melina inhaled the cool, fresh scent of the air, her senses feeling as if they were coming awake for the first time.

"You're quiet," Mac said.

"Sorry."

"No need to apologize."

He glanced at her as he opened the passenger side door to his black Challenger. The car was a welcome and familiar sight to her after so many months. Mac's clothes may have changed but at least his car hadn't. Maybe everything else hadn't either. She took her seat and waited as Mac got in before she faced him.

"I'm just trying to process everything. I didn't realize how much being locked up would affect me."

Mac started the car before he leaned over and kissed her cheek softly. "I'm sorry."

"For what?"

"For the way things had to be. I never wanted this for you, doll. Not in a million years."

"I know."

Mac pulled out onto the highway before he glanced at her. "Do you?"

There was a challenge in his voice. A question in both words and tone. Melina swallowed hard. "Of course, I do. Why would you even ask me something like that?"

"Because a man who loves his woman, knows her, and from the moment I saw you in that lobby, everything about you has been off. You're a spitfire on your worst days. But today—*today,* when I expected you to come at me with some smart remark or sexy quip, you looked at me as if you wanted to run. As if you thought you were safer behind concrete and steel than you were with me."

He'd read her.

Like a fucking book.

And she didn't like it, not one bit.

"You don't know what you're talking about."

"Don't I?"

Mac stopped at a red light and stared at her. A muscle moved in his jaw and there was a hard look in his eyes. She'd seen that look before, but it had never been directed at her. Her quiet restraint snapped.

"Well, since you think you know everything, did you know that every day that I was locked up in that miserable place, I was afraid? No, I bet you didn't."

"Afraid of what, doll?" His voice was gentler now.

"That I was a liability who would be eliminated. That … that I had nothing and no one to go home to when I was out."

"Is that what you thought? Seriously? After everything?"

"What did you expect me to think, Mac? I've seen enough of your … *lifestyle*, to know Cosa Nostra doesn't like loose ends. I'm a loose end. It would've been easier for everyone involved if I was out of the way permanently."

Before Melina could blink, Mac was pulling the car onto the far shoulder of the highway. Leaning across the console, he captured her face in his hands.

"I regret every single minute that you were in that hellhole. I can't even begin to imagine what you went through, but you were never in any danger from the family. Never. You could've sold me out to save yourself, but you didn't. Even though it cost you, loyalty means something to you. That was enough for Luca and everyone else to see the kind of woman you really are."

Melina swallowed hard. "You weren't there, Mac."

His thumbs caressed her cheeks. "I couldn't be. After

what happened the day of your sentencing, Luca wanted my head on a silver platter. I was supposed to stay hidden but I just couldn't do it. I had to let you know that I was there. That I cared."

"I get it. The last thing a boss needs is more attention on him and his organization. It didn't look good for you to be associated with me. I understand, but that doesn't stop the fact that it still hurt knowing that even if I called you, there was a high probability you wouldn't answer. It hurt never getting a letter from you and it damn near killed me watching the other inmates on visiting day, knowing that you'd never set foot inside that place. Not even for me. Even the messages you passed through the lawyer for me to get were small and vague."

Melina sniffled, doing her best to hold back the dam of emotion that was threatening to break loose at any moment. This was exactly what she hadn't wanted to happen. Mac didn't need her having a meltdown.

"Being without you was like stabbing myself over and over again. Staying away was a form of indescribable torture and I would rather slit my fucking wrists than do that again. But all that is over. We're together now, and nothing and no one is going to separate us again."

Melina sighed as she took in the sincerity on his face. He believed what he was saying with every fiber of his being. His eyes were soft and the hands that held her face were so gentle. A tear fell from the corner of her eye before she could stop it.

"That's still what you want?"

Mac's mouth crushed hers in a kiss so fierce it stole her breath away. His tongue teased the seam of her lips and her mouth opened, allowing him to deepen the kiss. Her body needed this. Craved this. Craved him. His tongue danced with hers and Melina leaned closer, suddenly desperate for his kiss. When Mac moved away, she found herself bereft.

"Does that answer your question?" he asked.

She nodded, unable to speak.

"Good."

He kissed her again, quickly, before he put the car in drive and eased back onto the highway. Mac reached for her hand and brought it to his lips. Melina smiled as the numbness that had become a daily part of her life started to ebb away.

"I love you," she said quietly.

"Whew, I can breathe a sigh of relief. For a minute there, I was scared."

Melina laughed. "Just a minute?"

"More than a minute."

"I thought so."

"Ah. There's the smart-mouthed woman I fell in love with."

"She never left," Melina replied, grinning.

Mac smirked. "Glad to hear it because I need her back and ready for action."

Melina cleared her throat, a small tendril of worry creeping inside her. "What kind of action?"

Mac flashed her a smile. "Dinner with my mother, for starters."

"Um, that didn't go so well last time and exactly how are you going to explain my absence?"

"She saw the papers."

Melina covered her face with her free hand. "Dear God. There's no telling what she must be thinking."

"Actually, she thought the picture of us together was very sweet."

"You're kidding?"

"Nope."

Melina squeezed Mac's hand. "Well, there might be some hope for me yet."

"And there's one more thing, doll."

"Oh?" she asked.

"Your presence has been requested at the Pivetti mansion."

Melina sank lower in her seat. "Just great. What does your boss want to do now? Grill me? Impress upon me the importance of keeping quiet?"

"Relax, doll. Nothing like that. Neeya has been pestering Luca about seeing you as soon as you got out. You've really made an impression on her."

"Oh. Neeya. It would be nice to see her again."

Silence stretched between them as Mac drove along the highway moving closer to the innermost part of the city.

"So what happens now?" Melina finally asked.

"Whatever we want."

Whatever they wanted.

Melina could think of a few things.

"If you stay in there any longer, you're going to turn into a prune."

Melina opened her eyes slowly. Mac was sitting on the edge of the tub, staring at her with undisguised interest.

"You let me fall asleep."

"Well, after I gave you that massage, you looked so relaxed and peaceful. I figured it would be rude to disturb you."

Melina moved closer to the side of the tub. "You could've joined me, you know."

Mac's eyes darkened as his gaze roved over her exposed arms and back.

"I couldn't have."

"Why is that?"

"Because the minute that happened, you and I would be locked inside this apartment for days, making up for all the time we've been apart."

"And that's a bad thing?"

"Fuck no, but it would be a bad thing to disappoint my mother and piss Luca off."

Melina rolled her eyes. "Yes. One must not keep the boss waiting."

Standing up in the bath tub she stretched, feeling revitalized after Mac's stellar massage and the restful nap she'd had inside the warm, bubble-filled tub. Mac cleared his throat and it was then that Melina noticed that her breast was barely an inch away from his face.

Melina smiled sweetly. "Something wrong?"

She lowered her arms back down and subtly thrust her chest forward, teasing him a little more.

Mac groaned. "Get dressed and meet me in the living room."

Before she could say another word, he was up and leaving the room, but not before she noticed the tell-tale bulge in his pants. Sighing, Melina got out of the tub and quickly dried herself off before she went into her bedroom.

That was when she noticed the boxes and bags on her bed.

"Mac?" she called out.

Reaching for the first white box lying on the bed, Melina lifted the top and looked inside before she lifted out the item. It was a wine-colored evening gown with strategic cutouts to showcase her slim waist and a long slit on the right hip. The gown was both sassy and elegant.

She loved it immediately.

Noticing Mac still hadn't ventured into the room, Melina yelled out, "I'm pretty sure that there's a whole new wardrobe in here, and that's why you're hiding. But don't worry, payback is coming."

Laughing, Melina looked through a few more of the boxes before she gave up and got dressed. Still nervous about making a good impression on Mac's mother, she settled on a black dress with a wide belt and four-inch black pumps. She left her hair loose and flowing. Adding wide, silver hoop earrings and a touch of mascara and red lipstick, she finally deemed herself ready. Walking into her living room, she found Mac sitting on the couch. He stood as soon as he noticed her presence.

"You look beautiful," he said.

"Thank you."

They stared at each other for a long while, simply soaking each other in, before Mac tore his gaze away first.

"Are you ready, doll?"

"Yes, but there's one thing."

Mac raised a brow. "What's that?"

"You went overboard with the gifts. You know that you don't have to buy me."

Mac came over to her and took her hand in his. "I know that, and I wasn't trying to. I told you once, a man takes care of his woman and after everything you've been through—after all the sacrifices you've made—you deserve to have anything your heart desires. And I'm going to do my damnedest to give it to you."

He brought her hand to his lips and kissed it. Melina tried to ignore the way her heart felt as if it were humming with joy.

This man loved her.

For better or worse.

Through the good and the very bad.

Mac loved her and if it made him feel good to express his love by giving her things, then she needed to make an effort to accept it.

"All right, but if you keep this up I just might get used to it," she teased.

"Maybe that's exactly what I want." He winked at her as he raised his hand to cup her cheek. "You're so damned perfect. How did I get so lucky?"

"Right place. Right time."

"Is that it?"

"I don't know. You tell me."

His thumb brushed over her cheek. "When we're

done with all these obligations, I'm going to remind you of what else you didn't mention. Now, come on. I've got one more surprise waiting for you downstairs."

"Mac …"

He smiled and shook his head before taking her hand, and leading her from her apartment. "Don't say anything. Just wait and see."

Mac closed and locked the door and then they were in the elevator heading down to the parking area. They'd only gone a few feet when Melina stopped walking. Directly in front of them was a silver, two-door Maserati.

"Mac. You didn't …"

Mac shrugged. "Your car was impounded and they refused to release it. You need a new set of wheels, doll."

Melina let go of Mac's hand and walked closer to the car, running her hands over the sleek body as she marveled at the rims. Shiny chrome with a small crown in the center of the hubs, there was no telling how much he'd spent on the wheels alone.

"But a Maserati, Mac …"

"You like it, don't you?" he asked.

"Of course I do. I love it."

"Then that's all that matters." He walked up to her and pressed the keys into her hand.

"You're letting me drive?"

Mac eyed her in that intense way of his, grinning sexily. "Why else would I buy you a car, doll?"

Melina wrapped her arms around Mac and kissed him hard on the lips. His hand palmed her ass, pressing her tighter against him. She'd missed this so much. The feel of his lips, the depth of his passion for her that he never tried to hide. She frowned when he ended their kiss.

"Can't we just stay in tonight?"

"You have no idea how much I wish we could. I promise I'll make it up to you," Mac said.

"I'm holding you to it."

"I'd expect nothing less. Now, let's see how this baby

rides."

Melina unlocked the car and Mac opened the driver's side door for her. He placed a quick kiss on her lips before he closed the door and took his own seat. Smiling, Melina started up the car and ran her hands over the smooth, black leather interior. The navigation system came to life, and Mac laughed softly.

"What's so funny?" Melina asked, facing him.

"It's cute to see you so excited about something. I could get used to seeing you like this."

"Don't get used to it, buddy. One way or another, I'm going to pull the reins on all this spending you've been doing."

"We'll see about that."

Buckling her seat belt, Melina put the car in drive and roared onto the highway. Mac took her hand and held it in his as they headed toward his mother's house in Amityville.

"I just had a thought," Melina said.

"What's that, doll?"

"What am I supposed to do now?"

"What do you mean?" Mac asked.

"I mean, you and I both know that I will never be able to hold a day-to-day job with my record. Hell, I probably won't even be welcome at the center anymore."

That last thought stabbed Melina right in the gut. In the time she'd started teaching kickboxing, she'd grown to love those kids. They were bright spots in her life when things had been so dark. Knowing she could probably never see them again hurt.

It hurt a lot.

"Melina, you don't have to work," Mac reminded her.

"Well, what do you expect me to do with myself? We've talked about this before. I'm not going to sit at home waiting for you and baking cookies."

"Can we discuss this a little later? Right now, the only thing I want to concentrate on is the fact that you're home and we no longer have to be apart. As far as the kids, don't give up on what you've built with them. People have a way of surprising you sometimes."

"I hope you're right."

"You never know until you give them a chance."

Deep in thought, Melina was silent as they drove the rest of the way to Amityville. The car handled like a dream. It was smooth and powerful beneath her hands and the desire to see how fast the car could really go was strong within her, but she checked the impulse. Mac had just given her this car. No way was she going to allow it to be taken away by the pigs who'd confiscated her other car.

In no time at all, they were pulling up into the driveway. Melina had barely parked the car when the front door opened. Cynthia Maccari rushed out of the house and was soon followed by Mac's sister, Victoria.

"Here goes nothing," Melina whispered to Mac.

"You'll be fine, doll. No sweat."

He kissed her softly before exiting the car and then opening the door for her. Melina stepped out, and was nearly rushed by Victoria.

"Melina, am I glad to see you. Finally, I've got some reinforcement to keep my brother in line."

Melina hugged Mac's sister as she tried to suppress her laughter. "Looks like I'm back in the nick of time."

Victoria stepped away and smiled. "Absolutely. You know how much work it is dealing with him."

She jerked her head toward Mac, who was hugging Cynthia fiercely.

"I heard that, Vic," Mac said.

"I meant for you to," Victoria said sweetly.

"Victoria, be nice to your brother," Cynthia said.

Victoria rolled her eyes. "See. This is what I deal with. Really glad you're back, Melina."

"Likewise. We'll have to schedule a girls' day soon."

"I'm always up for that," Victoria said.

Melina smiled, nerves fluttering in her stomach as

Mac's mom came toward her. "Mrs. Maccari."

"None of that, dear. I think we're on a first name basis now. It's so good to see you again, Melina. James has been worried sick with you not around. The poor boy would barely eat while you were away."

"Ma, must you?" Mac asked. He smoothed a hand over his face.

"Yes, I must. It's important Melina knows how important she is to you and to me."

Melina raised a brow. "To you?"

Where was Cynthia going with this?

"Melina, I wasn't sure what to make of you when James first introduced you, but now I am so glad he did. I always worried that he wouldn't find a woman who could take care of him and make him happy, but I was wrong. His eyes light up when he talks about you and he can't stop smiling. His happiness is my happiness, so thank you."

Melina swallowed hard, a sudden welling of emotion rising up in her. It took her a moment to gather her composure.

"You raised a good man. It's easy to love him."

"All right, enough of this love fest. Let's eat, people," Victoria said.

She motioned them toward the front door.

"Oh, yes. I wouldn't want dinner getting cold and now that you're back, Melina, perhaps we could discuss something important."

Cynthia linked her arm through Melina's and guided her toward the house.

"And what's that?"

"Why, wedding planning, of course. I'm sure that's on the horizon soon."

Melina's panic-stricken gaze flew to Mac who followed them. He winked.

Holy freaking hell.

Was Cynthia's comment an innocent one or was there

more to it than simply a desire to see her son settled down?

Had Mac said something to his mother about marriage? As Melina followed the Maccaris into the family home her thoughts ran every which way. Mac had told her once that when he loved it wasn't just for the moment. It was forever. As Cynthia guided them into the kitchen, Mac took a moment to slip close to her and kiss her cheek softly. The tenderness in his gesture nearly undid her.

Unknowingly, he'd given her something she thought she'd never have again.

A family.

"I love you," she whispered.

"And I love you."

Smiling, he slid back her chair to allow her to sit before he took his own spot beside her. Cynthia and Victoria started to bring out dish after dish. Melina's mouth watered.

Family and good food.

What girl could ask for more?

CHAPTER FOUR

The best things in life came free, Mac knew. Things like good health, happiness, purpose, family, and love. Sure, a person had to work for those things, but it wasn't the kind of work that drained a man of dignity and strength.

It was the most honorable kind of work.

Mac had never been more aware of that fact than he was in that moment, standing in the entryway of his mother's living room, watching Melina, his sister, and Cynthia flip through old family photo albums.

His girl was lit up—she probably didn't even realize it.

Bright eyes. A wide smile. Genuine happiness.

After the hell that was being locked up, he was grateful he had been able to provide this moment for Melina before real life came around to remind them of the outside world that was still turning … still waiting on them to get back to it.

For now, this would have to do.

"He didn't change a bit, huh?" Melina asked.

Mac grinned, knowing damn well she was talking about him.

"Not much in his looks," Cynthia said. "His attitude, however …"

"Ma," Mac said quietly.

Cynthia never even looked up from the pictures she

was showing off. "That attitude of his just grew and grew until it was too much for the rest of us to handle."

"I don't have an attitude, Ma."

"You do," the three woman said in unison.

"Although it's more like an arrogance," Melina added, shooting him a sly look.

Mac was a smart man—he prided himself on that virtue. Shit that didn't kill him only made him a hell of a lot stronger in the end.

This was one of those times, he knew.

No smart man would walk into the lion's den of three woman and write a check he had no way of cashing. And that was exactly what he would be doing if he decided to indulge his mother, sister, and Melina in an argument about what he acted like.

Besides, he was an arrogant fucker.

Mac wasn't about to deny that for a second.

He simply didn't think it was an *attitude* problem.

To each their own.

"James?" his mother asked.

"Yeah, Ma?"

"Get me the bottle of wine and a few glasses out of the cupboard, hmm? I think we all should celebrate Melina's homecoming."

Mac's gaze slid to his lover, and he watched the sweet smile bloom over Melina's features. Her dark caramel skin flushed in her happiness.

Homecomings were meant for those a person cared for—those who people wanted to know they were cared for.

Melina was adored.

Mac hoped she knew it, too.

She'd spent so much time either taking care of others, or surviving on her own. She deserved people who were willing to be a cornerstone in her life, regardless of what was thrown at her. God knew his family—his mother and sister, anyway—were the best kind of people for that job.

"Wine and glasses, James," Cynthia said, giving him a look that reprimanded him without even saying what for.

"Going, Ma," Mac said.

Mac found the chilled wine in the refrigerator, and the crystal glasses his mother always kept high and out of the reach of guests in the very top cupboard. Careful not to drop one of his mother's favorite wine glasses, he set them down to the counter when Victoria slid in beside him.

"Hey," she said.

Mac offered her an easy smile. "Hey. And thanks for earlier—letting Melina know there are other people who missed her—I think she needed that."

Victoria shrugged. "I'd miss your ass, too."

That was Victoria Maccari—always the blunt one.

"So," his sister started, glancing toward the entryway to the living room, "… has Ma said anything to you about you-know-what?"

"She's made it very apparent she would like to see me married, Vic."

Victoria's brow furrowed a second before a burst of laughter followed right behind. "Besides that, Mac. I guess I should have said 'you know who.'"

"No." Mac spun around slowly to face his sister fully. "Who, exactly, should she be telling me about and why?"

If someone was bothering his mother, they were going to have serious problems.

Like drinking through a straw for the rest of their miserable life.

"Apparently, James has been coming around lately, asking things."

It took Mac a second to realize who his sister was talking about—he'd gone months without having to deal with his father, and he really wished he could have gone a few more.

"What kind of things?" Mac asked.

"Ma said he was asking about you—but that's not the

important part."

Mac sort of thought it was. "Then what is?"

"He wanted to be here today—even showed up, but Ma made him leave. He was ..." Victoria trailed off, tipping her thumb up toward her mouth and pretending to take a fake drink. "You know?"

"Wonderful," Mac muttered.

He wasn't all too surprised that his useless, fuck up of a father was coming around. He was even less surprised that James was trying to get info on Mac.

He was surprised, however, that his mother made her estranged husband leave. Cynthia didn't indulge James Maccari, but she was never outright rude.

"She seemed really uncomfortable when he was here, Mac," Victoria added.

Fuck.

"I'll handle it," Mac assured.

"All right."

"And don't say a word to Ma that you told me about it."

Victoria gave him a wide, innocent look. "Told you about what?"

Exactly.

From across the large dining room, Mac sipped from a glass of Cognac as he watched Melina accept yet another hug from Neeya Pivetti. He let the liquor settle over his tongue before swallowing it back, and then he set the glass aside, done with the drink altogether.

It was all about compromise with Luca Pivetti.

The Don liked a good drink when he had guests in his mansion, and he preferred if they partook in the custom as well. Mac had settled his issue with not drinking by accepting whatever the boss offered, taking a sip—just enough not to be rude or refuse—and then being with done with the drink.

Luca never said a word.

Mac took that as a good thing.

"Seems jail did well for her," Luca said as he lifted his own glass for another drink.

"How so?"

"She doesn't seem any less of herself, I suppose."

Mac chuckled. "Melina? Less than herself?"

Even Luca smiled, the ever-cold and standoffish man that he was known to be. "You have a good point. I gather you would have much rather been at home with her than here, hmm?"

Mac had no shame. "A little."

Luca laughed. "I appreciate you indulging my wife. She worried."

Mac passed his boss a look, taking note of the content on the man's features. Luca didn't seem to notice Mac's surprise at the fact that his boss seemed a little happier than normal, for whatever reason.

And he'd *almost* thanked Mac.

He'd said he *appreciated* his actions, which wasn't entirely a "thank you" but it was damn close.

Luca Pivetti never thanked anyone unless it was well deserved.

It was all a little strange.

"So," Luca drawled, turning to face Mac fully, "… what of it? What have you figured out?"

"About what, boss?"

Luca tipped his head in the direction of the chatting women in a subtle way. "She's out—you've made yourself a name in *la famiglia* and earned a proper position. Don't you think you owe her the same respect?"

All over again, Mac did a double-take of his boss.

Was Luca saying what Mac thought he was saying?

Was he suggesting what Mac thought he was?

Marriage?

Luca's next words confirmed Mac's suspicions. "Wasn't it you who said you had been working on the wife thing before the arrest happened?"

"I did," Mac replied.

Months ago, Mac would have laughed someone out of his face had they told him that Luca approved of his relationship with Melina, never mind wanting to see it be a more permanent, proper thing. Luca had had little to no qualms with speaking against Melina when Mac had first started bringing her around, and even went as far as threatening her. He'd disapproved—vocally and often—on just about everything Mac had chosen to do with Melina.

Yet, Mac did his thing, knowing it pissed his boss off.

He'd needed to keep his lover safe, and he wanted her with him, no matter what.

"You amuse me when you're confused," Luca said more to himself than to Mac, smiling in that way of his again.

"I'm not confused."

Lies.

He was confused as fuck.

Luca only patted Mac's shoulder with one hand, turning to go back to the wet bar and have one of his maids pour him another drink. Before he went, he said, "She gave up a great deal to protect you—freedom is the one thing none of us want to have taken away, and hers was, for a time. I have no doubt in my mind that she didn't do it for my sake, or the sake of our *famiglia*, but I have to respect her for doing it, even if it was only for you. Do you understand, Mac?"

He did, finally.

Melina's loyalty was an admirable trait.

And God knew Luca liked to give credit where it was due.

"I'm still working on the wife thing," Mac said instead of replying to Luca's statements.

"Soon, yes?"

Mac didn't answer right away.

He wanted to agree, because that was what he needed. But he still wasn't sure on Melina's plans or desires, and that was where he always paused. He was just waiting on a sign from her so that he could put the ring burning a hole in his pocket to good use.

"Working on it, boss," Mac said instead.

Luca shook his head, slapped Mac on the shoulder once more, and made a beeline for the wet bar.

Mac didn't mind being left alone again.

Not when he could watch Melina from afar. He found her across the room; she was still talking to Neeya, but her gaze was only on him. She smiled wider at being caught staring.

She'd been watching him, too.

"Spent a lot of time here, huh?" Melina asked out of the blue.

"Pardon?"

"You seem to know where to walk, and we're not lost yet."

Mac pressed a kiss to the top of Melina's head. "We're not going to get lost."

"Yet."

Smartass.

Mac tightened his arm around her waist, keeping her close to his side as they strolled down the decorative stone pathway. It was just one of many pathways that led into the back property of Luca's mansion, weaving in throughout the two acres of woodland. It was a nice walk, as long as a person never left the path.

He'd learned that once …

"I did spend a lot of time back here over the last few months," Mac admitted after a few minutes.

Melina's stride slowed, forcing him to slow down his walk, too. "Why was that? Boss's new pet?"

Despite her teasing, he could hear the honest curiosity in her tone.

"It was more like Luca's way of punishing me."

She glanced up at him, her brow furrowed. "What, why?"

Sighing, Mac urged her to keep walking, and she did. He knew this moment had been coming, and he owed her the truth. "The day of your sentencing, I disobeyed him by making a fucking scene like I did. He wasn't impressed, to say the least."

Luca's way of punishing Mac had been to fuck him around with anything and everything he could. From interrupting Mac's time with his family, pulling him out of church, to even having Mac do what would be considered message runs that any fucking soldier could do. But no, Luca called on Mac.

A lot of the time, it forced Mac to lose time in his days.

Lost time meant work lost.

Lost work meant less money.

Then, when tribute rolled around, Mac would be left explaining why his money wasn't as good as it normally would be when he paid his boss. He was still over the minimum, but barely.

And of course, Mac couldn't blame Luca.

Nonetheless, Mac did what Luca wanted, and took his punishment without a fucking complaint. He didn't follow the rules all those months ago, so he had to answer for that.

Frankly, Luca could have dealt with Mac in a much more violent way than he had.

Mac was grateful.

"He had a fit over that?" Melina asked, anger heating

her tone.

Mac checked his impulse to smirk, because even when his girl wasn't pleased about something, he still found her anger hot as hell. Now was not the right time for that nonsense.

"Like I said, it caused a scene. The media was on that for days after. It was too much attention, and any sort of attention is bad for this business."

Melina frowned, her lips pouting in that way of hers. Mac didn't bother to check his impulse this time. He slid a finger under her chin, turned her to look at him, and pressed a fast, hard kiss to her mouth.

He fucking loved it when she pouted.

She probably didn't even know how hard it made him.

Melina grinned, sighing happily against Mac's kiss. His hand slid lower on her back, pressing firmly enough so that the curve of her body was tight to his form and she could feel his erection beginning to grow beneath his pants.

Though he didn't want to, Mac pulled away.

Luca had guards all over his property—Mac was not interested in giving people a show.

Melina smiled softly at him. "That was nice."

Mac winked. "Let me get you home and it'll get a lot better."

"Deal."

Before Mac knew what had happened, Melina turned on her heel and made a move for the grassy section just off the walkway. It would be a shortcut back to the mansion.

He grabbed her arm and pulled her back just in time.

Melina's eyes grew wide as growls echoed from deeper in the darkness where they had yet to walk. "What in the fuck is that?"

"Dogs," Mac said. "Stay on the path, okay?"

"Seriously?"

"They're not nice dogs."

Mac had learned that while Melina was away, too.

Melina stiffened a bit as the growling ceased. Not once had the dogs shown themselves. Mac had learned that they wouldn't unless Luca called them out—they would then proceed to act like overgrown Rottie puppies—or if someone stepped off the pathway while their master was not with the person.

Then, they acted like the guard dogs they were.

"Can we go?" Melina asked, still staring into the darkness.

"Yeah, let's go."

"Tired?" Mac asked.

Melina nodded, never taking her gaze off the passenger window as Mac drove up to the toll, digging out the change he needed to pass over the bridge. His girl had been tired, and didn't want to drive all the way back to their place, so Mac had taken the wheel.

"Doll?"

"Hmm?"

Mac's right hand left the steering wheel, sliding up Melina's thigh and just under the skirt of her dress. The warmth of her flesh heated his fingertips, and he felt her shiver work its way over her body.

"Are we good?" Mac asked.

Melina looked away from the window finally. "Good for what?"

"Us, I guess."

"Do we have a reason not to be?"

Mac shot her a sly smile. "Well, a man never really knows."

Melina pursed her lips before leaning over in the seat

and pressing a kiss to his jaw. "We're good."

"How good?" he asked.

She cocked a brow. "Are you trying to go somewhere with this?"

"I—"

"Because I am not giving you road head, Mac."

Mac couldn't have stopped his reaction if he tried, laughing hard and loud. Through his chuckles, he managed to say, "No, but never say never, Melina."

She opened her mouth to give a retort, but he squeezed her thigh roughly, quieting her. "Never say never," he repeated.

"We're not having this argument."

"It's not an argument, doll."

Melina slid back into the proper position in her seat, crossing her arms over her chest. "What were you trying to get at then?"

A bit of nervousness settled in Mac's gut.

He wasn't entirely sure why.

He adored this woman.

Loved her entirely.

Melina was everything, and more, he could have ever wanted in the person he chose to spend the rest of his life with. But they were driving in a car, going forty across a bridge, with cars all around.

It wasn't romantic.

Would she even want that?

Roses, a big night out, and all eyes on her when he asked?

Was that Melina's thing?

Mac didn't think so—he didn't think this was exactly right, either.

He felt silly.

"Mac?" Melina asked when he stayed quiet.

"What do you want after today?"

"I don't know what you're asking me."

Mac sighed, and ran a hand through his hair. "You

know, like kids or do you want to go back to school?"

Melina quieted for all of three seconds before she said softly, "Kids."

He wasn't sure if that was a confirmative reply or not.

"Yes, you do, or no, you—"

"Maybe … someday," she interrupted. "Is this about the whole wedding thing?"

Mac's head whipped to the side, and he took in the confusion on Melina's features before his gaze was back on the road. "What wedding thing?"

"Your mom said something about a wedding—Neeya mentioned a wedding. Is there something going on that I don't know?"

Somehow, Mac managed to laugh that off without the strain in his voice showing too much. "No, that is just people voicing their wishes."

"Oh."

A bit of sadness colored up the word.

Mac couldn't have missed it if he tried.

That sign he'd been waiting for—the one that told him Melina was ready for that question, if he decided to ask it—was glaring at him right in the face.

"But it's not just what *they* want," Mac said, giving her another look.

Melina was already back to staring out the window, her attention gone from him. He knew that was just her way of hiding her disappointment. "It's fine, Mac. It's not something people do just to please other people."

"Melina."

She didn't look at him.

Mac reached out to touch her thigh.

Again, nothing.

"Doll," he said, firmer than before.

Melina blew out a breath. "What?"

"Would you look at me?"

"For what? There's nothing to say."

But there was—and hurt filled her voice.

She could hide a lot of things from everyone else, but the woman couldn't hide a fucking thing from him.

Never.

"*Melina.*"

When she looked away from the window, Mac slowed his car to a stop, forcing the vehicles behind him to stop, too. Horns honked, and cars tried to maneuver out around their car to get past.

It didn't work, and it only left them gridlocked in a traffic jam on the middle of the bridge.

Mac didn't give a fuck.

He was far too busy staring at his girl.

"We should move," Melina said as someone else honked their horn.

"I have other shit to do."

Melina rolled her pretty brown eyes. "I wouldn't want you to do it—ask me—just because someone else wanted you to."

"There is no one else who ever had any opinion to voice about you that was important to me—except *you*, that is."

"Mac—"

He pulled the black velvet case from his pocket, quieting whatever she was getting ready to say. Opening his palm flat, he held the jewelry box up for her to see.

The horns kept honking.

Cars kept inching forward.

Mac never moved.

"I've had it for months," he told her, "just sitting there waiting …"

Melina's gaze flicked between the velvet box and Mac's eyes. "Waiting for what?"

"Apparently, nothing—I was being stupid and overthinking shit."

Humor danced on her beautiful features. "Oh?"

"I do that a lot with you. I never really know what you're thinking, even if I act like I do. But I love that, doll, because you keep me on my toes. You make me better—you've got my back."

"Always," Melina whispered.

Mac popped open the top of the velvet case, showcasing a princess-cut, two-carat diamond nestled in a crown of smaller stones on top of a white-gold band. Melina chewed on her bottom lip, a smile growing as she took the engagement ring in.

"You are—by far—the best thing to have ever graced my life. And I am—by far—the luckiest man because you picked me. Marry me, Melina."

"That didn't sound like a question. You're supposed to ask, Mac."

"I didn't really have to ask," he murmured.

Melina met his gaze again. "Because you knew I'd say yes."

"You still have to say it, doll."

"Was there ever any doubt?"

Mac grinned. "Not now."

Melina just stared at him, quiet and still.

"Do you want me to make a bigger show of it?" he asked. "Shout it from the rooftops—better yet, the roof of the car?"

"What?" she asked, laughing.

Mac pushed the driver's door open, already turning away and stepping out of the car. He ignored the blaring horns and the drivers giving him the finger as he had quite literally stopped three lanes of traffic on the bridge.

"Hey, asshole!"

"Mac!" Melina shouted from inside the car.

She scrambled out on her side just as Mac jumped up on the hood of the car, and then up to the roof. He spread his arms wide, looking down at Melina while people shouted and honked.

"Mac, get down!"

He did—on one knee.

Melina's eyes stretched even wider.

"Say you'll marry me, doll," Mac said as loud as he could, ready to shout it, if that was what she wanted. His hand outstretched toward her with the velvet box in his palm. "Make me even luckier—happier. Say you'll be my wife."

"*Yes*. Now get down!"

Mac did, flipping the cars behind him off as he caught Melina around the waist and pulled her in for a kiss.

The ring was a perfect fit.

Just like his girl.

Mac's eye caught the sparkle of Melina's engagement ring as she lifted her left hand for what seemed like the millionth time to look the diamond over. The piece caught the shine of street lights as they passed, and her smile grew wide.

"Do you like it?" he asked.

"Love it, Mac."

"I thought you would."

Melina shot him a grin from the side. "Who knew?"

"Only one person," Mac answered.

"Really?" Melina made a face. "Even though *everyone* felt like they had to mention something about us getting married?"

"Yep."

"Who, then?"

Mac chuckled. "My sister. And that was only for sizing purposes."

Melina let out a laugh, and as Mac pulled the car into the underground garage that belonged to their building, he took in the sight of her happiness. Because it was, after all, one of the most beautiful sights. With her eyes shut, a huge smile, and joy lighting up her features, he couldn't think of anything else he would rather see in that moment.

"Love you, doll."

She quieted instantly at his soft proclamation, her smile softening. "I love you, too."

"Do you have a date in mind?" he dared to ask.

Melina looked over the ring again as Mac parked the car in their allotted spot. It was a corner section, blocked off from sight by one cement wall and his Challenger on the other side.

"Soon," was all Melina said.

Mac cocked a brow. "How soon?"

"I don't … think I want to wait. I know what I want."

He couldn't have stopped his smirk from forming even if he tried. "Oh?"

"Yeah." She gave him another sweet smile. "I want you. Soon, Mac."

"Soon …" he trailed off, reaching out to hook a single finger in the collar of her dress. "But for now, I know what I want."

Melina leaned into his touch, and Mac let his palm wander over the smooth, delicate column of her throat, under her jaw, and over her cheek until his fingers could thread into her hair. He pulled her a little closer, watching the flickers of love and lust color her irises as her lips curved sinfully.

"And what is it that *you* want?" she asked softly.

"Right now, I'll settle for another kiss, doll."

Melina gave him what he wanted, leaning over the middle console to grab hold of his shirt and clench tight as her lips fell on his with brutal force. Mac answered the roughness back with his own, nipping at his girl's bottom lip before his tongue struck against the seam of her mouth, demanding that she open up for him.

She did, and he took that chance to deepen the kiss, their tongues warring, their mouths never breaking apart even as she climbed over the middle and fell into his lap.

Mac groaned long and hard as Melina's legs widened around his, the skirt of her dress pulling up around her thighs. He could feel that scrap of satin and lace keeping her sex covered grinding against the bulge beneath his pants.

His erection was damn-near painful.

He'd been semi-hard for hours and ignoring it.

Mac couldn't do that anymore.

"Doll," he mumbled against her lips, "we're at home. Let's go—"

Melina's fingernails dug into his pec, making him hiss. "Too far."

"Melina …" Mac swallowed hard when her other hand palmed the length of his erection through his pants, firm and insistent. Jesus. "I can't do a fucking thing to you in this car except let you ride me. Let's go upstairs."

"Right now," she demanded.

That breathy, high tone did him in.

Her desire was his unravelling.

He had no control when she sounded like that.

Mac never had.

"Fuck," Mac said in a half-snarl, letting his hands fall to Melina's waist. She was shifting her hips in just the right way that let her barely-covered pussy rub against his length. Each and every time she did that, his nerves snapped like crazy. "Lift the fuck up, then."

Laughing airlessly, Melina did what she was told without question. Mac fumbled with his belt and pants for longer than he wanted to, but he eventually got the offending articles undone and pushed down enough for Melina to free his cock from the confines of his boxer-briefs.

When her hand closed around him, and her fingers tightened to his pulsing base, Mac's air rushed from his lungs in a painful breath, his hips jerking up into her hold.

"So hard," Melina murmured, her hand stroking him slowly. "I missed feeling you. In my hand, my mouth, and my pussy. I missed that, Mac."

She stroked him again.

Firmer.

Harder.

Still slow, though.

Too fucking slow.

Achingly slow.

"Don't play the tease right now, doll," Mac warned. "You will regret it later when I get you upstairs, bend you over, and fuck you to the point you're about to come only to *stop*. And I will stop again and again until you are sobbing and begging to come. Do. Not. Tease. Me."

Melina's gaze snapped up to meet his, desire dancing in her eyes. "Promise?"

Jesus.

This woman would kill him someday.

Mac would welcome that moment with open fucking arms.

Threading his hands into her wavy hair, Mac pulled Melina down for a bruising kiss as he growled against her lips, "You know it."

In the darkness of the car—the only light provided was from the illuminated dashboard—Mac caught sight of just the sliver of Melina's lace and satin thong as she lifted her skirt higher, and one of her hands disappeared between her thighs.

Above him, her lips parted with a shaky sigh.

Pure bliss.

That was what she sounded like as she touched herself.

"Are you wet for me, doll?"

"Mmm," she hummed back.

Mac let her continue with her hand between her legs as he kissed a path over her jaw and down her neck, his teeth nipping every so often, and his tongue striking out to soothe the bite right after. He could hear the sounds of Melina's fingers sinking into her sex—wet, noisy sounds that made his cock ache even more.

She trembled when his fingertips ghosted over her thigh and in between their bodies, her hand still on his cock stuttered in its movement.

"Keep going," he told her softly.

Sliding his hand further in between her thighs and under the lace trim of her thong, he slipped a finger in with her two already fucking her pussy. It stretched her a little wider, filling her fuller. Melina whimpered, her pelvis grinding harder into her own hand and his. Mac pulled his hand away a bit, just enough to start circling her throbbing, hot clit with the pad of his fingertip as her own fingers started moving faster.

"You going to come, doll?" Mac asked. "Fucking your fingers on my lap while I touch you, yeah? Are you going to come and then ride me?"

Melina answered him back with a whine that seemed to claw its way out of her throat. All of her sounds were like life to him—electric, even.

He'd not forgotten what she sounded like, of course, but he missed it.

Constantly.

Melina fell into his chest, shaking and panting her way through an orgasm with his name right on the tip of her tongue. "*Mac.*"

He slowed his hand between her thighs when he felt hers stop, and wrapped an arm around her back, letting his hand tangle into the hair at the nape of her neck, keeping her rooted against him.

Just for a second, he wanted her closer.

Still.

Free and happy.

Mac always wanted her like that.

Melina didn't let him keep her like that for long, though. Her head lifted and their mouths crashed together as she shifted her hips and positioned his cock along the seam of her wet slit. There was no warning before she dropped down—just the hitch in her breath and her wide, blown-out pupils as she watched his face while she sunk down his length.

She was heaven around him.

A tight, hot heaven that took away his breath and blinded him.

Sensation ran on overload as her fingernails scored over his neck and her fingers dug into his thigh.

"Shit," Mac managed to say through his clenched teeth.

Melina's forehead found his as his hands met her waist. The waves of her hair created a barrier of sorts, locking them into a staring contest as she began a slow, smooth rhythm on top of him. Her hips lifted and lowered, her pelvis rotating every time she came down on him, grinding her clit into the muscles of his groin.

"And this," Melina mumbled quietly

Mac pulled her harder onto his cock with her next movement, making her shiver beautifully. "This?"

"I missed this."

God, he did, too.

Melina's hand slid from his neck to his jaw, her thumb stroking his skin in the tenderest way. Mac turned his head, kissing the skin of her palm and feeling the engagement ring on her finger brush his cheek.

Her rhythm never stuttered.

He felt fucking weak.

But she didn't even slow.

He shuddered, her name falling from his lips like a prayer.

She was Godlike to him.

And he already worshipped her.

CHAPTER FIVE

She was getting married.

She was getting married.

Even thinking the words twice did little to dispel her current reality. Melina looked down at the sparkling engagement ring Mac had given her two months ago. It was even more beautiful now than the night he'd given it to her. A symbol of his love and his commitment to her. Even now, on the threshold of starting their new life together, she was still amazed.

A year ago she had been struggling in more ways than one. Coping with the illness of her father and doing her best to survive in a profession that changed people in the worst of ways. Things hadn't been easy and more than once, she'd wanted to give her burdens to someone else, but there'd been no one else to take them. Now she had someone.

Mac.

There wasn't a doubt in her mind that the man would crawl over broken glass for her or deal with any threat that came her way. He'd proven that in his own quiet, unassuming way more than once. And now he was about to prove before God, *la famiglia* and those who mattered to him, just how important she really was to him. Tears threatened to fall but with sheer force of will she held them back.

Today was a happy day.

Today was the day that little girls dreamed of when they grew older.

It was the day women dreamed of even as they grew older and were faced with the harsh reality that life was not the fairytale they'd grew up believing it to be.

Melina had been one of those women.

Until Mac had proven her wrong and dared to make her believe in happy endings again.

Now they were about to start living one of their own.

If only … Shaking her head, Melina pushed those thoughts away. There was no point in dwelling on the past. On things that could never be. But still, a part of her wished that things could have been different.

Standing before the full-length mirror in the room that served as her bridal chamber, Melina smiled at her reflection. Her long, glossy hair was curled, pulled atop her head, and secured with pins. A thin silver and diamond studded diadem was the centerpiece of her veil.

And her dress.

Her dress was something she might have never picked for herself, but there was a first time for everything. The gown she wore was cream and made of lace. Off the shoulder with small sequins around the bodice and a tapered waist that trailed down to a long train. It was beautiful.

She looked like a bride out of a glossy, couture magazine. From the ornate headpiece she'd reluctantly allowed Neeya Pivetti to talk her into choosing, to the long veil embedded with more Swarovski crystals than she could even dare to count, she looked every inch a princess.

Melina Morgan Maccari, mob princess.

She laughed at the thought. For better or worse, she was about to tie her life to a man who moved in shadows. To a man whose first loyalty would always be to a family that hadn't initially been welcoming to her. To a family that would always come first, even above their own. Was she ready for everything their lifestyle would entail?

"Melina?"

She turned at the sound of the soft voice and found Cynthia Maccari standing hesitantly in the doorway.

"Come in," Melina told her.

"You look beautiful, dear. Absolutely breathtaking. James isn't going to be able to take his eyes off of you."

Melina smiled beneath her future mother-in-law's praise.

"I can say the same. You look wonderful. There's a glow about you."

"I was expecting to see the same glow about you. What's wrong?"

Melina shook her head. "Nothing. Just a bit emotional is all. Never thought I'd be getting married."

Cynthia's eyes were soft. "That may partly be true, but there's more that you're not saying. It's your parents, isn't it?"

Melina turned away in an effort to get her warring emotions under control. She felt Cynthia's hand touch her shoulder and the tears she'd been fighting slipped down her cheeks.

"Yes," the word tore from her suddenly raw throat.

"They're here. In spirit. In your heart. In your memories."

Melina faced Cynthia. "It's not the same."

"I know. Loss is never an easy pill to swallow but it's on days like today that we appreciate what we still have left. I know that somewhere, your parents are smiling down, so happy that you are finally about to have all the things they ever dreamed of for you."

"I would give anything to hold my dad's hand. To have him walk me down the aisle."

"He'll be right beside you every step of the way."

Cynthia took a tissue from the holder and carefully wiped Melina's tears away.

"I don't know how to be a wife. Mac needs …"

"Mac needs you and only you. Everything else will fall into place. Besides, you've already got a head start."

"And what's that?" Melina asked.

"You've learned to cook decent food. That's half the battle."

Melina laughed and Cynthia joined her as she fidgeted with Melina's veil, making sure it was perfectly in place.

"Well, when you put it like that," Melina admitted.

"See. Now no more tears."

"I'll say. You'd better not be messing up my makeup job, Melina."

Victoria entered the room, clutching a bouquet of white tulips. Her gaze went suspiciously back and forth between Melina and her mother.

"Leave her alone. This is an emotional day for all of us," Cynthia said.

"I realize that, Ma, but someone has to keep it together. Everyone can't be a blubbering mess."

"I'm fine, Victoria. Really."

Mac's sister came closer and gave her face a quick glance. "No, you're not. Ma, what did you do?"

Victoria quickly put down her bouquet before she ushered Melina back to the bench seat in front of the vanity.

"I didn't do anything. I was just giving her some words of encouragement," Cynthia said.

"Well, her mascara is running and now she has tear trails down her foundation. It's good I came to check on things."

Opening up the three stacked make up case, Victoria went to work re-touching Melina's makeup.

"I appreciate this Victoria," Melina said.

"You can appreciate me more by not ruining your makeup again," Victoria scolded.

Melina pinched her lightly. Mac's sister had a rough exterior, but deep down when she cared for you it meant everything. Today Melina just wasn't marrying Mac, she was gaining a sister, and for that she couldn't be more grateful.

A knock at the door drew the three women's attention.

"Who could that be?" Cynthia asked.

She went to the door and opened it, sticking her head out. "Yes."

"Delivery for Melina," a man's voice said.

"From who?" Cynthia asked.

"Your son, ma'am."

Melina waited as Cynthia closed the door and came over to where she and Victoria were. She was holding a large rectangle-shaped, black velvet box.

"Here," Cynthia said. She handed the box to Melina.

"Hurry. We only have five minutes," Victoria urged her on.

"All right, Miss Bossy."

With trembling hands, Melina lifted the lid of the box and gasped. He didn't. Yes, he had. Nestled inside the lining of velvet was a four-strand diamond choker.

"It's beautiful," Cynthia said.

"No one can ever say my brother doesn't have style," Victoria said.

"I can't believe he'd buy something like this. It's so … so …"

"It's you, Melina," Victoria finished for her.

"What makes you say that?"

Victoria pointed. "This is a piece of jewelry that a queen would wear and you carry yourself as a queen in every sense of the word. This is just Mac's way of giving you a little extra bling to cement your status as his new queen."

"My daughter finally says something that makes some sense. Today is truly a day of miracles."

"Very funny, Ma."

Melina lifted the choker from the box and held it out to Victoria. "Will you do the honors?"

"Absolutely."

Melina held her veil out of the way so that Victoria could fasten the jewelry around her neck. It fit perfectly.

"Every inch a queen," Cynthia said softly.

"Yes, now let's get this queen to her king," Victoria said.

Melina rose and allowed Victoria to flip her veil down to cover her face.

"This is it," she said.

"No turning back now. You're stuck with us," Victoria said.

"I wouldn't have it any other way."

And Melina meant every word of it.

The sounds of organ music filled the air, loud and strong. Even standing behind the massive wooden doors that would lead inside the sanctuary, Melina could hear the music clear and strong. She clutched the bouquet of white tulips tight in her hands as she waited for the doors that separated her from the interior to open. She was really about to do this. When those doors opened, there would be no turning back and it was exactly what she wanted.

Slowly, the massive doors opened and Melina walked through them. Everything was decorated so beautifully. From the white and silver ribbons that twirled elegantly from the Cathedral ceiling, to the large arrangements of white tulips. Not to mention the covered white altar at the very front of the church.

For a moment, she was momentarily stunned. St. Matthews was filled with people and she didn't know even a third of them. As she gathered her composure and walked down the long aisle that lead to the man she loved, she dared to risk a glance at the people who stood and watched her pass. These had to be members of *la famiglia* out and in numbers to show support and respect to one of their own.

Once, Melina might have wondered what they thought about her. About the woman that Mac was daring to introduce into their world. But today, it didn't matter. The only thing that mattered was the man standing at the altar next to the priest with his gaze fixed squarely on her. In her belly, butterflies fluttered and she tried to quell the sudden rapid beating of her heart. And then she suddenly felt cold.

Her gaze turned to the right and then she saw him. Smirking, with arms folded, James Maccari Sr. stared at her the way a man looked at something he wanted to consume. What was the man even doing here? She knew Mac hadn't invited his father. He couldn't stand the man, but yet here he was in the flesh, acting as if he belonged. Melina narrowed her eyes before she returned her attention to the only man in the room that truly mattered.

Mac.

Wearing a fitted black tux, his hands were clasped together in front of him and she saw something in his eyes she thought she'd never see.

Anxiety.

He was just as nervous about today as she was.

Though he couldn't see her well behind the veil, she offered him an encouraging smile.

A few more steps brought her up to the raised altar where Mac, the priest and the others in their party stood. Melina handed her bouquet to Victoria as Mac stepped forward and reached for her hand. The second they touched, that familiar warmth spread through her body. With only the priest separating them, Melina watched as Mac's mouth tugged into a sly grin as he looked at her from head to toe. When he reached forward to touch her veil, the priest swatted his hand away like an errant child.

Melina stifled a laugh as Mac's gaze narrowed on the

one man separating him from what he wanted most.

Her.

"Dearly beloved, we are gathered here today to unite this man and this woman in Holy Matrimony. Today James and Melina are taking the next step in this journey called life and they are taking it together. Love is the ultimate commitment because it challenges us to give the very best of ourselves and be all that God intended for us to be. Let us have a moment of prayer for this couple."

Melina and Mac got to their knees at the altar and allowed the priest to pray over them. Melina barely heard a word of what the man said. Her eyes were on Mac.

Then he winked at her and she melted inside.

A few minutes later, the prayer was over and the priest motioned for Mac's best man, Bobby Dinazio, to step forward. He handed Mac the ring and then re-took his place.

"Take your bride's hand," the priest instructed.

Mac took Melina's hand in his, every fiber of his being focused on her.

"Repeat after me."

The priest's instructions were lost to her as Mac said his vows.

"I, Mac, take you, Melina, to be my lawfully wedded wife. I promise to be true to you in good times and in bad, in sickness and in health. I will love, cherish and honor you all the days of my life."

And then he slipped the diamond-studded infinity band onto her ring finger. It was a perfect match to the engagement ring he'd given her months ago. The man really had thought of everything.

"Melina," the priest said making a motion.

Victoria stepped forward and offered Melina the band she'd picked out for Mac. She held his hand tight as she prepared to say her own vows.

"I, Melina, take you, Mac, to be my lawfully wedded husband. I promise to be true to you in good times and in bad, in sickness and in health. I promise to love, cherish and honor you all the days of my life."

Melina slid the thick silver band on Mac's finger. Tears blurred behind her eyes, so she closed them, lest they fall and ruin Victoria's makeup job.

"What God has joined together, let no man put asunder. If there be any that have reason that James and Melina should not be wed, let them speak now or forever hold their peace."

Melina didn't look at the crowd, but Mac did briefly. A glare daring anyone to risk their life by ruining his wedding. A minute or two passed by but only silence remained.

"Then if that be all, by the powers invested in me, I pronounce you man and wife. James, you may kiss your bride."

Mac wasted no time lifting the veil away. He smirked when he saw her and Melina couldn't help the tears that fell. Cradling her face gently in his hands, Mac kissed her. The crowd erupted inside the sanctuary, but all Melina could feel was the sweetness of Mac's kiss.

It was a promise of forever.

When he finally pulled away, her tears came even harder.

"Ladies and gentlemen, I give you Mr. and Mrs. James Maccari Jr.," the priest said.

Mac frowned and opened his mouth to say something, but Melina pressed a finger to his lips.

"I don't care if your name is James, Mac or the man on the moon, I love you."

"And I love you."

And then Melina wrapped her arms around Mac and kissed him with every last ounce of love she had in her heart.

"Why do you keep glancing at me when you think I'm not looking?"

Melina took a sip of her champagne before she spoke, suddenly shy and having a hard time meeting Mac's eyes.

"Doll," Mac said softly.

"Part of me still can't believe that you're really my husband. It seems surreal."

Mac grinned, an easy relaxed smile. "Get used to it, Mrs. Maccari. You're stuck with me now."

"That's the same thing your sister said to me this morning."

"It's a Maccari motto."

Melina laughed. "Yeah, right." She smiled and then her expression turned somber.

"What is it? That beautiful smile should never leave your face today."

She hadn't wanted to say anything, but the more she considered it, the more she knew that it was important not to start their marriage with secrets between them.

"Did you know your father was at the church?"

Mac's gaze hardened. "Yeah, I did."

"Oh."

"It wasn't my choice, Melina. By the time I realized he was there, it was too late to do anything about it."

"And besides that, it wouldn't have looked good to make a scene," Melina surmised.

"That, too."

Melina reached for Mac's hand. "Are you okay?"

"I'm fine. Am I happy that he had the nerve to show up on a day that had absolutely nothing to do with him? Hardly. But James is nothing. He matters to no one."

"He looked at me when I was walking down the aisle and there was something in the way he looked at me. It was like …"

"Like what, doll?"

"The way a predator watches their prey."

A muscle in Mac's jaw moved and his eyes grew cold. Melina started to move her hand away from his, but he didn't allow her to.

"I don't know what game he's playing at, but I don't want you to worry. I'm going to take care of it."

"Mac, I'm not trying to cause any more issues between you and your father. I just want us to start our marriage off right. I don't want to keep things from you, even if it might not be important."

Mac held her face in one hand and kissed her softly. Melina responded with eagerness, never tiring of the way he showed his adoration for her.

"Mac," she whispered against his lips, "people are watching us."

"Let them."

Mac kissed her again, one hand slipping around her waist to bring her closer to him. Melina's body heated beneath her wedding gown. What she wouldn't give to bid everyone *adieu* and head off to be alone with her handsome husband.

"Have you two forgotten the rest of us might like to enjoy your company?"

Melina and Mac broke apart to find their hostess, Neeya Pivetti, standing next to them.

"Sorry, Mrs. Pivetti. We meant no disrespect," Mac said.

Neeya laughed. "Of course you didn't. No one here can blame you two for being all over each other. I don't remember the last time I've seen such an attractive couple."

"Thank you, Neeya. That means a lot."

"You can thank me, my dear, by coming with me. I have something for you."

"Haven't you already given us enough? You've let us

use your gorgeous home for our reception," Melina said.

Neeya waved a hand. "Nonsense. I won't hear of it. Now come."

Melina smiled and turned to her husband. "I'll be right back." She kissed him quickly.

"I'll be waiting."

Mac helped her to her feet and Neeya took Melina's arm leading her from the massive ballroom where the reception was still in full swing.

"I promise he'll be there when you get back. No business today," Neeya said.

"Are you sure?"

"I made Luca give his word. Nothing is going to ruin your day."

"I appreciate that more than you know. My nerves are already at an all-time high."

Neeya led them deeper into the house, before stopping in front of two paneled doors and opening them. She motioned for Melina to follow her inside.

"And why is that?"

"I never expected this. Any of this. And now I'm someone's wife and not just any someone, a very important someone. Any mistake I make will reflect not only on me, but him as well. I just don't want to mess up."

Walking over to a large painting, Neeya carefully removed it, revealing a small black vault. Melina turned away to give the woman her privacy.

"You're worrying for nothing. You went to jail for that man. You kept your mouth shut and that has proven the depth of your loyalty to any who might have doubted it."

"But what now? How do I balance that fine line between supporting him and not butting into things that aren't my business?"

Neeya came over to her, a red velvet box in her hand.

"Very carefully." Neeya placed the box in her hand. "Open it."

Melina did as she was instructed and found inside a small silver band. In the center was a purple princess-cut diamond.

"This is beautiful."

"Glad you like it. I wanted to give you something special. Everyone has white diamonds but a purple diamond, now those are rare."

"Thank you. Thank you so much."

Melina hugged Neeya, a wave of emotion coming over her. For so long she'd been alone and now her life was suddenly filled with people that cared about her.

That cared about her happiness.

It was almost too much.

"You're very welcome, dear. Now let's get back. We have so much more celebrating to do."

Melina moaned as Mac fed her a piece of their wedding cake.

"That good, huh?"

"Buttercream frosting is my absolute favorite."

"Well eat up, doll. We've got eight layers to eat through."

"No way. I'll be as big as a house."

Mac opened his mouth to say something, but before he could a loud chiming interrupted him.

"Excuse me. May I have your attention please?"

Mac's best man, Bobby stood up in the middle of the ballroom floor, a glass in his hand.

"Thank you," he continued once the room became quiet. "I almost can't believe it. Mac finally found someone crazy enough to put up with his arrogant ass."

The room erupted into laughter and Mac pointed a finger at Bobby, a mock scowl on his face.

"No, but seriously, I've known Mac since we were kids and he's a good man. I'm glad that he's finally found someone to share his life with. Melina, I hope you know what you're getting yourself into. You're in for a wild ride. *Saluti.*"

Bobby raised his glass and around them all the others did the same.

"All right. Now let's party," Bobby said.

He made a motion toward the DJ and the sounds of music filled the air.

"It's time for us to wow the crowd, Melina."

As Mac led her to the dance floor, Melina smiled as the song she picked for their dance began to play. Tears blurred in her eyes. *Ribbon in the Sky* by Stevie Wonder. It had been her parents' wedding song.

Kissing her forehead, he pulled her close and they danced as Stevie sang. This was a glimpse of heaven. A promise of the happiness that had finally found its way to her.

"I love you," she whispered near his ear.

"And I love you. Now and forever."

CHAPTER SIX

Bobby slapped Mac hard on the back as he passed him a shot of whiskey with his other hand.

"You know I don't like to drink," Mac said, although he took the shot from his friend.

Bobby shrugged, and tossed his own shot back. "Maybe so, but this is a night to be celebrated. The least you could do is do so with a drink or two."

Mac passed Bobby a look. "Or enough to get me hammered?"

"Or that."

Knowing he wouldn't get anywhere arguing with his friend, Mac tipped back the shot and let the burning liquor slide down his throat. As soon as a server walked past their spot, Mac got rid of the empty shot glass as to discourage Bobby from demanding Mac have another round.

He had plans for the evening.

Plans for Melina.

Those plans did not include having whiskey dick.

Leaning back against the fountain, Mac found his girl out on the floor, dancing with guests. She radiated happiness—pure joy.

His wife.

That word felt almost surreal.

Almost.

Except it wasn't, because Mac had been waiting for

this day from the very moment he knew that he loved Melina. There was no one else for him—just her.

"You know," Bobby started to say, grinning in that sly way of his, "what I said earlier was true."

"What's that?"

"Never thought I would see the day Mac Maccari settled down and married a woman."

Mac laughed. "It just took the right woman, man."

Bobby nodded, his gaze roaming over the crowd of guests, but he didn't reply. Mac didn't really need him to, as his longtime, childhood friend was not of the same mentality Mac was where women were concerned. Bobby enjoyed the game of women—he liked females that could play him as well or better than he played them.

It was all about the chase.

And once Bobby caught a girl?

His fun was over—he moved on.

Mac didn't begrudge his friend's ways, as far as that went. Bobby never strung a woman along; he was upfront with his motives. A man had to respect that—Mac did, simple as that.

"You'll be good for the next week, yeah?" Mac asked.

Bobby was reaching for a glass of wine off a server's tray as she passed. "I'll handle your crew while you're gone on your honeymoon."

"Good."

Because as much as Luca assured that another Capo could handle Mac's men for the week, he didn't trust a fucking soul. As it were, Mac had to work twice as hard because of his age and newness to the family just to get any sort of goddamn respect from the other Capos.

Especially ones like Anthony Corelli.

Speak of the devil and he shall appear ...

The Capo in question was making a beeline for Mac from across the room, the man's dark eyes looking like there was something on his mind.

Mac knew he should probably chat with the man.

It was never good to leave bad blood to sour.

God knew he and Anthony didn't see eye to eye on a lot of things.

"It's my wedding," Mac said more to himself than to Bobby.

Bobby was listening, of course. He was a good friend in that way.

"Yeah," his friend said. "It's your day, man."

"No business on my day, right?"

Bobby finally caught sight of the approaching Capo, and sighed. "He's a fucking asshole."

That Anthony was.

"Melina's waving me over," Mac said, using another passing server to drop his staring contest with Anthony and move toward his wife on the middle of the dance floor.

Melina hadn't been looking at him, or waving him over.

But she was now …

Good enough, Mac thought.

"What if he wants to chat?" Bobby asked at Mac's back.

"He doesn't want to chat," Mac assured. "He wants to irritate the living shit out of me because he's got himself ten years on my button, and he likes to remind me every fucking chance he can."

All of that was true.

Mac would handle Anthony another time, and give the asshole the respect he was due for his position and time in *la famiglia*. But at the same time, Mac wasn't a liar, and he wasn't going to pretend to be interested in Anthony's nonsense.

And he was in no mood to play Anthony Corelli's games—not tonight. It was his wedding, and that was far more important than any stupid shit Anthony wanted to talk about with Mac.

Melina was more important.

This whole day was *far more* important.

"Could I interrupt?"

Mac felt Melina's lips curve into a gentle smile at the sound of his mother's voice. She had tapped Melina's shoulder, stopping their dance.

Melina stepped away from him, and he immediately wanted to bring her closer, but his mother looked far too happy for him to refuse the hand she was holding out. He took Cynthia's hand in hers, giving Melina a wink over his mother's shoulder.

"Don't go too far," he told her, "we're not finished, doll, we've got a long night yet."

Cynthia laughed, but Mac couldn't find it in himself to be embarrassed that his mother had heard the underlying promise in his words to his wife. Why should he be embarrassed?

The sweetest pink flushed Melina's cheeks, however, and as much as she tried to give him a stern look, she failed.

"Where's she going to go?" Victoria said, sliding in beside Melina. "She needs to have a family dance, too. And that's why I'm here. Melina?"

The song changed, keeping that slow tempo.

Spotlights from up above came on, lighting the dancefloor with a giant circle, and drawing in the attention of the guests to the four people dancing in the middle.

Mac with his mother.

Melina with Victoria.

Cynthia's hand brushed Mac's shoulder, like she was wiping away invisible dirt. "I didn't get the chance to tell you earlier, but you look very handsome."

Mac grinned. "Don't I always look that way, Ma?"

"That arrogance of yours is going to get you into trouble someday."

Probably not.

Mac didn't tell his mother that, though.

"And Melina looks beautiful," his mother continued.

"She does," he agreed, giving his wife a look.

And she did.

Everything about her—every inch of Melina—screamed beauty, grace, sex, and *his*.

Entirely his.

Mac focused his attention on his mother for the moment, knowing the end of the night would come soon enough, and he would have the next week on a white-sand beach to show his wife just how beautiful he thought she was.

Cynthia watched Mac with a soft smile and even gentler eyes. The very tips of her fingers patted his cheek in that way she used to do to him when he was child and had done something sweet that made her happy.

"What, Ma?" he asked quietly.

"I did something right—in my life, with you and Victoria, I did something right, James."

Mac almost stumbled in his steps, surprised at his mother's confession. "What would make you think any differently, Ma?"

Cynthia patted his back, almost like she wanted to wave away his words or soothe his concerns. "Maybe for a long while, I had assumed somehow that I failed. I wasn't a good enough wife—not good enough to keep your father home, or away from a bottle, or even to keep him from pissing his life away."

"None of that was your fault. He chose those things, not you. Your worth is not determined by his mistakes, Ma."

"It was for a long time," she replied softly. "And then I had to worry about you and your sister, too. I thought I was failing you two. You had no real father, we struggled all the time, and where could we possibly go?"

"Ma." Mac stopped their dance, wanting his mother to look at him instead of focusing on the wall behind him or the tapestries that had been hung for the wedding reception. "You were—*are*—the best mother. You survived, and that's not failing, Ma."

She nodded. "But do you know how long it took me to figure that out, James?"

"How long?"

His mother patted his cheek again, teary-eyed and smiling. "This moment. I was going to tell you to treat your wife well, and to love her like she deserves."

"I wouldn't dream of doing anything different, Ma."

"Exactly. I did something right, and that is not failing."

Because she had taught him those things. How to love, how to care, protect, and cherish.

Cynthia Maccari had done that.

Not anyone else.

His mother.

Mac smirked up at Melina from his spot kneeling at her feet. "I don't know, doll, this dress is pretty damn tight. It's going to be—"

"I swear to God, if you flash my lingerie to these people, Mac …"

His grin only deepened. "You'll what?"

Melina pressed her lips together in a shitty attempt to hide her laughter. "You are terrible—wicked terrible."

"Yes, but you married me, sweetheart."

"Damn lucky I did. Nobody else would put up with your arrogant ass."

Mac smiled wide. "But you get to."

Melina didn't even bother denying it that time. "Hurry up."

"Yes, hurry!" someone shouted from the crowd.

Mac flashed his teeth at his wife, his hands flipping up the bottom of her skirt just enough to show off a bit of her smooth, dark caramel legs. His wife shot him a warning look, her brow cocked high.

He just chuckled as his hands traveled up her calves, under layers of lace and tulle. With one last wink at Melina, Mac dipped his head down, and flipped the skirt of her dress over his shoulders. Her giggles rocked them both, and the chair she was sitting on.

This one tradition had been something Melina hadn't wanted to do at first. She didn't mind throwing the bouquet for all the single ladies, but she had not wanted Mac to go searching for her garter in front of a large crowd, only to emerge from between her thighs with it stuck between his teeth.

But ... tradition was tradition.

And fucking right, Mac wanted to do this one.

Melina conceded.

He tickled Melina's thighs with the tips of his fingers, and kissed the insides of her knees, letting his tongue slide along her sweet tasting flesh. No one had to know what he was doing, after all. It wasn't like they could see him.

Still, Melina knew.

She could feel it.

Mac figured that was all that mattered.

Her giggles increased the higher he moved, until he found that stretchy scrap of lace and satin around her mid-thigh. He nipped onto the fabric and tugged, letting it snap against her thigh before biting onto it again.

Even being under her heavy skirt, and the sounds of the people being muffled, he could still hear the raucous laughter and cheers.

"Oh, my God," Melina said through bouts of laughter.

Mac pulled the garter down and emerged from his wife's skirts with a wink and the item between his teeth. Tugging it from his mouth, he put one end of the garter around his index finger, and pulled the other end hard before letting it fling into a group of waiting men.

Never once had he taken his eyes off his wife.

He never even saw who caught it before he was leaning down to press a kiss to Melina's smiling lips.

"Did you have to make such a show of it?"

"Goddamn right," Mac replied.

"Terrible," she repeated.

"You picked me."

Giving his wife another lingering kiss, Mac then helped Melina up from the chair. But while he should have been focusing on her for the moment, his attention was on something else.

Or rather, someone else.

In the far corner of the ballroom, he watched a confusing scene unfold. No one else seemed to take notice of Luca Pivetti and his two closest men standing nearly toe to toe with one another.

Matthew, Enzo, and Luca all looked ready to throw a fist or two.

Mac was shocked—the men were, for all purposes, best friends.

He had rarely seen them publically disagree.

Luca waved a hand, like he was shooing away dirt.

Enzo's posture softened.

Matthew, on the other hand, nodded, his face a mask of bitterness. Then, just as fast, he was walking away. Enzo moved toward Luca, but the boss lifted his hand again, keeping his other man away.

And just like that ... it was over.

No one had seen a thing.

But Mac had.

What was happening?

The night was finally over and Mac couldn't be more grateful for that fact. No one had thought to tell him that weddings were fucking exhausting. A person never stopped moving, or eating … or *something*.

Add in the fact it was a *famiglia* wedding and the night had just seemed to go on and on with no real end in sight.

Just when Mac thought he would be able to pull himself or his wife away from the crowd for long enough to announce they were going to depart for the airport, someone else would approach them, smiles on their faces, congratulations on their tongues, and gifts in their hands.

That gifts were almost always money.

Envelopes of money, actually.

Bobby had been good enough to keep hold of the *gifts* for Mac.

Luca had even jokingly said it would be the only money Mac made in his life that he wouldn't owe tribute on.

It was a lot of money.

Too much money, maybe, but that was a mafia wedding. Their whole wedding had been the perfect example of what wealth could and would do for a person. No matter how many times Melina and Mac asked for the planning not to go overboard, it still somehow managed to do just that.

But he was grateful all the same.

He'd been able to give Melina her one day to show off the queen she truly was.

It wasn't a day they would soon forget.

"My feet hurt," Melina said in his ear.

Mac chuckled, and kissed her temple. "Almost to the car, doll."

Hopefully, she would sleep their plane trip to

84

Barbados away. A white, sandy beach and private residence was just a few hours away.

After the crazy day and night they had, he couldn't wait.

"Did you say goodbye to your mother?"

"Fifteen times," he said, shaking his head.

And everyone else, too.

"Is my bag—"

"Stop worrying, Melina," Mac interrupted, still keeping her close as they strolled through the throng of people who had come to the front of the Pivetti Mansion to see them off. "Everything is taken care of. Victoria made sure your bags were in the car, and you have an outfit to change into. This is now relax time—so *relax*, doll."

She did.

A little.

The guests finally quieted as they reached the Challenger. Mac was just pulling the passenger door open to let his wife slide in the car when the silence was shattered by loud pops coming from the shadows the mansion created near the side of the house.

Where the walkways were ...

Where the dogs were ...

Melina's hand on Mac's wrist tightened, her fingernails digging right through his suit jacket like she was going to keep him right where he was no matter what.

The people began to scatter back into the mansion when more gunshots rang out, and the shouts from the guests almost drowned the pops out.

Almost.

That sound was far too distinguishable to ignore.

While a lot of people went toward safety, others didn't. Capos, the boss, and a large group of Luca's security bolted toward the back of the Pivetti property.

Snarling and vicious barking filled the air.

Mac got Melina into the car, despite her protests and

85

clinging and still refusing to let him go. Once he had the door closed, he turned fast on his heel, searching for his friend in the moving crowd.

"Bobby!"

"Right here, Mac," his friend said, pushing through the wall of people moving toward the mansion.

"What is happening?"

Bobby shrugged, and while he seemed cool and unruffled, fear still colored up his gaze.

Because that was what the sound of gunshots did.

It brought fear.

Even when a man was told to ignore it.

He never really could.

"I don't know what—"

Bobby's words cut off as a group of men rounded the side of the mansion.

Luca headed them all—hands outstretched.

"He was on the path," he heard Luca said. "They didn't attack—he was on the path!"

Mac heard his boss's words, but his gaze was stuck on something else. Despite the shadows, he could plainly see the red coating Luca's hands.

Blood.

But who did it belong to?

Police stations were cold as fuck.

It was even worse when the first thing the cops did when pulling the guests to the wedding into the station was separate them all as much as they possibly could.

Mac watched his wife be shuffled away with his mother, sister, and a few other men and women that weren't entirely affiliated with the Pivetti Cosa Nostra.

So was the way with the pigs, he knew.

They were far more likely to separate the people they thought were the weakest in the bunch first—the ones they assumed would talk.

No one was going to talk.

Nobody fucking knew anything.

Mac certainly didn't.

Scrubbing a hand down his face, Mac passed the clock on the wall a look, checking the time. Frustration thickened his blood as he realized they had missed their flight for Barbados by an hour.

And that just pissed him off.

No woman wanted to spend her wedding night in a fucking police station.

Despite his anger, Mac couldn't ignore the anxiety simmering through his nervous system. He didn't have a clue where his wife was, and while he knew that Melina was more than capable of handling a police detective's questioning, he still didn't like the idea of it.

Simply because she was his wife—nothing more, nothing less—she would be treated like a criminal.

He also wondered where the hell his mother was, and his sister.

Or why the hell he'd been shoved into a room the size of a goddamn sardine can.

Mac briefly considered why his lawyer hadn't been called as well, but given he wasn't under arrest, there was no need for the man to make his way down town to the station in the middle of the night. Because even when the man wasn't doing actual work for Mac, he just had to be *thinking* of doing some kind of work, and he was charging by the damn hour.

Giving the time another glance, Mac's back straightened in the hard, metal chair as the interrogation room's door flew open. A detective strolled in, and Mac looked toward the mirrored window on the left wall.

"Is your partner going to sit this one out to learn, or what?" Mac asked.

Cops didn't work alone.

They always had partners.

The plain clothed detective barely passed Mac a look, and he didn't react all that much to his attitude, either. He wouldn't usually be so nasty to the police unless they'd provoked him.

He kind of figured dragging him away from his honeymoon was sort of like provoking.

"Where's my wife?" Mac asked when the man took a seat.

"In a sec," the detective replied, glancing through a folder.

He had his arm placed just so on the table that Mac couldn't even get the slightest glimpse at what had the detective's attention otherwise occupied.

Mac's irritation jumped a notch when another two minutes passed by without the detective even looking at him. "If you have no questions for me, asshole, I'm going to find my wife and get the fu—"

"In a minute."

The detective's blasé attitude rankled Mac's hackles. Something was going on here …

He just didn't know what in the hell it was.

"What can you tell me about … Luca Pivetti?" the detective asked, finally glancing up from the folder and staring Mac right in his eyes.

"Nothing."

The detective smirked. "Just like any good made man."

Mac didn't bite onto that chain. "It's my wedding night—so if you don't mind, get the fuck on with whatever it is, or let me get on with my evening. There is no doubt in my mind that you are well aware I was walking my wife to the car when whatever happened, happened."

The detective still didn't blink. "What about Matthew Corvi?"

Hesitance stabbed in Mac's spine, but he answered

carefully, as was the way of any made man. "If you're talking about Luca's lawyer, that's all I've got to tell about him. He's a close friend to the boss."

A scoff answered that back. "Right—*close*."

"I don't have much else to say."

"Not even about this?"

The detective tossed out the folder, and pictures spread across the table between them.

Bloody pictures.

Pictures that showcased *violence*.

The man was nearly unrecognizable.

But not entirely.

Matthew's face look like it had been blown apart all across one of Luca's walkways.

"Do you happen to know why this may have happened?" the detective asked.

Mac's gaze flew down to the grotesque shape of Matthew's mouth, as if he had opened it to shout for help … or something.

But even as he stared at the picture, Mac's thoughts flew back to the scene he'd witnessed earlier that night between Luca and his two men.

"Well?" the detective asked again.

"No," Mac said, "I don't know a fucking thing. Now, where is my wife?"

CHAPTER SEVEN

The room was colder than an icebox and Melina was well aware that it was intentional.

Sitting at the gray table with arms folded, she leaned back in her chair, waiting for the interrogation that she knew was sure to come.

None of this was new to her.

Still, she wondered what the hell was going on.

One minute, she and Mac had finally been ready to leave their wedding reception and the next, all hell had broken loose. Now she was alone and waiting.

At the mercy of pigs once again.

Her gaze flicked to the clock on the wall, the loud tick-tock once again drawing her ire. Another fifteen minutes had passed.

Fifteen minutes, she should have been in Barbados.

Fifteen minutes, of sticking her toes in the sandy beaches.

Fifteen minutes, of making love to her husband.

Her husband.

She had no idea where Mac was.

Once the police had descended on the Pivetti mansion, they'd quickly separated the men and women. For a short time, Melina, Cynthia and Victoria had been together and then she'd been taken away from them.

Isolated.

Alone.

Prime for manipulation.

Too bad for the pigs, Melina had no intention of being manipulated.

"Ah, the blushing bride."

Melina cut her eyes toward the door as two men entered the room and closed the door behind them. One of the men held a manila folder in his hand. Melina watched the men warily as they came toward the table where she sat.

"You'll have to excuse my partner, he's new. I'm Detective Peterson."

Melina said nothing.

Detective Peterson carefully put the manila folder on the table close enough that Melina could reach it if she wanted to.

She didn't.

"Just married, huh? I'm sure the police station is not where you wanted to spend your first night as a married woman," the younger detective said.

"You think?"

"Well, Mrs. Maccari, we don't want to inconvenience you any longer than necessary but we need some information."

Melina leaned forward and placed both hands on the table. "I have nothing to say."

"Melina, Melina, I thought we were going to make this smooth and easy. You help me, I help you."

"I guess you didn't hear me the first time. I have nothing to say and if you're not going to charge me with something, then you need to let me out of here."

"All right. John, show her the pictures," Detective Peterson instructed the younger man.

Nodding, the man opened the manila folder and placed a sequence of photographs in front of Melina.

"I think you might want to reconsider," he said to her.

Rolling her eyes at the detectives, Melina reluctantly looked at the pictures in front of her. She recognized the man immediately.

Or rather, what was left of him.

Matthew Corvi, consigliere to Luca Pivetti.

The man's face looked as if it had nearly been blown to pieces.

Melina shook her head as she quickly glanced at the rest of the pictures. When she was done, she leaned back in her chair.

"Can I go now?" she asked.

Detective Peterson's face turned a mottled red. "A man has been murdered and you're going to sit here like you don't give a damn?"

"See no evil. Hear no evil. Speak no evil."

Melina smiled at the men and both of them looked at each other, seemingly at a loss as to what strategy to try next.

"I'm taking my wife home. Now."

Melina rose from her seat when she saw her husband standing in the doorway. His eyes were cold and she could see the familiar tic moving in his jaw.

He was pissed, and royally.

"We're not done," Detective Peterson said.

"Yes, you are and if you attempt to keep my wife here any longer under false pretenses, this department will be hit with the biggest harassment suit you've ever seen and both you pricks will be lucky if you can find jobs picking up trash on the streets," Mac said.

Melina smirked. "Gentlemen."

She walked over to her husband and took his arm and together they left the interrogation room. Mac was quiet as she walked with him through the police station.

"I didn't say anything," she whispered.

Mac gave her a look. "Trust me, that was not one of my worries. You know how to handle yourself."

"I just wanted to be sure you knew that. Where are

your mom and Victoria?"

"They were released a half hour ago. They've already been taken home."

"Mac, what the hell is going on?"

"I wish I knew."

Together they exited the police station and Mac ushered her toward a black Bentley. Mac opened the back passenger side door and helped Melina inside. Once she was settled, she slid over to make room for him. When he didn't join her, she frowned.

"Mac?"

"Stefan is going to make sure you get home safely. I'll be along as soon as I can."

"Okay. I'll see you when you get home."

Melina smiled but she knew it didn't quite reach her eyes.

"I'm sorry, doll. I'll make it up to you. I promise."

She nodded and then Mac closed the door. A few seconds later, the car was moving away from the police station and her husband. Melina sighed. She knew that being married to a made man wasn't going to be a walk in the park, but she never expected to be spending their wedding night being chauffeured home … alone.

Melina sat in the middle of the king-sized bed, eating a bowl of cookies 'n' cream ice cream drenched in chocolate syrup. It was nearing midnight and Mac still hadn't arrived home. She still couldn't believe that someone had actually been bold enough to murder Luca Pivetti's right-hand man at her wedding reception.

What had started out as the happiest day of her life had turned into an evening of bloodshed and chaos. Melina wished she could get her hands on the son of a bitch who was responsible for murdering Matthew Corvi and putting her honeymoon plans with Mac on an indefinite hold. And what about Matthew's family? Melina was sure the man had a wife and children. Their lives would never be the same and her heart ached for them.

Finishing up the bowl of ice cream a few minutes later, Melina left the bedroom and headed toward the kitchen to wash the bowl and put it away. When she was done, she headed down the hallway that lead to the small office Mac kept. Turning on the lights, she looked in the room and noticed that it was impeccably organized, except for the array of papers scattered across the small desk. Curious, Melina walked into the room and picked up the papers. Her eyes scanned over the contents.

"Interesting."

Apparently, Mac's new position hadn't just come with a new title, it had come with some properties as well. A few warehouses, and a dry cleaner's, among other things. But it was the last paper she held that caught her attention. It was a deed from Luca Pivetti to Mac for a place called The Playpen.

It was a whorehouse.

Melina didn't need it spelled out for her. Some things you just knew.

A whorehouse previously owned by Mac's former Capo, Guido, that was apparently hemorrhaging money.

Interested now, Melina took a seat at the desk and poured over all the details relating to The Playpen. It wasn't long before ideas started to quickly form in her head. Reaching for a blank sheet of paper, she furiously wrote, lost in her thoughts.

"Well, this isn't how I expected to find my bride on our wedding night."

Melina jumped at the sound of Mac's voice. Turning around she smiled at him as he leaned against the door way.

"I didn't hear you come in."

"I noticed. What has you so engrossed that you're here in my office and not waiting for me in bed?"

Melina glanced at the clock before she answered. "Well, considering it's after one in the morning and you're just now coming home, I think I should be the one asking the questions."

"Is that so?" Mac asked.

Entering the office, he placed both hands on the arms of the chair effectively trapping her.

"Yes," Melina whispered.

Her pulse raced and she could feel a familiar ache start to build.

"Hmm. Looks like I need to do something to change your mind, then."

"I'm not easily moved," Melina said.

Mac raised a brow. "We'll see about that."

Before Melina could read his intentions, Mac was lifting her out of her chair, pushing the papers off the desk and laying her on the flat surface. Her breath quickened as he reached for her gown. There was a hunger in his eyes that excited her. Leaning over her, Mac kissed her slowly as if he had all the time in the world. Heat started to build in her belly as he kissed her. Melina tried to wrap her arms around his neck, but he deftly evaded her grasp, chuckling.

Pulling away, Mac reached for the hem of the black, silk spaghetti-strapped nightgown she wore and eased it up her thighs. The pads of his fingers ghosted over her skin, touching just enough to make her want more. Mac watched her with darkened eyes as he inched the gown up further and further. When the gown eased past her hip bone, Mac groaned.

"Fuck."

"Guess I was waiting for you after all," she whispered.

Mac parted her thighs and rubbed her clit slowly. "Thank God you were."

He eased a finger inside her as he continued working

her clit. Her thighs opened wider as Mac stroked her. The flames of desire continued to build as his strong, nimble fingers touched every aching part inside of her.

"*Mac.*"

"Shh," he whispered.

And then he lowered his head and replaced his thumb with his tongue. Melina arched off the desk, pressing herself eagerly against his torturing mouth. He licked her clit slowly with the tip of his tongue before sucking softly on the sensitive bundle of nerves. Every touch made her desire burn for him hotter and hotter. When he scraped his teeth over her clit, Melina came hard and fast. Her fingers tangled in his hair, holding him to her as the orgasm rocked her body.

"Oh my God."

Melina's arms fell limply to her side as her husband stood to his full height and gave her one of his trademark grins.

"God had nothing to do with it, doll."

Mac easily maneuvered Melina so that she was sitting on the edge of the desk.

"You're incorrigible, you know that?" she said.

He nodded. "Yeah, but that's one of the reasons you love me."

"Is it? I didn't know being a smart ass was on the list of loveable qualities," Melina teased.

Mac laughed. "And the pot calls the kettle black. Wife, what am I going to do with you?"

Melina looked into Mac's eyes, beautiful hazel pools. She would never get tired of looking at him, of appreciating his masculine beauty. Emotion lodged deep in her throat.

"Love me."

Mac cupped her face gently. "Always."

He kissed her lips softly before he pulled away. Melina's eyes traveled to the telling bulge in her husband's pants and she rubbed him softly.

"How about me returning the favor?" She licked her lips.

"We have plenty of time for that and other delights, but first I want to apologize."

"For what?"

"For us missing our honeymoon."

"Mac, you had nothing to do with that. It's not like you could have predicted someone would commit murder at our wedding reception or that we'd all be dragged down to the police station."

"I know, but you and I should be in Barbados. You, running across the sand in a string-bikini or dripping wet from the water as we fuck on a beach. I wanted all that for you, Melina."

"We have a whole lifetime for that," she assured him.

"You're being very understanding."

"Isn't that what a good wife is supposed to do? Besides, I knew that when I married you our life together was going to be unpredictable."

"Tonight was more unpredictable than anything I could've imagined."

"You'll get no disagreements from me about that one."

Mac ran his hands from her shoulders down the length of her arms. "You're not going to ask me anything?"

Melina shook her head. "No. If there's something you can tell me or you want to tell me, you will."

Mac's eyes narrowed briefly. "No one was expecting this and we have no idea who would be bold enough to kill the consigliere of a boss of Luca's status."

Melina was quiet for a minute before she spoke. "Someone with nothing left to lose or someone with a potential for gain. I'd start there."

"Perceptive and beautiful. You never cease to amaze me, doll."

"I'm glad you appreciate it. Now there is something I

would like to talk about."

"Well, before we get too engrossed in conversation, let's go to the bedroom. I have a feeling I'm going to need to be lying down for what you have to say."

Melina rolled her eyes. "Whatever."

Hopping off the desk, she pulled her gown back down and prepared to exit the room. Before she could take a step, Mac scooped her up in his arms and departed the room.

"What do you think you're doing?" Melina asked.

"Carrying my bride across the threshold, of course."

"Your bride can walk just fine you know," Melina said.

"I'm well aware that my bride can do just about anything, so why not indulge me this once?"

Melina pressed her lips together as Mac carried her into the bedroom and deposited her gently on the king-sized bed before flopping down beside her.

"That was super graceful."

"Your husband is tired, doll. Adrenaline doesn't last forever."

"I know."

Melina grew quiet. Lying on his back, Mac reached for one of her hands.

"Talk to me. What's on your mind?"

Melina pushed a lock of hair from her face. "I know this isn't the best time to bring this up, but I want to have a job. I need something to do all day when you're away from home."

"Melina, you don't have to work."

"I know, but I'm not like the wives of the men you're constantly around. I need something to do every day, other than spend your money and be a pretty little housewife who has your supper on the table when you get home."

Mac cleared his throat. "If you were to get a job, it might look to some as if I couldn't provide for you. It wouldn't be a good thing."

Melina frowned. "Mac, I'm not interested in the appearances foolishness that others care so much about. I can't just sit at home. I'm used to making my own money."

Mac sat up. "What about college? Isn't there something you would like to study?"

Melina pulled her hand away from him and folded her arms. "I'm not interested in wasting money on a bunch of useless classes for a degree that isn't even worth the paper it's printed on."

"So no to higher education. All right, throw me a line, doll. I'm drowning."

"I want you to give me The Playpen."

Mac scowled. "How do you even know about that place?"

"I saw the pile of papers on your desk and I looked through them. I know the place is bleeding money, but I'm sure that I can make it a profitable venture for you."

"The Playpen is a whorehouse and not a very nice one at that. Frankly, only the lowest of the low tend to frequent it."

"And that explains why it's not making a profit. But I can turn it around. I have a vision for it."

Mac rubbed a hand over his face. "It's our first night as a married couple and instead of begging me to fuck you until you can't see straight, you're trying to convince me to let you run a whorehouse. You're truly one a kind, doll."

"If you didn't want a challenge, you would've married someone else," Melina said.

She leaned close and ran her tongue along the shell of Mac's ear. He sat up straighter and reached for her, drawing her into his arms so that she was straddling his lap.

"Since you're determined to not play fair, tell me your vision."

"For starters, a name change. The Playpen just screams sleazy. I think the place would have a lot more potential as something with an underground feel to it.

Remember the old-time Speak Easies that were popular in their era?"

"Yeah. It was a place men would go to hang out, gamble, have a few cigars and maybe enjoy the company of a certain female," Mac said.

"Exactly. It was classy and sophisticated, but at the same time it appealed to a man's basic nature, catering to all his vices. That's the vision I have."

Mac was silent for a moment and Melina watched him, biting her lip and wondering what her husband would say to her proposal. After a few minutes, he finally spoke.

"I think you might be on to something."

Melina smiled. "See. And here you thought I was just coming up with some crazy scheme."

"I never said that."

"But you implied it."

"If I did, it wasn't my intention. But I do have one question, though. Now, suppose one of your male patrons is interested in the company of a certain woman, and she's not interested in him, what then?"

"No means no. Simple as that."

Mac nodded in agreement. "I really think you're on to something, but I have to tell you I haven't had a chance to check out the property or even see what's really going on now that it's mine."

"That sounds like something we need to rectify as soon as possible then."

"I agree, but right now I have more important things to concern myself with."

Melina raised a brow. "And what might that be?"

"Fucking my beautiful wife."

Turning her so that he could lay her down on the bed, Mac's lips met hers again in a hungry kiss of passion and for the moment nothing else mattered.

Business and subterfuge could wait.

Their desire for one another could not.

CHAPTER EIGHT

Melina pointed at the far wall of the bottom floor and said, "I want the whole length of that wall to be the bar. Custom-made shelves behind it, floor to ceiling. Mirrored glass behind that, too. It'll make the bottles shine and stand out on the shelves. Specialty lighting within the shelves and pot lights will help that along as well."

The man—someone Melina had contacted about renovating and re-designing The Playpen—nodded his head and jotted something down in the notebook attached to the clipboard he held.

"Any specific colors?" the guy asked.

"Black and royal purple," Mac said before his wife could get a word in edgewise.

It was a classic—if not regal—combination.

Melina paused, giving Mac a thoughtful glance as she considered his one request. He'd actually managed to keep quiet as she walked through the place with the contractor, letting Melina do her thing and make her choices without much of his own input. It was intended to be *her* place, after all.

But this ... this he wanted.

"Black leather and crushed velvet," Melina said to Mac.

"*Perfetto*, doll," he replied.

She just smiled and went back to her task. Mac didn't

mind all that much—he didn't have very many requests where The Playpen was concerned.

As it were, he hadn't wanted very much to do with the place at all. But when Luca handed something over to someone—a gift or otherwise—a man couldn't just tell the Don "no" and be done with it.

The place had been, for all purposes, a whorehouse that couldn't keep a steady stream of money coming in. It was seedy-looking with its ripped, stained furniture sporting suspicious marks and spots that Mac had little desire in learning how, or rather *who,* had put them there and which bodily fluids they might actually be. The walls had holes all over, never mind the smell that reeked from the place when the front doors were first opened.

It seemed like no matter where Mac walked in the place, the floor was sticky. And the backrooms and upstairs section with its private rooms and bare, old, and stained mattresses?

Fucking disgusting.

Unfortunately, the women who had worked within The Playpen had been just as rundown and unappealing as the building itself. None had particularly seemed to be forced into the place, but all of them had been working to feed an addiction of some sort, whether it be smoking, shooting, or snorting something into their bodies.

Just a sparse glance at their barely-clothed, unclean bodies with track marks and sunken-in faces had told Mac that story when he visited The Playpen after Luca had handed the deed to the business over.

It seemed that the fool of a man that had been running the joint for Luca was in just as bad of shape—if not worse, than the girls—where addiction was concerned. And he'd certainly had a rampant supply of drugs to use while he should have been doing his job.

Mac figured he might have understood why the place was just pissing out money, instead of turning any kind of decent profit. It was practically impossible to make money in the business of sex and drugs, if a person was too dependent on the business itself to sustain a man's own addiction.

And so, a random visit to The Playpen to see why one of his many businesses that should have been lucrative and profitable was ready to break, Luca decided to wash his hands of the place.

Now, Mac's hands were fucking filthy with it all.

He sighed loudly, glancing at Melina across the floor.

Well, he supposed his wife was the one dirtying her hands with it all, but Mac wasn't quite sure how he could possibly refuse Melina—or if he even wanted to, given her interest in turning the place from a shitty little whorehouse into something that might actually be … goddamn amazing.

Mac certainly couldn't deny that Melina had more knowledge in the business of sex and money than he did. Even though his wife hadn't worked as a prostitute, she still had once had her hand in the trade of escorting. She understood what would draw in the right class of men, who would be willing to spend money. She had access to a number of girls who would certainly be willing to do the job. She was capable of doing it all—so he chose to let her.

There was little doubt in his mind that Melina had come across more than enough men that were willing to cut a check to get whatever they wanted, just like she had probably met a few women who had a price waiting for those same men.

It could work.

Mac passed the dank space another look. His girl could and would do whatever she put her pretty, sharp mind to. He wasn't the least bit concerned about that at all. Melina would likely have the joint looking classy and beautiful while throwing back mentions to a time long past, if her plans were followed through to the letter.

He knew they would be.

No, it wasn't Melina's plans at all that had Mac

BETHANY-KRIS
ERIN ASHLEY TANNER

worried.

Well, not entirely.

Women working in business alongside men never really sat well with Cosa Nostra—never mind made men in general. The Playpen was intended to be a place Mac was expected to pay tribute to the boss from the profits made. That meant the boss, and others, would be watching the business.

There would be no hiding Melina's involvement.

Someone would have an opinion.

They always did.

Mac wasn't sure how he was going to handle all of that backlash when it eventually came his and Melina's way.

Because it *would* come.

That was a given.

He could hear the bullshit that would be spewed already.

No respectable made man …

No respectable wife …

Rules.

Mostly unspoken ones.

Their whole fucking lives were smothered in those fucking rules.

Melina, however, had no time for the mafia's rules or politics, and especially not for their expectations of wives. She hadn't been brought up in Mac's world, having constant demands and constraints thrown at her.

No, his wife had been given an entirely different set of roadblocks to conquer. Ones that certainly weren't any easier than his had been.

So maybe he understood why she would scoff and toss a middle finger up high when told she couldn't do something because *men* wouldn't approve.

Melina was far too independent and stubborn to let any man—regardless of his status in *la famiglia*—tell her what she could or couldn't do.

It was one of the many things he loved about his crazy wife.

And he would not be one of the fools who told his wife no, or God forbid, said she couldn't do something because she was a woman.

Yet, Mac was a little concerned that this whole thing might not be as well-received as Melina wanted it to be. But what could he say?

"It would be cheaper—and easier—option to just go with refurbishing the old bar."

The contractor's statement brought Mac from his thoughts into reality once more. He found his wife staring at the contractor like the guy was the dumbest thing to have ever graced her presence.

And shit, maybe he was.

Not many people made an effort to argue with Melina Morgan—Maccari, now—once they got to know her.

"If I wanted cheap or easy," Melina drawled with a sardonic smile, "I'd have made a run to Ikea. You can either do the job the way I want it done, or I can find another contractor who won't work my nerves at every goddamn turn. Which would you like to go with, huh?"

Wives of made men were expected to be a list of many things.

Quiet mannered.

Polite.

Able to turn cheek when needed.

Respectable at every turn.

Compliant to men …

Melina didn't give an honest shit if she was any of those things.

The contractor passed Mac a look that silently pleaded for any sort of help. Mac simply shrugged and offered nothing in response.

He'd tell this fool the same thing he would tell any made man that had a problem with Melina's plans.

She's not like every other woman.

She's a hellion, through and through.

A good ol' gangster's moll.

And she didn't have to be what *they* wanted her to be. She just had to be his.

"Three months, four at the most, and we'll have the place opened for business," Melina told Mac as they exited the old building.

Wrapping an arm around his wife's side, he drew her in close to his side and kissed her temple. Melina smiled up at him with a softness in her gaze she rarely showed to anyone else, and almost always reserved solely for him.

"I have all the faith you will get The Playpen up and running again in no time at all," Mac said.

Melina made a sound under her breath, the disgust ringing out as clear as day.

"What?" Mac dared to ask.

"That name," she muttered, her nose scrunching up. "It's the first damn thing to go."

"I don't think the name was meant to really hide the kind of business that was going on inside, sweetheart."

Melina smirked. "Well, it certainly succeeded in not doing that. It screams 'whorehouse.' Just saying."

Directing his wife toward her car that was parked just one spot ahead of his Challenger, Mac scanned the neighborhood. It wasn't exactly a shoddy part of town, but it wasn't the high-class kind of place, either. But it was a good location for the kind of club-slash-entertainment that Melina wanted to bring forth.

A discreet location.

Little noise.

No outside markings on the building.

People kept quiet about the goings-on.

The cops weren't necessarily frequent in the area.

Not that Melina particularly cared for the police, or Mac, for that matter. They had both had more than their fair share of attention from the pigs.

A sudden, gentle tug on Mac's sleeve brought his attention back to his wife. Melina frowned at his raised brow.

"Where did you go?" she asked. "Am I boring you that much?"

Mac only laughed before kissing Melina's pouting lips with enough force to make her grin grow and a sigh echo.

"You could never ever bore me, doll," he told her, winking. "You are far too entertaining for that."

Melina didn't look like she believed him. "Well, I must be. You just dazed off while you were staring across the street."

"Melina, you always have all of my attention, even if it seems like you don't. You already know this, *donna*."

Melina pursed her lips. "I do, but—"

Mac caught his wife under her chin with his forefinger and thumb, quieting her rebuttal instantly as he tipped her head up to make her look him in the eyes. "Always, hmm?"

"What were you thinking about that could have possibly been related to me, then?"

He waved a hand high, gesturing around them. "I was thinking you couldn't get this place in a better location than it is for what you want to do."

Melina's smile bloomed instantly. "You think, Mac?"

Mac held his wife a little tighter. For all Melina's strengths and stubbornness, there was still a small part of her that was like any other human being, craving approval, even if she only wanted it from him.

He was more than happy to give it to her.

"I know, doll," he murmured.

She stared back to the building, her happiness quickly replaced by a look of consideration. "About that name, though …"

"I am all ears."

Mac was sure Melina already had something in mind for the place, and if she had thought about it, she probably had already decided.

"What about The Dollhouse?"

Melina turned to look at Mac, likely gaging his expression for any signs of disapproval on her pick, though he was sure his face betrayed nothing about how he was feeling.

On purpose.

His wife began to fidget the longer he stayed quiet.

"I know it's sort of similar to the original name," Melina started to say, "but it's different *enough*. And it's got a bit more class to go along with the old world feel we're trying to go for."

When she finally stopped rambling, Mac pulled his wife in close, letting her wrap her arms around his middle as he stared down at her.

"And is that the only reason?" he asked.

Melina flashed her white teeth in a sinful smile. "Not the *only* one."

"Do tell, wife."

"Maybe it's a little for me and you, too."

Mac cupped Melina's jaw in his palms and tilted her head back. "A little, *doll?*"

"A lot," she whispered.

Yeah.

That was what he thought.

Uncaring of the cars passing them by or the few strangers watching, Mac kissed his wife hard and deep, his tongue snaking into the sweet heat of her mouth the very second she parted her soft lips to war with hers. They stayed like that, connected together, for a good while … until Melina finally pulled away with a shake of her head.

"I have to stop you now, or you'll have me naked in the car before I know it," she told him, a hint of chiding in her tone.

Mac chuckled. She was right. "You know you would damn well love every second of it, too."

Melina didn't even bother to try and deny his statement.

He was glad his wife enjoyed sex, considering he had one hell of an appetite where she was concerned. He couldn't seem to get enough of Melina. The more he had her—the more she gave to him—the more he wanted from her, and *of* her.

Like a fucking drug being shot straight into his veins.

Now, if only he could get his wife on board with stopping her birth control.

Another time, Mac told himself.

Today was not the right day for all of that, not to mention the crazy it might bring when he finally made the request to his wife. But he did want that with Melina— soon, preferably. Two-point-five kids, the white fence, and maybe a dog, too. As long as it didn't bite his ankles or chew his shoes. Hell, he was already working on the white fence thing in a way, although he had yet to tell Melina. He wouldn't, not until he had everything settled and the ink was dry.

As for the babies … well, Mac wasn't the only person in the equation. Melina had to want those sorts of things, too. He knew that she did want them eventually, but probably *not* anytime soon.

Especially not now, with The Dollhouse in the works.

Mac could wait.

For a little while, anyway.

"You have to let me go so I won't miss my spa day with Victoria," Melina said.

Reluctantly, Mac did as she said, releasing her and stepping back. With a wave of his hand at her car, he said, "Go, and get pampered. I like the taste of you after, anyway, all soft and sweet."

Melina laughed. "There's no helping you, is there?"

"Nope."

No shame.

Mac had none where Melina was concerned.

Melina was just sliding into the driver's seat when she called out, "Do you want to do something specific for supper? Or are you even going to be home in time for it?"

"I should be. Or do you want to meet up somewhere?"

"How about I bring something home?"

Mac nodded. "Sounds gr—"

His words were cut off when a familiar jingle sounded from his slack's pocket. The unmistakable ringtone belonged solely to Luca's private number that he used to contact his men. Melina heard it, too, as she glanced down at his pocket from the driver's seat.

"Sorry, doll," he said.

Melina just shrugged—she was getting used to their conversations and time being interrupted by Cosa Nostra, but that didn't mean it was easy. "Give me a call if our plans need to change for tonight, all right?"

"Will do."

Melina mouthed her "I love you" just as Mac answered the call on the second ring. He greeted the Pivetti Don while watching his wife pull out of the parking spot and head back toward the heart of Brooklyn.

"Boss," Mac said, phone to his ear. "What can I do for you today?"

"Mac—Timothy's Diner, thirty minutes."

Shit.

Luca didn't sound very pleased, but then again, it had been less than a week since one of his best friends and right-hand man was killed. That was sure to do some kind of number on even the coldest of men.

Even if they hid it well.

"Sure, boss," Mac replied. "What's happening?"

Tribute was another two weeks away yet, so that wasn't it. Mac hadn't done anything that would warrant him getting in shit or earning him a personal call from Luca to have a chat about it. And as far as the killing thing went, Luca had kept everyone and their fucking mothers at arm's length ever since Matthew was gunned down on the night of Mac's wedding.

Things were strange.

People were talking.

That was never a good sign.

Mac had a feeling that Luca wouldn't let the nonsense go on for long.

The Pivetti Don's next words confirmed Mac's thoughts.

"It's time to talk about Matthew," Luca said, "and what we're going to do about it."

Mac was already heading toward his car before Luca had even finished his sentence.

Mac strolled through the front doors of Timothy's Diner, and walked straight into a shouting match.

As was usual for the small, hole-in-a-wall diner, it was void of patrons that were not in some way connected to the Pivetti Cosa Nostra. So was the way with their businesses and the streets they ran like kings. It was not uncommon for an establishment to become claimed by mob affiliation in some way, shape, or form. Automatically, word would travel to the streets that the joint was not very welcoming to outsiders. Then, made men could safely come and go from those businesses to discuss whatever needed discussed without fear of someone overhearing. The owners of the joints were always well compensated for their … *cooperation.*

Timothy's Diner was just one of many places.

And it was good for business.

"Those fucking savages, likely," one Capo shouted.

Mac checked his watch, noting that no, he wasn't late for the meeting. He'd made it in lots of time, just as Luca demanded during his short phone call. Tardiness was not in any way acceptable to the Don.

But even though he clearly wasn't late, the meeting had obviously already started without him. It also seemed like everyone else was already there.

Mac didn't mind.

Taking a seat in the back, he was determined to stay out of the drama as much as he could—God knew Mac had enough problems with a good majority of the Capos attending the meeting.

He wasn't the least bit interested in getting into yet another verbal sparring match with one of the Pivetti Capos. It didn't even seem like it was optional with some of these men. Mac only needed to open his mouth and someone else would be at the ready with an argument, wanting to disagree with him simply because he had an opinion to share.

Mac didn't know if it was because he was the youngest Capo in the family, the way he had come about getting his button, his father's shitty past in *la famiglia*, or the interest the boss had shown in him months ago.

Or hell ... maybe it was a mixture of all four things.

Who fucking knew?

Mac didn't have any desire to poke that bear today. Not with the boss watching, anyway. It wouldn't lead to anywhere good.

Another shout brought Mac back to the conversation at hand. It was a new Capo this time with another opinion to share, apparently.

"The Albanians have been causing us one problem or another for a good decade or more. And those fucking scum don't need a damn reason to come in on any of us. You just have to look at them while driving by and they're ready to kill. Bastards."

Luca sighed heavily, rubbing at his temples with two fingers and looking like he was entirely over the day and the men surrounding him. Through his fingers, he glared at the man throughout his entire tirade, saying nothing, and not once stopping the man from talking.

That was Mac's first clue that something was wrong with Luca.

That, without a doubt, Luca was close to reaching his limit before he exploded.

By nature, Luca was cold, cool, and calm. But he never tolerated disrespect of any form from his men. Shouting and going on like the men currently were was certainly something Luca would not normally allow to happen.

Yet, there the boss was, doing just that.

It was all a little strange.

"It wasn't the Albanian syndicate," Enzo said quietly from his spot in a corner booth. With a coffee resting on the table in front of him, the underboss never took his attention away from the steaming mug as he spoke. "They have a habit of making a show and claiming a kill. It's been almost a week, and not a single word has come out of their side. Regardless of past issues between our organizations, we can safely assume they were not the people behind the bullets that killed Matthew."

"And therefore, not our target," Luca added firmly.

"But—" the Capo from earlier started to say.

"*Not* our target."

"What about the Russians?" Anthony—a Capo that regularly tested Mac's patience and good nature—asked. "We had that scuffle two months ago down in the Coney. They're known for their patience. They like to wait, to make you think all is well again, before they strike and have their revenge. It wouldn't be the first time."

The room grew quiet as the suggestion was considered. Glances and silent questions passed between men, wondering but never speaking out loud.

But while the men were looking between one another for answers, Mac looked to the only man in the room whose voice truly mattered above the rest.

Luca.

The ever-calm, always regal Don seemed tired.

Worn down, maybe.

A darkness lingered in his features.

An emptiness colored his gaze.

Grief, Mac realized suddenly.

Luca was grieving for his friend who had been killed on his very property—a home that Mac would consider to be one of the safest places, with its security.

Except apparently, it wasn't the safest place.

Mac had to wonder—did Luca blame himself?

His thoughts drifted back to the argument he'd witnessed between Luca, Enzo, and Matthew on the night of his wedding. Whatever had caused it couldn't have been good—it had been heated—and Luca rarely, if ever, publicly fought with anyone. Especially if others who were not a part of their lifestyle might be watching.

Mac had, for a short while, his suspicions about Matthew's death and Luca's possible involvement. It wouldn't be unusual for Luca to kill someone, even if that someone was a friend, should they give him a good enough reason. But it hadn't really been Mac's place to say anything or ask questions. No made man demanded answers from their boss. That was not the way things worked in Cosa Nostra.

So, yeah, Mac had wondered.

Who wouldn't after what he'd witnessed?

Still, as he watched a look of sadness pass between Luca and Enzo, a look that was missed by the other men, Mac wasn't so sure Luca had done something to Matthew.

But of course, if there was anything Mac had learned in this life, it was to trust no one.

Grief was not just subjective to loss.

For some men, it was also a reflection of regret and

guilt.

"The Russians …" Luca trailed off as all eyes turned to him again, conversation ceasing. "That's unlikely as well."

No murmurs passed between the men that time. No one questioned Luca's statement at all.

"If not another syndicate," Anthony said, "then the only plausible explanation is rather simple, isn't it, boss?"

Luca didn't respond.

But he really didn't have to, Mac believed.

The boss's silence was answer enough.

Enough to make them all question.

To allow them to wonder.

… to look between one another and let the suspicion burn.

If not from the outside of their organization, then there was only one other possible explanation.

It must have come from the *inside*.

That probably concerned Mac the most.

Suspicion bred fear.

Fear would breed contempt.

Contempt was known to breed unrest.

Unrest meant a lack of stability.

The strongest of organizations could and would crumble under that sort of mistrust.

And Mac knew that if *he* had been able to witness the disagreement between Luca, Enzo, and Matthew the night of his wedding … it was possible that more men had seen it, too.

All it would take was a thought turned into a word, and then to a rumor.

It was a dangerous game.

But Mac wasn't sure if Luca knew it was one he was now playing with the men.

Shortly after, the men began to trickle out of the diner once Luca had dismissed them. As Mac stood to leave with the rest, the raising of Luca's hand stopped him.

It was only then that Mac noticed a young man—maybe a couple of years younger than him—sitting in a corner booth with his attention on the window.

Mac did a double-take of the kid.

He looked like ... Luca.

"I have a request to make of you, Mac," Luca said once the diner had cleared.

"I'm open to whatever, boss," Mac replied.

Luca nodded, but his smile was fleeting. He waved at the young man. Mac passed the guy a look, unsure of what Luca wanted from him.

"I want you to take him under your wing and have him work with you for a bit—as an apprentice of sorts," Luca said.

Mac wasn't as ready to agree to that as he had previously said once the order was out in the air. Taking on an apprentice to his Capo position and his crew was a great deal of work and time. Time Mac really didn't have.

"I'm a bit new to my position for that, aren't I?" Mac asked.

Luca shrugged like it didn't make much of a difference to him. "But I asked it of you, and of course, I trust you."

"With what?"

Luca gestured to the quiet young man whose attention was back on the windows like he didn't have a single damn to give about the entire conversation and day. "Enric Pivetti. My son."

Well, then.

Fuck.

CHAPTER NINE

"So, tell me, how's married life treating you?" Victoria asked.

Melina smiled at her sister-in-law as they enjoyed their pedicures. "No complaints."

"You aren't going to get all boring and sappy on me now, are you?"

"Don't get it twisted. Just because I'm married, doesn't mean I'm going to lose my edge."

Victoria smirked. "We'll see. Next thing you know, my brother will have you barefoot and pregnant in the kitchen."

Melina's eyes narrowed as Victoria laughed.

"Sweet sister, you must have forgotten your brother didn't marry a nice little Italian homemaker. I'd have his balls if he tried that shit."

The dark-haired woman doing Melina's pedicure gasped and Victoria laughed harder.

"See. This is one of the reasons I love you, Melina. You're the perfect woman to keep Mac's ass in line."

"Hey, give your brother some credit. He's a remarkable man."

Victoria rolled her eyes. "Okay. Now you do sound all lovesick and sappy."

"Don't be a hater, Victoria. Wedding bells could be ringing for you before you know it."

"No, thank you. I'll pass. Besides, I don't need Ma breathing down my neck for grandbabies. I'm surprised she hasn't said something to you and Mac about it."

Melina admired the opaque, dark-blue color on her toes before she answered.

"We haven't been married that long."

"You've been married long enough to be pregnant by now. Big Italian family, remember?"

"Whatever. Your mom only has two kids."

"That's because it became evident sooner, rather than later, that my father is a piece of shit. Ma wasn't going to bring another child into the world to have to suffer. But Mac is nothing like James."

"Trust me, I'm well aware of just how little Mac and James have in common," Melina said.

"So then you see my point. You and Mac are the future of our family and Ma is ready to see that future."

Melina was quiet as she digested what Victoria had just shared with her.

Cynthia Maccari wanted grandkids.

Preferably, now.

It was a lot to take in.

"Mac and I haven't even discussed children since we've been married. We've just been enjoying each other," Melina confessed.

"Do you want kids?"

Melina swallowed. "Yes, but ..."

"But what?"

"Sometimes I'm afraid of bringing them into a world that is so unpredictable."

"I can understand that, especially with Mac's lifestyle."

"It's not even necessarily that. Life can be a real bitch, all on its own."

"You said a mouthful there, Melina, but don't let that get in the way. Mac would move heaven and earth for any child the two of you had and you'd be a great mother."

"You sure have a lot of faith in my parenting skills. Faith I'm not sure I have."

Victoria tapped Melina on her forearm. "And why is that?"

"I lost my Mom when I was eight and there's so much in life that I was left unprepared for. Motherhood definitely fits in that arena."

"Melina, I'm sure that everything will come to you whenever the time comes. Now, no more excuses. I'll give you and my brother a little more time and then I'm going to be looking for a niece or nephew that I can spoil."

"Oh, Lord. More pressure."

Victoria's phone rang and she answered it, leaving Melina to her thoughts as she waited for her toenail polish to finish drying.

A baby.

She wondered if Cynthia had said something to Mac about it and if he'd just chosen not to share it with Melina.

She wasn't naïve.

Mac was a man.

A made man.

He'd want a son to carry on his name.

To continue restoring dignity to the Maccari name that James had nearly sullied beyond repair.

Mac would want daughters too.

Little princesses that he could spoil.

And there was no doubt in Melina's mind that Mac would be an amazing father, devoted and loving.

But now wasn't the time.

Not with everything that was going on.

It wouldn't be fair to bring a child into the world, in the midst of uncertainty.

But still, Melina couldn't stop herself from smiling as she imagined the pitter-patter of little feet running around. Resolving to speak with her husband about the expansion of their family at a later time, Melina carefully put her shoes back on and paid for the services she and Victoria had received. After hugging and promising to meet up again soon, Melina left the spa and headed toward the lot where she'd parked her car.

"Well, if it isn't my beautiful daughter-in-law."

Melina stopped walking and turned. To her right was James Maccari Sr., watching her with a smirk on his face.

"Mr. Maccari."

He shook his head as he walked closer to her. "None of that. Call me James. After all, we're family."

His eyes roved over her in the most inappropriate of ways.

Melina itched to slap the hell out of him.

"I don't think my husband would see things that way."

James shrugged. "My son always was a bit of a hot head, but sometimes he gets things right. Like marrying you."

Melina raised a brow. "Is that so? I had the distinct impression you didn't find me worthy of your son."

"Maybe I did, but then I didn't think he could handle a woman like you."

The double entendre to his words was not lost on Melina.

Mac wasn't man enough to satisfy her.

"A woman like me." Melina folded her arms. "Pray tell what you mean, James."

"You've certainly got a mouth. You're nothing like the woman his mother would've picked for him, that's for sure. I just didn't think my boy would go for something like that."

"Well, let me debase you of your ridiculous notions. Mac doesn't need to handle me, because unlike you and the chauvinistic pigs of your time, my husband sees me as his equal. He values me and most importantly, he respects me. So why don't you take your bullshit to someone that gives a fuck, because I don't."

James frowned and took a step closer to Melina. "Is

that how you talk to your father-in-law? Who the hell do you think you are?"

Melina lifted her hand in front of James' face. "Melina Morgan Maccari. Don't forget it."

And with a tight smile, Melina left James Maccari where he stood.

The man was a creep. Sometimes it was so hard to believe that James could actually be Mac's father. The two men were nothing alike. She hadn't seen James since her wedding day when he'd all but ogled her as she walked down the aisle. He'd done the same today, eyeing her as if he'd like nothing better than to have his way with her.

She didn't like it and she wasn't going to stand for it. Mac was going to have to handle his father. She had enough things to deal with, like renovating The Dollhouse and making sure she didn't do anything that could undermine the position her husband had worked so hard to obtain. James Maccari was one problem that neither of them needed.

Melina hated funerals.

How could you celebrate someone's life, when it had been senselessly lost?

And how could you hope for the future, when you had no idea what could possibly come next?

Melina asked herself those questions as she sat next to Mac in the limousine that would take them to the grave site. The Catholic service for Luca's underboss was ostentatious, to say the least. A silver and platinum casket was the centerpiece of the service and sat directly in front of the altar. The sheer amount of floral arrangements that had filled the church was staggering. Almost as staggering as the number of people that had filed in on this dreary day to pay their last respects.

Leading the way was Luca Pivetti. In the short time she'd known the man, Melina had seen him as a ruthless man in total control. Today, she'd seen him as just another grieving person. Holding Neeya's hand, he'd stood for a long time before his dead friend's closed casket before taking his seat on the front row. His three daughters had accompanied him, looking every inch the proper mafia *principessas*.

Melina hadn't known Matthew Corvi. Hell, she didn't know hardly anyone that Mac worked or did business with. But after hearing the priest eulogize Matthew and watching his widow break down in front of her husband's coffin, Melina understood a few things better than she ever had before.

What a man did for a living didn't define who he was.

Real love was forever.

The world may have seen Matthew Corvi as a criminal, but to the family he left behind, he had been their everything.

With Matthew gone, his wife, Amelia, would be left to raise their three children alone. Melina had been unable to hold back her tears as Matthew's youngest son, Bryce, had touched the casket and cried. It was too much. Beside her, Mac had blinked his eyes in rapid succession, showing that he too was affected by the younger boy's anguish.

The tears of a child could break down any man.

As they neared the cemetery where the underboss would take his final resting place, Melina glanced at her husband. He stared straight ahead, unseeing. She touched his thigh.

"Mac," she whispered.

"Yeah, doll?"

He faced her and for the first time, Melina noticed the faint worry lines under his eyes. The uncertainty was taking a toll on him. She couldn't believe she'd just now realized it.

"How many?" she asked.

"How many, what?"

"How many funerals have you been to?"

"One too many."

"Oh."

The honesty of his answer wasn't unexpected. It was the way he'd said it that struck a nerve in her.

"His children ... my heart just broke for them. Children that young shouldn't have to lose a parent," Melina said.

"No, they shouldn't."

Mac took her hand and held it tight.

"And his wife—it looked as if she'd lost another piece of herself."

"Amelia has a strong support system around her. She won't have to deal with all this alone."

"A support system isn't going to help when you lie awake at night and want your husband. It won't help when you want to hear his voice or feel his touch. Some things a support system just can't help."

"Melina, what aren't you saying?"

She swallowed hard. "I couldn't bear it if anything happened to you. I don't know if I'd be strong enough to handle it."

Mac's eyes grew soft as he pulled her close. His mouth met hers in a kiss that was sweet and tender. She melted into him, wrapping her arms around his neck as they continued to kiss. When he finally pulled away, she rested her forehead against his.

"Nothing in this life is guaranteed, doll, but I promise that I will do everything in my power to make sure that I come home to you always."

Melina smiled. "I'd burn this city to the ground if you didn't."

Mac laughed as he drew away from her. "I'd expect nothing less from you."

"Just so you know."

Mac lifted her hand and held it up. Her wedding ring and engagement band sparkled. "For better or worse. Through thick and thin. We're going to be all right."

Melina nodded, momentarily at a loss for words as the car rolled to a stop. "Yeah, we are," she finally said.

Mac gave her a fleeting smile. "When this is over we'll have a quiet evening at home. I promise."

"Sounds like heaven."

The door was opened by their chauffeur and Mac exited first before turning to help her from the car. It was time to put her brave face back on. She had to put away her secret fears and stand stoically beside her husband once again.

Appearance was everything.

"Mac, where are we going? You know I don't like surprises."

It had been nearly a week since Matthew Corvi's funeral and though Mac was starting to come home before dinner now, things were still tense.

So tense that they still hadn't been able to go on a proper honeymoon.

Melina thought Luca was being a little paranoid by not wanting them to leave the country. But she knew Mac had no choice but to abide by his boss's wishes. She still didn't like it, but she understood the way things had to be. For now.

"It wouldn't be a surprise if I told you."

Mac smiled and patted her knee as he drove the Challenger through the evening traffic.

"That's exactly my point."

"Relax, doll. You trust me, don't you?"

Melina rolled her eyes. "Why would you even ask me

a stupid question like that? Of course I do. I married you, didn't I?"

"Yeah. I seem to remember a lot of begging and pleading on my part."

Melina thumped her husband on the forehead. "I see someone's got jokes today."

"Maybe just a few," Mac said.

He turned off one of the main highways and Melina glanced at their surroundings. She had no idea where they were.

"I don't recognize any of these landmarks."

"I wouldn't expect you to."

She waited for him to say more and when he didn't she sighed.

"Okay. I'll play along, but this had better be an awesome surprise for all the cloak and dagger you have going on."

"I think it's really going to be special to you. At least, that's what I'm hoping for."

Melina smiled at his soft tone. "Anything you do is special, Mac. It's one of the main reasons I married you."

"And what are the others?"

Melina tapped her finger on her chin, mischief already creeping into her mind.

"Your exquisite cock. Oh and you're not bad to look at either."

Mac made a cutting motion across his chest. "You wound me, doll. I haven't heard you mention a word about my stellar personality."

"You know that's hit or miss sometimes."

When Mac glared at her, Melina laughed, before she leaned toward him and kissed his cheek.

"You know I'm just playing. There is so much about you that I'm grateful for, especially your patience."

Mac nodded. "Yeah. Who else could put up with you?"

Melina's mouth dropped as her husband laughed.

"You know what, you're about to make me remind you who is the boss in this relationship."

"Now that promise has some merit, but give me a bit, doll. We're here."

Melina looked around as Mac drove them down an asphalt road. A yellow Dead End sign stood on her right side as they passed. A minute later, they pulled up to a cul-de-sac and Mac killed the ignition.

"Mac?"

"I'll explain in a minute."

Before Melina could say anything, he was out of the car and opening the door for her. Melina stepped out and shut the door, leaning against the car.

"Mac, I don't see anything out here but wide-open space."

He shook his head. "Yes, but it's more than that. This is our future."

"Okay, you lost me."

Taking her hand, Mac led her away from the car and toward the grass in front of them.

"Every king and queen need a castle. This is where we're going to build ours."

Melina was silent as she took a moment to process what Mac was saying to her. This was their homestead. This was the place they were going to build a home.

"This is a new subdivision?" she finally asked.

"No. Everything you see around us is ours. Ten acres of prime real estate."

Melina looked at her husband. "When did you have time? You've been so busy lately."

"A man makes time for what's important."

"Ten acres? What are we going to do with all this space?"

"I want you to have your dream house, doll. Whatever you want."

Melina took Mac's face in her hands. "I don't need all of this to be happy."

"I know you don't and that only makes me want to give it to you even more."

"But Mac, I'm fine with the apartment for now. Besides, your mother needs a new house more than we do."

"Oh, she's getting a surprise of her own. I just haven't sprung it on her yet."

"There's no talking you out of this, is there?"

Mac shook his head. "No. I've worked hard and I'm finally starting to reap some of the benefits. As my wife, you're entitled to all of them. This is our fresh start."

Melina looked away, lest he see the tears that were threatening to fall. Her husband was so considerate and so romantic. As if buying her a Maserati wasn't enough, now he'd purchased what looked to be a small subdivision so she could have the house of her dreams built.

"I must've done something right in another lifetime to end up with such an amazing husband."

Mac's arms circled her waist, bringing her closer to him. "You think so?"

"Yes. If you're like this with me, then I can't imagine how you'll be with ..." Melina trailed off.

"With who, doll?"

"With our children."

A light came on in Mac's eyes. "I ... I hadn't even connected the house to kids. I just wanted to do something to make you happy."

"I know, and I love you for that, but we both know we can't put off that discussion forever."

"Nothing could possibly make me any happier than us having children together. A little girl with your smile, your beautiful skin and eyes ..."

"A son that looks like you would make my heart melt," Melina said.

Mac smiled. "It seems we've both been thinking about it."

"I have. I love you and we're building a life together.

I want children, but there are some things I'd like to do first before we take that step. Is that okay with you?"

Melina knew that she was asking a lot. Mac had damn near spit out rainbows and sparkles as he shared his longing for a daughter that looked like her. Without a doubt, if she gave him the word, they would immediately start trying to conceive a child. But the timing needed to be right.

"If and when we decide to have a child, it will be about us and what we want."

Melina giggled as Mac lifted her off her feet and swung her around. This was all she needed. Happiness wasn't about the things you had. It was about the people you loved. And as Mac put her back on her feet and kissed her, silently Melina vowed she wouldn't deny them what they both wanted much longer.

CHAPTER TEN

"Come on, doll," Mac said, giving Melina's smiling lips one more kiss as he tangled their fingers together. "I have one last surprise for you today."

Melina gave him *that* look. The one that said she was excited but didn't quite know how much more she could take. His wife wasn't overly romantic. Mac knew it could sometimes be hard for her to appreciate that trait in him when it wasn't the type of thing she was accustomed to.

But Mac, on the other hand, lived for Melina's happiness and her smiles. It was even better if they were caused by him.

So, maybe, he didn't care if she was overwhelmed with his gifts, attention, and love. Melina would get used to it, one way or the other.

"What else could you possibly have for me?" Melina asked. "Wasn't this enough?"

Mac shook his head, saying nothing as he guided them toward the trunk of the car. He'd already hit the trunk latch when he parked, though Melina hadn't seemed to notice. He lifted the trunk to showcase the items waiting inside.

A small shovel, four wooden stakes, a roll of neon orange ribbon, and a bottle of champagne.

Melina's brow furrowed at the pile of stuff. "What is all this for?"

"You'll see," Mac answered vaguely, giving her one of his usual smirks.

His favorite part of giving gifts to his wife was the surprises he mixed into them all. They always had Melina's eyes lighting up in a way that made him know she thought he was her king. And damn, he wanted to be that for her.

So much.

Mac grabbed the ribbon and stakes in one hand, and the shovel in his other. Then he nodded at the bottle of champagne and said, "You can handle that, right?"

Melina laughed as she grabbed the bottle and then closed the trunk. She was indulging his little game, he knew, but Mac had a feeling that she was enjoying it, too.

"What now, Mac?"

"Now," Mac said, leading the way to the end of the cul-de-sac before he stepped into the overgrown field, "we mark it off."

Melina still seemed like she didn't understand what Mac was trying to do. "Mark what off?"

"Where we want our house to be, doll."

"Right *now*?"

Mac turned to face his wife, throwing his arms wide in the air. "How about right here?"

"But shouldn't we look at land maps or something?"

"You have ten beautiful, raw acres to do with what you wish, Melina. You can look over the surveys at any time and say whether you want this here or that over there. You want a pond? Let's do that. A pool? Okay. But right now, at this very moment, we're going to mark off the spot where they'll dig for the foundation of our house. And when we're done …"

Melina couldn't stop the smile from spreading. "What then, Mac?"

"Then," he told her, waving the shovel he held, "we're going to stick this shovel in the dirt. We'll be the first to break ground on *our* home. Together."

"And the champagne?"

"Celebration, of course."

Melina nodded. "Of course. Only you."

"It's only proper," Mac joked. "Are you going to help me, or leave me to do this alone?"

Melina didn't keep him waiting for long, thankfully. "If we start here, we'll have no damn driveway. The road will end right at our doorstop, basically."

Mac jogged a good fifty feet further into the field. Turning back to Melina, he yelled, "Here?"

"Could we have a gate, too?"

"Anything you want, doll."

She didn't even have to ask, really.

"There is ..." Melina's words trailed off, her expression softening.

Mac was pretty sure he understood why his usually vocal wife was all of the sudden so quiet. It was probably for the same reason he had been the first time he'd come out to check the plot of land to decide whether or not the price was worth it.

It had been worth every single damn penny he paid.

Mac had seen his home here—the one he would share with his wife; a home they would build to raise their family in—before his very eyes.

And yet, it didn't even exist.

The place was that great.

"What is it?" Mac asked.

Melina stepped off the end of the cul-de-sac and finally joined him in the field. "It's perfect."

Mac let out a breath he hadn't realized he'd been holding in, the relief was sweet. "I had hoped you would say that, doll."

"Did you honestly expect something different? You know me too well, Mac."

Once Melina was in front of Mac, he dropped the items he was still holding so he could grab his wife and bring her closer. "Sometimes you keep me on my toes and make me wonder, Melina. That's all."

Melina winked and then kissed him quickly. "Here is perfect, Mac."

"Yeah?"

"I want our home to dominate the place. It needs to be the first thing someone sees coming up the road."

"Then it will be," Mac promised.

He'd make damn sure of it.

Whatever Melina wanted, she would get.

"Let's break some ground, Mac."

He was already picking up the shovel before she had even finished her sentence.

"Where are we going, James?" Cynthia asked from the passenger seat.

Mac offered a smile in response, the same thing he'd been doing every time his mother asked that question. It earned him yet another one of her sighs and an eye roll. She had never been one for surprises. She liked to plan things and be prepared ahead of time.

Mac supposed he got that from his mother.

But today, well, today, she would have to deal with it.

"I hope this is going to be worth making me miss cooking supper," Cynthia mumbled to herself.

Mac chuckled.

Only his mother.

"Stop fretting, Ma," Mac said. "You'll still get to cook, if you're feeling up to it. Or we could order something—"

"You shut your mouth. That is *blasphemy*. I don't *order in*."

She'd said the words as if they were dirt she was spitting out.

"Sometimes I do," Mac replied.

Cynthia clicked her tongue. "I don't know where I went wrong with you."

"I look at it like you went completely right with me, actually," Mac said, never taking his eyes off the quiet, upscale suburban street. "I can cook for myself, or not if I choose."

"Your wife knows how to cook."

"We're busy a lot, Ma. It's not fair of me to put all of that on her, on top of what she already has, when I am more than capable of feeding myself."

Mac caught his mother's slight smile out of the corner of his eye before Cynthia reached over to pat his cheek lightly. He swore he could feel all of his mother's love and pride in the tender action. Cynthia had never been very vocal about her affections—something Mac had always attributed to her strict upbringing and then her failed marriage—but she never made Mac or his sister feel unloved.

In fact, it was the exact opposite.

Mac knew what love felt like *because* of his mother.

He was damn grateful to have Cynthia.

Cynthia patted his cheek again. "My good son."

Mac laughed, giving his mother a sidelong look. "Good to you, Ma."

"To your *family*," she replied just as fast, "and that's what matters most."

Well, Mac wasn't about to argue with his mother on that point.

Finally, Mac's destination came into view and he pulled the car into a freshly paved driveway of a two-level home with an attached garage. It also sported a large backyard, and a three-foot high, newly painted white-picket fence all around the front of the property to protect the beautifully maintained grass and blooming flower beds.

Flower beds that were filled with newly-planted flowers that were just waiting for a tender pair of hands to care for them.

Hands like his mother's, he knew.

Mac took the home in again as his mother stared curiously at the house, too. It was three times the size of her current home, with a second level on top of that. The pale yellow siding and rich brown shutters gave the place a welcoming feel. There was no leaking roof, no holes in the walls, and no mortgage owing. The cherry hardwood floors it had throughout the halls and rooms were a style his mother had always silently admired in other people's homes.

It was a new home for Cynthia.

It was everything she deserved and more, but Mac was well aware his mother would never ask him for it.

Cynthia had raised her children in a home that was just fine for them. But over the years, his mother had always put her children and their needs first before anything else. And so when her home had begun to fall apart, she never complained, but rather, made due with what she had.

It made her happy.

Now, it was Mac's turn to give back something to his mother and make her happy with more than simply being her good son.

"What is all this?" Cynthia asked. "Who lives here? You should have told me if we were going to be visiting someone, James."

Mac chuckled.

His mother would never change.

Not that he wanted her to.

"Why don't we go see," Mac suggested.

He didn't give his mother a chance to argue. He pushed out of the car and walked the rest of the driveway, right up the steps, and stood in front of the door. A flower pot rested beside a clean, brand-new welcome mat.

Eventually, Cynthia made her way up to join Mac, her purse under her arm. She admired the things she passed, and once she was at his side, looked to him expectantly.

"Are you going to stand there all day, or knock?" she asked.

Mac shrugged. "Go for it, Ma."

Cynthia gave him a displeased look, but reached out to press the decorative doorbell. Mac listened as chimes rang a familiar tune from within the home. He waited a few more moments, knowing damn well the whole time that no one would answer.

His mother didn't know that, however. She pressed the doorbell again, and Mac didn't stop her. When no one answered yet again, Mac looked to his mother.

"No one is home," she said.

"Oh, I guess I forgot to mention that, huh?"

Cynthia's brow furrowed. "Why come to visit if you knew no one would be home?"

Mac pulled out a set of keys from his pocket, and handed them to his mother, even as she tried to refuse them. "Because, Ma, I was coming to visit *you*."

It took Cynthia a good minute or two of staring between Mac's grin and the keys in her hand before an understanding began to dawn on her features. Her eyes watered.

"Welcome home, Ma."

"Oh, Mac."

Mac smiled widely. He was always James to his mother no matter what, so to hear her use his nickname with such affection was more than enough thanks for him.

"Unlock the door," he said. "Let's have a look inside."

Cynthia unlocked the front door with trembling hands as she shook her head at the same time. "You shouldn't have done this. It's too much and—"

"Nothing is too much for you, Ma."

Soon, she had the door wide open and they stepped inside, standing in a large foyer painted the welcoming, warm beige his mother favored. Cynthia didn't stay still for long, dropping her purse and the keys to a side table and waiting glass bowl. She was off with a smile, exploring and chattering, even as Mac kept a few feet of distance behind her to let her enjoy her new home.

Her favorite spot?

The kitchen, of course.

And that's where Mac found himself, watching his beaming mother dig through the cupboards for mugs as a kettle whistled on the stainless steel, flattop stove.

"Well?" Mac asked. "Do you like it?"

"You don't really have to ask, do you?"

"I figured I should, Ma."

"I love it," his mother said softly, still happy and smiling. "It's a bit to take in, though."

"We knew it would be, and that's why I brought you alone. We'll have a dinner or something to celebrate, when you're not as high-strung and can find everything in the cupboards."

Cynthia laughed lightly. "We?"

"Me, Vic, and Melina. They helped a bit."

His mother seemed overwhelmed, but Mac figured that was to be expected.

She sighed, glancing around her kitchen as she stirred Mac's coffee. "Thank you."

"You don't have to thank me, Ma."

"I know, but I *should*."

Mac didn't argue. "No one else knew but us."

Cynthia didn't look at him a she pushed his cup across the island. "No one?"

"No."

"Huh. Well, that's good, I suppose."

Mac didn't like the lilt coloring his mother's tone. "Would it matter if someone had known?"

Cynthia waved his question off like it didn't matter. "No, no. I was just thinking out loud, James."

"Sure. But *why*?"

His mother wouldn't meet his gaze, and it was at that point Mac knew that she was trying to keep something from him. Cynthia Maccari was not a liar. She couldn't tell a lie to save her life, and made it a habit to correct her children when they were caught in lies.

Cynthia was about to lie to him.

Mac knew it.

"Ma," he said quieter.

"It's nothing," she replied carefully. "But having a new home will certainly save me some headaches."

Now, Mac really didn't like the sound of that. "Keep going, Ma."

Cynthia sighed and rubbed at her temple—a sure sign of her distress. "Your father has been coming around more often, and when he does come around, he asks about things."

Rage simmered through Mac's blood, but he managed to keep calm. Somehow. "This is beginning to feel like pulling teeth."

"The house—the deed. His name is on it, too. It always was. He just never cared."

Mac chose his next words carefully. "Did you tell him to leave?"

"Asked," his mother corrected. "And he did."

"But?"

"He came back. It's not as though I can kick the man out of his own house."

Right.

A house James Maccari Sr. had never paid for, taken care of, or anything else for that matter. Cynthia had done all of that, including raising her children without a husband and father to help them through life because he was too busy fucking himself up on drugs and street women.

Mac counted backwards from ten in his head to chill the hell out. He couldn't be angry at his mother, even if she should have told him that James was giving her problems. Besides, this was intended to be a happy day. One for his mother to enjoy. He wouldn't ruin that with nonsense.

"Give him the house—we'll get your name off the mortgage and deed as soon as we can," Mac finally said once he was calm enough to talk without anger heating his words. "It'll be one less problem for us all."

Cynthia frowned. "I have a feeling that if your father wants to cause problems, I will be the last person he goes through to cause them."

"What's that supposed to mean, Ma?"

Again, Cynthia's gaze shifted away. "Nothing."

"*Ma.*"

"He might have mentioned the last time he came around that he happened to *bump* into Melina. It sounded a lot like he meant to do it, and that it was not accidental."

Mac's rage blew out of control again.

He was off the island stool before his mother could say a thing to stop him.

Fucking hell.

His mother was one thing. Cynthia was a good old Catholic woman who didn't believe in divorce and would put up with her estranged husband's stupidity to the bitter end simply because she thought she had to for the Church and God.

But Mac's wife?

James Sr. knew better than that.

And better yet, why hadn't Melina told him?

"Get the fuck up."

Mac's order was punctuated with a slap to the back of Enric Pivetti's head. The crack of his palm landing to the younger man's skull echoed through the quiet, empty warehouse. As Enric cursed a blue streak and blinked crazily in the chair he'd been sleeping in, Mac continued walking back to where the office was. He had shit to get before he could go pay a visit to his old man.

Mac certainly hoped James got the goddamn point after tonight.

One of the benefits of being a made man, and a Capo, was that Mac could lay whatever lesson he wanted down on another man, so long as they weren't made. It was a little tricky when it happened on someone else's territory, but Mac figured he was justified enough in this without making a call to the Pivetti Don.

"*Cazzo*! What the *fuck*, man?" Enric snapped, his army-style boots hitting the floor hard as he stood straight from the chair.

Mac barely gave him a glance before he disappeared into the office. For the most part, Enric was a good kid— young in his early twenties, though—and did what Mac told him to do when he was told to do it. For being as young as he was, Enric knew how to follow orders and didn't rile shit up.

That was a point in his favor.

But Enric had a mouth on him. And he liked to use it.

"I was having a damn nap. *Merda*."

"Stop your whining," Mac muttered as he pulled open a drawer on his desk. Enric came to stand in the doorway with a scowl that could rival the devil's as he rubbed the back of his head. Mac rifled through the drawer, pulling out a small pocket knife he liked and an extra round of bullets for his gun. "We have shit to do."

"You slapped me awake, asshole."

"You talk too much—like your father," Mac said.

Enric quieted at that statement.

It was a strange quirk, but Mac had quickly learned that if there was anything Enric hated more than most everything else, it was being compared to his father. He respected Luca Pivetti, he liked him even, and talked well of his father. That didn't mean Enric wanted everyone to see him as *just* his father's son.

Mac respected that a great deal.

"What kind of business?" Enric asked.

A chuckle escaped Mac, dark and sadistic. "*My* father, actually. Seems the bastard needs an update on my feelings, because all the other ones must have fucking expired."

Enric made a sound that came off as both concerned and interested at the same time. Everybody who was anybody in the Pivetti Cosa Nostra, made or just affiliated, knew who James Maccari Sr. was, and exactly what he was worth as a man.

Fuck. All.

"What happened?" Enric asked.

Mac shrugged, his anger bubbling to the surface all over again. "I don't know. Why don't you call my wife and ask? She didn't even tell me."

It wasn't like Mac to blurt out information about his wife, even if it was in anger.

It was a good show of how irritated he currently was.

Sadly, some of that was directed at his wife.

A larger portion was directed at his father.

James would get the brunt of it.

"Fucker has earned it," Mac said under his breath.

"Huh?" Enric looked to Mac, waiting for an explanation.

"Nothing. Let's go."

It took a few calls, but Mac eventually got a lead on where he could find his asshole of a father. Unsurprisingly, James was apparently enjoying his time at a shoddy stripper joint that was also used as a billiards bar. Mac learned that his father also paid rent for a bachelor apartment above the business.

Mac supposed his father didn't have to go very far to feed his addictions.

Enric kept a couple of paces back from Mac as they passed by the bouncer at the door, who looked like he was already three sheets to the wind and would fall over if someone flicked his fucking ear. The guy barely passed him or Enric a glance, never mind sparing any attention to the baseball bat Enric was swinging to and fro at his side with every step.

"Are we going to kill him?" Enric asked.

"Not today," Mac replied.

But that could still happen.

Mac wasn't ruling it out.

If not today, then someday.

Mac ignored the scratched tables, ripped booths, the dancing women, and the bar filled with shady-looking characters. He side-stepped a stripper as she approached, making it clear he wasn't there for whatever she wanted to offer.

All too soon, he found his father in a corner booth, a girl that looked no older than eighteen, but blitzed out of her mind, was grinding her ass against James' groin.

It just pissed Mac off even more.

His mother had never entertained another man.

Never stepped out on his fuck up of a father.

James could never say quite the same thing.

Mac's father didn't notice his approach until he was right on top of them, grabbing the stripper by her forearm, and yanking her backwards. The girl screeched, stumbling in heels that were far too high and looked a little wobbly. She cursed at Mac, but he was already focusing in on his drunken father.

Mac barely noticed the two bouncers coming up behind him, likely reacting to one of the girls being handled in a way that wasn't allowed in the club.

Who gave a shit?

Mac sure as hell didn't.

Besides, that's what Enric was there for.

"Take another fucking step and I'll blow your goddamn kneecaps out," Enric warned the men. "Test me—I've got a hell of an aim."

Mac held back his smile. He would never tell Enric, because it would only deter the kid, but when he got in one of his moods and talked like he did, he sounded just like his father. Luca would be all kinds of proud, surely.

"James," Mac greeted quietly, staring his father down.

James Sr. blinked up at Mac like he was just seeing him for the first time. "Son?"

Mac almost laughed—*almost*. "Since when have I ever been *that*?"

"You've always been my boy."

This was not the time for Mac to be getting into this old argument with James.

"I told you, didn't I?" Mac asked calmly. "I thought I'd made it perfectly fucking clear that I didn't want or need you around. Your mess is better left hidden away in whatever hole you've dug for yourself. You keep me the fuck out of it—and by me, I mean every single part of *me*, James."

"I—"

"I might not be able to do much for Ma because she's stubborn as fuck, but my *wife*. My wife is a whole other story."

James sat up straighter in the booth, gaze flicking between Mac and Enric behind him. "Come on now, Mac. There's no need for you to be going and making a scene in this establishment because of a woman. Besides, you know better—this isn't your territory."

Was that supposed to matter?

It didn't.

"You're sorely mistaken if you think I give a single fuck. One last warning before I put you in the ground like the dog that you are. Stay the hell away from me and mine. I've got nothing for you—I never have, and I never will."

GANGSTER MOLL

James stood, his mouth opening to say something as his hand rested on the wooden top of the booth's table.

Mac didn't give him the chance to speak a single word before his pocket knife was in his hand, the blade flicked out and gleaming, and then it was brought down too fast for James to react. The blade drove into the back of James' palm with enough force to cut straight through and stick into the table. Blood welled instantly, spilling from the wound to the table.

James shouted, his immediate reaction being to pull his hand away from the cause of the pain, but that was impossible to do with it being embedded into the wood now.

Mac pulled his gun out of the holster at his back, flicked off the safety, and cocked the hammer. He pressed the barrel of the gun straight at James' forehead.

"Breathe in my wife's direction again," Mac said with a cold smile, "and I'll have your skull boiled and bleached so I can use it as an ashtray."

James didn't say a word.

Mac figured that was to his father's best benefit at the moment.

When Mac walked out of the club without his favorite knife in hand, he heard the first *thwack* of the bat being brought down against bone.

Screams echoed. Female. A shout from a man. Glass shattered.

Another plea from James Sr.

Mercy, he wanted.

No other sound had ever been more satisfying.

Mac rolled up the sleeves of his bloodstained dress shirt as he rested back against a purple velvet couch accompanied on both sides by black leather chairs. He took a look around The Dollhouse, noting the changes that had been made since the last time he'd checked up on his wife's progress.

It was almost ready for opening night.

Another week, Melina had said when he asked that morning.

He was proud of his wife.

The place looked hauntingly beautiful with an old world feel, dark colors, and a sexy appeal. The place was going to do just fine.

Mac, on the other hand, was still trying to swallow the rage on the back of his tongue. It'd been hours since he'd sent his father a very up close and personal message. He'd gone back to his warehouse office, taken a few swings at a punching bag, shouted at Enric for a while, and then he'd gone home.

He thought that would be enough to get rid of any lingering anger.

It hadn't been.

It didn't help that his wife wasn't home.

Melina was pulling late nights at The Dollhouse to get it finished on time for opening night. She had women ready to work, girls she trusted and knew. A bartender ready for the bar, and a backup, just in case.

It might have been that Melina was so busy she forgot to mention James' show. Or maybe she hadn't thought much of it at all.

Mac didn't know.

It still irritated him to no end.

Melina stood across the room from Mac, waving at something at the back of the bar. She hadn't noticed he'd come in, but he was perfectly fine with that.

For now.

The woman at her side nodded, agreeing to whatever Melina was saying.

With a final wave, Melina turned away and was off,

moving toward the back hallway that Mac knew belonged to her new office space and a few private rooms. Mac was off the couch and following his wife's direction before he had even thought it through completely.

What was he going to say to her?

Mac didn't even know, but it had to be *something*.

Melina just opened her office door when Mac's hand landed to the small of her back and guided her inside with him right behind. He let the door shut with a soft click as Melina turned in her tight dress and sky-high heels to face him. Her surprised but happy eyes at seeing him was enough to make some of his anger ebb away.

But not all.

"Doll," he said. "Before I say anything else, I just want to give you the chance to tell me whatever you need to tell me. *Anything*, Melina, that you think I might need or want to know. Important shit, okay. Go for it."

Melina's brow furrowed. "I beg your pardon?"

She didn't get it.

Mac figured that was half of the problem.

"I know you're used to handling shit on your own, problems or whatever, but even when you do that, you need to include *me*."

"Mac, what is fucking wrong with you?"

Ah, there she was.

Claws and all.

Melina's eyes lit up with her anger, but she didn't back down when Mac took a step forward, crowding her body with his.

"Who approached you?" he asked.

"Nobody."

"Wrong answer, doll."

Melina's lips drew into a tight line. "I don't know what has gotten into you, but I've already had enough. Go home. I'll see you when I get there later."

"No."

"What—*no*?"

"No," Mac repeated simply. "My father. A while back, you two had a run in, and you didn't bother to tell me. Why not?"

Melina's shoulders stiffened. "After I calmed down, I didn't think it was that big of a deal. We barely spoke. And it's not like I give a flying shit about him. He's not too fond of me, either."

"Not the point. James only comes around when he wants something—I've explained this to you before, Melina. The man is a fucking snake. You should have told me."

"Nothing happened for me to tell!"

"Yet!" Mac exploded right back. "Nothing has happened *yet*."

His wife blinked in the face of his rage, her gaze dropping to the bloodstains on his shirt and the bruises on his knuckles. "What happened to you?"

"Me?" Mac scoffed. "Nothing. Fuck all happened to me."

"Then, who?"

"Someone who knows better than to bother me and mine."

Melina frowned. "Your father?"

"He earned it."

"Mac! It wasn't anything important. I would have told you if—"

"You should have told me *this* time, Melina."

Melina didn't look like she was ready to back down on the issue, but still asked, "You didn't kill him, did you?"

Mac sneered. "Not this time."

CHAPTER ELEVEN

Mac had a control complex.

Now, more than ever, Melina was firmly convinced of it.

It had been nearly a week since Mac had showed up at The Dollhouse spoiling for a fight and they'd barely spoken more than a few words to each other since then. Mac had thrown himself even more into his "work," and to Melina, his paranoia levels were at an all-time high. She didn't understand it. All she had been trying to do was keep the peace and as a result, her husband was pissed at her because she hadn't run to him and whined like some damsel in distress.

She'd never been the girl who needed saving and she wasn't about to start now.

What was so wrong with her handling the situation herself?

James Sr. had gotten the message because she hadn't seen him since.

No doubt, he'd crawled back under the rock he'd slithered out from in the first place.

So why was her husband giving so much of his energy to someone who didn't matter?

She didn't know, but she meant to find out because this … whatever this was going on between her and Mac had to come to a stop. They were still newlyweds, for fuck's sake. They should still be basking in the ambiance of being married, not still stewing over a situation that was not even worth arguing over in the first place.

Melina loved her husband and she understood that he had an image to maintain.

After all, Cosa Nostra was all about appearances.

It wouldn't be good if word got out that a man like James Sr. had no fear of approaching the wife of a made man and making insinuations. It would look like Mac wasn't capable of protecting his family.

In short, he would look weak.

So from that part, Melina could understand why Mac thought she should have told him.

On the other hand, she thought Cosa Nostra tended to make a mountain out of a mole hill.

So James Sr. had made a few slick comments. Big whoop. It wasn't like he was the first man to do so to her and before her time was finished on this earth, Melina was certain he wouldn't be the last.

She was a big girl, who could handle herself.

Perhaps Mac needed reminding of that.

Melina's eyes narrowed as Mac opened the door to their bedroom. She glanced at the clock on the wall.

"Do you know what time it is?" she asked quietly.

"Yeah."

Another one word answer. He took off his jacket and threw it on the bed without looking at her. Melina's ire was piqued but she squelched her inclination to throttle him. Tonight wasn't about re-igniting their fight. She had plans to re-ignite something else altogether. Melina rose from her seat at her vanity and walked over to her husband. When she stepped in front of him, he looked at her for the first time.

"We need to talk."

"About what?" Mac folded his arms.

Still looking her husband in the eyes, Melina slowly undid the belt to her black silk robe, giving Mac a subtle peek at what she wore beneath. His eyes narrowed.

"About the fact that we're mature adults who need to be able to talk things out. About the fact that this distance between us isn't good for a healthy marriage."

"Neither is keeping secrets, doll."

Melina sighed. "Mac, I wasn't keeping secrets from you. Will you please listen to me?"

Mac took a seat on the side of the bed. "The floor is yours."

"Look, when James Sr. ran into me, I fully had intentions of telling you. I thought to myself that you'd want to know he was still on the radar somewhere."

"Your first inclination was right. What changed your mind?"

Melina sat beside Mac on the bed. "I didn't want to cause any more problems than we already have."

"How could you telling me that he accosted you cause more problems, Melina? You're my wife. My *most* important job is to keep you safe!"

"Mac, you and James already have a contentious relationship and that's putting it lightly. If I'd come home and told you exactly how the conversation went down and the way I felt afterwards, there's no doubt in my mind you would have come unglued. If your father's blood has to be spilled, I don't want it to be because I enflamed an already volatile situation."

Mac's nostrils flared. "So you're saying, there was more to it than you told me?"

Melina tucked a strand of hair behind her ear. "Yes. He made me feel really uncomfortable."

"In what way?" Mac's voice was low.

"He didn't look at me the way a man should look at his daughter-in-law and he made some insinuations about you."

"What. Did. He. Say?"

"He said that he didn't think that you were man enough to handle a woman like me and that perhaps someone like him was."

Melina bit her lip as she regarded her husband. His eyes closed and his hands curled into fists. When he opened his eyes, and looked at her, Melina swallowed hard. She'd expected to see the cold, detached man she'd glimpsed when it came to dealing with business. What she saw before her was a man on fire. His hands relaxed and Mac touched her face, gripping her chin between his thumb and his forefinger.

"You're mine and any man that thinks he can do and say whatever he wants to you without consequence has signed his own death warrant."

His words were soft, like a silken caress and despite his veiled threat of murder. Melina couldn't deny it turned her on.

"I don't want you to …"

Her words were cut off as Mac pressed his thumb against her lips.

"Shh. Don't go there, doll. Whatever decision I make will be mine and mine alone."

She nodded as his other hand tugged open the side of her robe. His hot gaze scorched her and Melina's body burned for more.

"You are so damned beautiful. So fucking sexy. So damned stubborn. A man couldn't want you more than I do, doll."

"I want you, too. I've missed you," she whispered.

Mac leaned close and pressed his forehead against hers. "I'm sorry."

"I'm sorry, too."

"I appreciate that you didn't want to make things worse between me and James. And I have no doubt that you put him in his place when he got out of line."

"I did."

"But next time, tell me, even if you think it's nothing. Or even if it might make things worse, tell me. You and I can't afford to have secrets."

"You have my word. From now on, I'll tell you everything, even if it bores you to tears."

"I don't think you could ever do that, doll. Now tell me something, is there a reason you're wearing nothing but lace?"

Melina smiled as she leaned away so that she could look her husband in the eyes. "I planned on seducing my husband."

Mac raised a brow. "Is that so?"

"Absolutely. Don't you recall me saying your exquisite cock was one of the reasons I married you?"

Mac laughed. "I do seem to recall that."

"Then what do you say we do something about that?"

"Absolutely, doll."

Melina's arms wrapped around her husband as he maneuvered them on the bed so that he was lying on top of her. Their lips met and the first touch of Mac's mouth on hers ignited a spark deep inside. Melina's legs opened, eager to welcome him into a place that belonged only to him. His lips trailed down her neck, sucking the sensitive spot behind her ear that made her toes curl. When he caught the lobe of her ear between his teeth and bit down softly, Melina's fingernails dug into his shoulders.

Her moan echoed.

His tongue traced the shell of her ear before Mac grabbed the neckline of her nightgown and ripped it down the middle, exposing her naked body.

"Perfection," Mac said.

"You owe me a new gown."

"Next time, just be naked and we won't have this problem." He winked at her.

"Smart ass."

Any further response was lost as Mac's mouth engulfed her nipple, sucking it hard in his mouth. Her sensitive nerve endings were on fire. As his tongue swirled around the soft tip, Melina's hand eased between her thighs. She rubbed the tight bundle of nerves that were crying out for relief for but a moment before her hand was roughly jerked away.

"What the hell?"

"Hush," Mac said.

And then his mouth was there. Melina's thighs opened wider as he licked and sucked at her hot, aching flesh. No one knew her body like her husband. Mac knew just what spot to kiss, lick and suck. Wetness seeped from between her thighs and Melina held tight to Mac as she rode the wave of pleasure that coursed through her body. She couldn't hold back the scream that tore from her throat as she came hard, hot and loud.

Mac leaned over her, reaching for the buckle to his pants. Together they worked until his pants were off and they were skin to skin. His hard, hot body on hers was everything she'd been missing. Mac slipped inside her easily, filling her completely. The thick, velvety drag of him inside her was like an ember that gradually grew to a flame. His hands were in her hair, holding her tight as their bodies tangoed in a dance as old as time.

"Ah, fuck," Mac said.

The pace of his strokes increased and Melina's thighs tightened around him as she came closer to the precipice of pleasure that awaited them both.

One.

Two.

Three.

Melina and Mac's grunts and groans of pleasure filled the air, before Mac rolled to his side, taking Melina with him. He was still buried inside of her. They lay entwined together, their breathing rough and irregular as they both struggled to catch their breath.

Fire and passion.

It was like that every time the two of them came together. As if the world could burn down around them and nothing else would matter but the pure primal desire they had for each other. Minutes passed before they could finally speak.

"Doll, we are going to have to kiss and make up more often. That was something else."

Melina laughed. "It always is."

"Give me a few more minutes to recover and we can make up some more."

"That sounds like a fine idea."

"Mac, what's the meaning of this?"

Melina stood in their bedroom, clad only in a black strapless bra and matching thong. The dress she'd picked out to wear to the opening of The Dollhouse was nowhere in sight. Mac entered the room, casually adjusting his tie.

"What are you yelling about, doll?"

"Don't be cute. What did you do with my dress?"

"I put it back in the closet."

Melina put her hands on her hips. "Why?"

"Tonight is a special night for you and I wanted you to have a little something that reflects that. Go ahead and open it."

Melina turned her attention to the large silver box that lay on the bed. Opening it and moving aside the tissue paper that was covering what lay underneath, Melina pulled out the garment. Her husband was something else.

"You really know what I like."

"I'm your husband. I'm supposed to. Now, if you don't hurry up and put that dress on we're going to be late."

Holding the dress up in front of her, Melina smiled at her husband.

"And why would we be late?"

"Because I'm a half second away from throwing you down on the bed and fucking you for at least another hour," Mac said.

"How can you not be tired?"

Mac came over to where she stood and cupped her chin in his hand. "I'm never too tired to love you properly."

Then he winked and sat on the edge of the bed, waiting for her to get dressed. Standing in front of the full-length mirror, Melina unzipped the back of the dress and stepped into it easily.

"All right, zip me up."

Melina waited as Mac zipped up the dress and pressed a soft kiss to her nape.

"Perfection," he said.

"You think so?" Melina asked.

She admired herself in the mirror. Though she had a special love for bodycon dresses, there was nothing wrong with trying something a little different every now and then. Mac had chosen for her a dark purple cocktail dress. Two straps crossed her right shoulder and there was a strategic cut out just above her cleavage. The soft silk of the material clung to her body and ended just below her knees. She looked the part of hostess at an exclusive event, especially with her hair styled in an elegant updo.

"I know so. Go on. Admit you like it."

"Of course I like it. Thank you for the dress."

"My pleasure. Now why don't you slip on those Prada spiked heels I like so much and we can get out of here," Mac said.

Melina faced her husband and smiled, "You and those heels."

Mac shrugged as she went into the closet. "What can I say? Spikes turn me on."

"Is there anything that doesn't turn you on?" Melina asked.

She sat down on the bed and strapped on her spiked heels.

"That was a low blow, doll. I'm a peculiar sort of

man."

Heels on, Melina stood and touched the cross that hung around her neck. Since Mac had given it to her on that fateful night, she'd done her best to never take it off. The simple cross was a subtle reminder that strength sometimes came from unexpected places.

"Yes, you are and I'll always love you for that."

Mac brushed his fingers over the cross. "You nervous?"

"Just a little bit," Melina confessed.

"No worries. Tonight is going to be a success. We have nothing to worry about."

"Maybe you're right."

"Of course I am. Now let's go, Cinderella. Your chariot awaits."

Melina couldn't contain her laughter as Mac took her hand and lead her from the room. Cinderella indeed.

"You mean my carriage awaits?"

"Yeah."

Melina smiled. Her husband was something else. With Mac, the surprises never stopped coming.

The Dollhouse was filled with people. Melina could only help but wonder how word had gotten out to so many people about the grand opening. It wasn't exactly like she'd been able to advertise the grand opening through some of the normal channels for a business opening. Especially a business like The Dollhouse. But somehow or another, it seemed that the night was off to a roaring success.

Unsurprisingly, the number of men far outnumbered the woman in attendance. After all, sex was something that would always sell, whether it was explicitly advertised or not. Standing near one of the large bars, Melina surveyed the crowd again. She'd noticed more than one of her girls discretely slip away with a well-clothed gentlemen. Tossing them a subtle nod as they'd disappeared, Melina was mentally counting the money that would be made this evening, not only from the bar but with the girls as well.

"Champagne?" a passing waiter asked.

"Absolutely."

Melina took a glass from the tray and took two long sips of the cold bubbly, liquid.

"Melina, there you are, dear."

She turned when she heard her name called. Melina nearly choked on her champagne.

"Neeya?"

The tall, elegant woman wrapped Melina in a warm hug. "Why the surprise?"

"This is not the sort of place I would expect a Don's wife to be."

Neeya laughed. "This is a completely different establishment than it was before. You've done wonders here. Why wouldn't I be here to support you?"

"Again. You know what kind of place this is," Melina reiterated.

"Nonsense. I couldn't be prouder. I knew from the first time we met you would turn things on their heads and you have done exactly that."

"I just hope I haven't pushed things too much with this place."

"What do you mean?"

"I'm supposed to be the quiet little wife, not running a business. I don't want this to reflect negatively on my husband."

"There will always be those who have something to say, but they don't matter. If anything, you are proving to everyone that you are your husband's equal in every way."

Melina fingered her necklace absentmindedly. "That's all I want to be. An enhancement to Mac, not a detriment."

Neeya grabbed her shoulders. "You are. Now enough of this self-doubt. Let's toast to a profitable new venture."

"I'll second that notion."

Luca Pivetti eased next to his wife while motioning for a waiter.

"Thank you," Melina said. "This is unexpected."

"It shouldn't be. This place was bleeding money and now it will be raking it in. A smart man can appreciate business savvy, no matter who it comes from."

"You couldn't be more right, boss."

Mac appeared, sliding an arm around Melina's waist as the waiter came over with drinks. He, Luca and Neeya each took a new flute of champagne. Melina drained the rest of her glass and took a new flute as well.

"A toast to my beautiful, hardworking, ambitious wife and a stellar opening night."

Mac raised his glass.

"I'll drink to that," Neeya said.

Luca gave a rare smile before raising his own glass. Melina followed suit and breathed a sigh of relief. Her worries had been for nothing. If Luca Pivetti had given the okay to The Dollhouse, then things were going to be fine. She wasn't breaking some unwritten mob rule. She wasn't shaming her husband. She was just a business owner.

The four of them enjoyed their glasses of champagne and made small talk before Melina was motioned over to the bar by one of the bartenders. Excusing herself, she headed behind the counter and then stopped in her tracks.

Pop.

Pop.

Pop.

Melina's blood froze in her veins.

She'd know that sound anywhere.

Gunfire.

The Dollhouse descended into chaos. People were running everywhere. Half-naked men and women emerged from the private corners of the club. Shattering glass mixed with the sounds of gunfire. Melina turned, eyes searching the crowd for her husband. Her heart rate increased when she couldn't spot him the crowd.

"Mac! Mac!"

Before she could yell again, he was at her side.

"I've got you, doll."

Pulling his gun from his waistband, Mac grabbed her hand and navigated them through the maze of people rushing to the front of the club. Melina looked for Neeya Pivetti in the crowd but spotting one person in the mass of people was impossible. Melina held tight to her husband's hand as one of the back door entrances to the club finally came into view. Flinging the door open, Mac went through first, gun raised before he pulled Melina behind him.

Descending the concrete stairs that led down, Melina scarcely dared to breathe as she followed her husband down the alley. In the distance, sirens could be heard. Damn. No doubt the cops were already on their way. When Mac abruptly stopped, Melina crashed into his back.

"Mac?"

"We have to get out of here. Now."

Before Melina could react, he was half dragging her out of the alley and toward a side street behind a neighboring building. But Mac wasn't fast enough. As they ran, Melina saw what had captured her husband's rapt attention.

A man lay in the alley. What had once been his face was unrecognizable.

Holy fuck.

Death had found them once again.

Melina knew that one way or another, the storm they thought they'd been facing was about to get worse.

Much, much worse.

CHAPTER TWELVE

"No comment," Mac said to Melina. "That is always your response, doll."

Melina gave him a look from the side, questioning and exhausted at the same time. "Is that—"

Another knock on the apartment door interrupted her question.

Mac wanted to reassure his wife as much as he could before he opened the door. He wanted to tell her things were perfectly fine and that it would all be figured out without any sort of trouble.

He'd be lying.

Mac didn't want to lie to his wife.

He didn't know what the fuck was going on. He didn't know why yet *another* person was killed at an event that had been planned around something he and his wife had done. He'd gotten Melina out of there the night before, only because he didn't want police backlash on her during business hours, and he figured it was a buffer zone between Melina and the activities going on inside the place.

Just in case …

However, they couldn't stick their heads in the sand forever.

Luca had already called. He wanted a meeting—soon. Another Capo had called, confirming Mac's suspicions that the police had been all over The Dollhouse the night before. Enric also called, thankfully with the news that no one was arrested.

The body, on the other hand, had been identified, according to Enric.

Luca Pivetti's *new* lawyer, hired after Matthew had been killed, Kyle Reeves.

Mac didn't know why the lawyer had been at the club, never mind in the back alley, but apparently, he had been and that's where he'd ended up dead.

The who, why, and what were still the questions of the hour.

"Answer the door, Mac," Melina said softly.

Mac blinked out of his daze, losing his thoughts in the process. He could plainly hear the police detectives behind the front door announcing their presence and asking if anyone was home. He should have ignored them, but he knew it wouldn't do him any damn good. If not today, they would be questioning them tomorrow.

He wanted to make sure that fucking *no one* questioned his wife when he or a lawyer wasn't present. It was her business, so there was no doubt they would come for her.

Finally, Mac pulled the door open. He faced two familiar police detectives, the same ones that had questioned him the night of his wedding. That in itself, just seeing their snide smiles, was more than enough to make Mac's blood boil.

He almost slammed the door right in their faces.

Melina's hand curving around his shoulder was the only thing that stopped him.

"Mr. Maccari, beautiful morning, isn't it?" the shorter of the two asked.

Both men flashed their badges, not that they needed to. The stench of cop was as clear as day, even if Mac hadn't recognized them.

Mac's jaw clenched involuntarily. "I wouldn't know."

"May we come in?" the other one asked. "We have a few questions about the incident last night at your wife's establishment."

"Say what you mean," Mac replied coolly. "You want to speak with my wife because she owns the joint."

"And you, too."

Fucking wonderful.

"Mac," Melina said behind him, soft and sweet, "let's just get it over with."

"Make it quick," Mac said, stepping back to allow the detectives into the apartment. "I have somewhere to be."

"Ah, yes," the tallest detective said, moving inside like he owned the place. That probably pissed Mac off the most, if he was honest. "Luca's let out the war cry this morning, hasn't he? Time to gather all of his little soldiers so he feels a tad safer on the streets."

Mac hesitated, grip tightening around the edge of the door as he took in the detective's words. Melina seemed oblivious to the blatant statement that essentially admitted the cop had inside knowledge of Luca's orders. Something no one outside of the men in the family should know.

Already, the detectives had moved onto questioning Melina about the club and the events of the night before. Mac stayed quiet through it all, only speaking when spoken directly to, and answering as vaguely as he could. Melina did the same.

They'd practiced this.

Talked about it all.

She knew what to say.

Mac was still on the detective's statement.

He knew Luca had put out an order.

That only meant one thing.

La famiglia had a rat.

Mac ignored the stares as he strolled into Luca's library, trying to appear as unbothered as he possibly could be, given the situation. It was never good to let another made man see that you were concerned about something, even if it was widely known they were all concerned about the same thing.

The fear of the unknown would always be better.

"Great of you to finally join us," Luca said, a cigar sticking out of the corner of his mouth.

"Detectives," Mac said in explanation.

He didn't offer more; his words were more than enough to get the point across.

Luca's lips curled up at the edge, showcasing his teeth biting into the end of the cigar with enough force to mark the tan, tapered end with indents of his bites. He looked as though he'd smelled something bad all of the sudden.

"And?" the boss asked.

More than a dozen pairs of eyes landed on Mac, all questioning at the same time.

"And nothing, they're gone."

Enzo scoffed from his seat at the window bench. "The bastards will be back."

Probably.

Mac wasn't concerned about that at the moment. There was bigger fish to fry.

"Who else had a face to face with the police last night or today?" Luca asked the men in the room.

Hands flew up. Murmurs passed around, confirming they too had been approached. Luca's face grew progressively redder with each person who admitted they had needed to talk to police.

"*Cazzo*. They're gonna put us in the ground," Luca said, more to himself than the room.

Nonetheless, Mac knew every man had heard it. Especially as they had all turned into stone statues of themselves.

Mac understood the boss's frustrations, and the men's hesitance. Having police attention was never on Cosa Nostra's high list of priorities. It was better to keep officials looking away from you rather than focusing in on *only* you.

At the moment, it seemed like every cop in New York was all up in Pivetti business in one way or another.

That was bad all over.

"Why don't we address the real elephant in the room?"

The question came from the corner. It'd been posed quietly, and nothing else was offered from the stoic Capo that sat on one of the many leather chairs against the wall.

Anthony Corelli.

"What elephant is that?" Luca asked.

Without missing a single beat, Anthony tipped the drink in his hand toward Mac and said, "The one standing right in front of you."

Irritation and stress tightened Mac's shoulders. God knew he had enough bullshit going on and things he needed to handle without adding Anthony to the pile. The Capo was always looking for a reason to give Mac hell. This wasn't even a surprise.

Luca leaned forward on the edge of his desk, his fingers drumming against hardwood as a billow of smoke clouded his features from the cigar. "Explain yourself, Anthony."

"Two separate incidents. Two men dead. Both close to you, boss." Anthony shrugged. "Seems kind of obvious."

Luca's face lost all emotion, turning blank as slate. "Then I must be the only one with 'Idiot' tattooed across my forehead, because I'm not understanding what you're implying. Explain, or get the fuck out."

Anthony's gaze turned on Mac, cold and violent. "I'm not the only one who thinks it, boss. I'm just might be the only one that'll say it, though. Seems whenever Mac and his wife have something going on, someone shows up dead. It's a little strange is all. He's like a bad luck charm—that, or it's just … *coincidence*."

Mac schooled his features, refusing to let Anthony's statement get under his skin. "Is that so?"

Luca stayed quiet, his stare passing between the two men.

"Well," Anthony drawled with a smile, "you know what we say about coincidences, Mac. In this life, they don't exist. You're two for two. What does that tell you?"

Mac didn't give Anthony a response, knowing it wouldn't do him any real good to argue with the older Capo. He had been listening, however, and Mac had to wonder how much of what Anthony said was true. Were there other Capos that were blaming Mac for these issues? Were they assuming it was connected to him?

Was it all because of him?

The stillness in the room—the quietness of the men surrounding him—told Mac that it was very possible their suspicions were being placed at his feet.

"It is odd," Luca finally said to Mac. "You have to admit that much."

"I think we have bigger problems," Mac replied.

Luca seemed even less impressed than before. "Oh? Do tell. What other problems do we have that need attention as much as my men being slaughtered?"

All eyes turned on Mac again.

He focused on the boss instead of the men.

Luca was the most important one in the room. If Mac's suspicions were right about the police having a rat in their family, it could be anyone sitting in that office.

But it wouldn't be Luca.

And it sure as fuck wasn't Mac.

"One of the detectives that showed up to question my wife this morning said something," Mac started to say, carefully choosing his words as he went along. "Somehow he knew that you'd put out a very specific order for the men in the family to be here today."

Luca stiffened on the desk. "What are you saying, Maccari?"

"I think we have a rat."

The silence was deafening.

That word—*rat*—was poison.

It bred contempt, suspicion, and fear, all in one fell swoop.

It didn't need help.

It spread like a fucking airborne *virus*.

Luca met Mac's gaze as he said, "A rat and a killer. This is a delicate time to be a Cosa Nostra man, it seems."

Apparently, it depended on who that Cosa Nostra man was.

The unknown bred fear.

After all, the men were still watching Mac like he needed to be watched.

Even Luca.

"You could at least explain to me why you want me to stay at Ma's for a week or two," Victoria grumbled from the passenger seat of Mac's Challenger.

"It's a favor, nothing more. Can't you leave it at that and stop looking for more?" Mac asked.

"Yeah, but—"

"She's also our mother. It won't hurt you to keep an eye on her for a bit."

Victoria pressed her lips together tightly, her annoyance evident. "Pretty sure that's always been a job you took care of, Mac. And I'm busy with work, you know that."

"And partying," Mac said, adding what his sister didn't. "Clubbing four nights a week, even nights when you have to work the next morning. Running with a couple guys."

"Don't even start."

Mac had hit a nerve with his sister, it seemed.

"Listen," he started to say, "I don't care what you do, Vic. It's your life, really. Do what you want. But right now, I am asking for one simple thing, nothing more. You can do that without questioning me to heaven and back."

"I just want to know *why* or what is wrong," Victoria replied.

From the backseat, Enric flicked his cigarette ash out the window. "Shit may or may not be happening. Mac wants his people to be safe just in case. Be grateful, not annoying."

Mac wavered between being thankful for Enric opening his mouth, or scolding the man for talking to his sister that way. He decided to go with being thankful, seeing as how Victoria had quieted in the passenger seat and was watching Mac with less irritation than before.

Of course, that didn't mean she felt the same way for Enric.

Turning a cold eye on their passenger in the back, Victoria said, "And who the fuck are you exactly?"

Enric let out a slow stream of smoke, smooth and unbothered. "Now that, Vickie, isn't any of your concern."

Mac chuckled at that one, knowing what was coming.

"Don't call me *Vickie*, asshole."

"Rhymes with bitchy, right?" Enric asked.

Mac chose to step in before Victoria clawed Enric's throat out. It wasn't such a crazy idea, considering his sister looked damn ready to do murder.

"All right, that's enough," Mac said, never taking his eyes off the road in front of them. "Act like children on your own time."

He should have known that with these two, given their entirely opposite personalities, having them close together would only end badly. Enric was too aloof, and didn't mind telling someone to cut out their bullshit. Victoria was loud and sometimes her personality was a bit much.

Maybe this was a bad idea.

Mac sighed, knowing he didn't have very many other options at his disposal.

Hopefully, his mother would keep Enric and Victoria from killing each other.

That was his piss-poor plan.

"I get the Challenger, right?" Enric asked from the back.

Victoria's eyebrow cocked at Mac. "What's he talking about?"

Shit.

So maybe Mac hadn't told Victoria *everything* just yet.

Mac waved a hand, dismissing Victoria's bitter question. "It's nothing—just a secondary precaution while I figure some things out."

"*What precaution*?" Victoria practically screeched.

That migraine was beginning to make its appearance again.

Awesome.

"Oh, your brother forgot to tell you?" Enric asked, smirking at Victoria in a way that said he was going to enjoy this.

"Enric," Mac warned.

The younger man didn't even act like he heard him.

It seemed like Enric was enjoying teasing and torturing Victoria. Maybe a little too much.

"I'll be keeping an eye on your mother … and you," Enric said, his grin deepening. "For a little while. Should be fun."

Victoria turned her burning eyes on Mac.

He pulled into his mother's driveway at the same time.

Pulling the keys out of the ignition, Mac tossed them back to Enric and opened the car door to get the hell out before Victoria could say another word to him. Was it cowardly? Hell yes.

He was not in the mood to deal with his sister, though.

"Call me if you need something," Mac said over his shoulder, heading for the road. He hadn't directed his statement to one particular person in the car. Already, he could hear them arguing behind him again.

He'd call a fucking cab to get home.

This was for Victoria and his mother's own good.

Yeah, that's what he was going to keep telling himself.

Mac had gone back to the apartment first, thinking his wife would be there waiting for him. After the day they had had, together and separately, he figured she would want nothing more than a quiet night in with some good food, a movie or two, and him.

The apartment was empty when he had arrived.

Melina was nowhere in sight.

He found the note she left behind, scribbled in her familiar feminine scrawl.

The tape is off The Dollhouse.

Be home after supper.

Love, Melina.

It would have been better—*safer*—had Melina stayed home and waited to go into work once Mac was back, but that wasn't the way his doll worked. She intended to keep that business going, and make it a fucking success, no matter what it meant or cost them to do it. He couldn't even find it in himself to get annoyed that she had gone as soon as the tape had been taken off the place.

Mac had passed the clock on the kitchen wall a look.

It showed that by the time he had gotten home, it was well beyond supper time.

Melina probably didn't even realize the time.

So, he'd locked up their apartment, and gone to her.

Keeping his mother and sister safe by making sure they were together, quiet, and had someone watching them was one thing. But Melina? That was not as simple. His wife wouldn't go quietly into the night to hide out in an apartment until he had shit straightened out and gotten done whatever else he needed to do in the process.

Frightened, Melina was not.

Mac didn't even think the word was in her dictionary.

That only left him with one real option, as far as he was concerned. He would have to keep his wife close— closer than he normally would. Usually he did his business, and she did hers, and they were almost always apart because that was their nature of works. Mac had to be everywhere at once, all across the city, visiting men, collecting money, and seeing to his crew and their activities. He couldn't just sit in one place and wait for the money to come to him. That wasn't how a Capo's job worked.

The Dollhouse was sometimes the exception.

When things were quiet, Mac could chill out there while Melina did her thing before it had opened. Even now, he suspected he could still hang out there with his wife if he wanted.

And that was probably what he would need to do now.

At least for a little while.

Melina likely wouldn't think much of Mac being around more, especially after the second shooting. But he wasn't sure on how much of the other stuff he was going to let her in on. It wasn't that he didn't trust his wife.

God, he trusted that woman with his *life*.

He just didn't think it would do her any good to worry about things she couldn't control.

Not yet.

The bigger, most obvious, problem was that Mac was doing all of these things proactively with no real reason or obvious threat to justify his actions. No one had actually threatened him, per say. It wasn't his right-hand man or second lawyer that had been killed.

No one said *he* was the one that pulled the trigger.

Still, something didn't feel right.

Anthony—as much as Mac hated that fucking *cafone*—had a point when he said it had been two incidents, both involving Mac in some way.

That, to Mac, was threat enough for him to act proactively like he was.

Just in case someone was trying to make a point of something, and decided Luca wasn't getting them anywhere. Mac—or his wife and family—wouldn't be the one whoever it was came after next.

Not if he could help it.

Instead of having a cab take him back across the city to The Dollhouse, Mac only took one half way, opting to get out at a storage place. Since Enric would be using his Challenger for a week or two—the guy refused to get a car, though he did have his license—Mac would need something else to use. Melina had her car, but he wasn't about to take the keys from her.

Mac found the storage container that had a large number nine painted on the front. It was small enough that a car couldn't fit inside, but large enough for him to keep safe the one thing he only brought out occasionally. He made quick work of unlocking the padlock and pulling up the metal door to expose his metallic, navy and red Ducati Superbike waiting for him. The full-faced helmet hung off the right side of the handlebar.

Damn, he'd missed this bike.

It wasn't often he used it—it wasn't practical when his car could haul things if needed.

The bike would do, and when he drove it, Mac found

he didn't have to focus on anything but the sound of his bike and the road ahead of him. It relieved his stress in a way his car couldn't.

It wasn't long before Mac was on the highway, face hidden behind his helmet as he passed car after car, his bike pushing three times the legal speed limit. It took him half the time it usually would to reach The Dollhouse. He'd just parked his Ducati alongside the front in an available spot as his phone began to buzz in his pocket, and three women stepped outside of The Dollhouse's front door.

He recognized them as girls that his wife had hired, and didn't pay them any mind as he tugged his helmet off and then pulled his cell phone out of his jacket pocket to answer the call.

Mac didn't check who the caller was as he put the phone to his ear. "*Ciao?*"

"How is Enric doing?"

Mac's brow furrowed at Luca's calm tone. "Boss?"

He was the last person Mac expected to hear from, after what had gone on earlier that afternoon, never mind a friendly chitchat about Enric.

"Who the hell else calls you from this number?" Luca asked.

Mac decided to answer Luca's first question. "He's doing well. A little mouthy sometimes, but he's good at what he does. That says a lot. He's good."

"Good," Luca echoed.

Passing the front door to his wife's business a look, Mac said, "Was that all?"

"No. A rat, you said."

Mac stiffened on the bike. "I thought you weren't listening."

Luca chuckled dryly. "Or did you think I was more interested in what that fool Anthony was saying?"

"Honestly?"

"Let me have it, Mac."

"A little bit of both," Mac muttered.

"We all have to be careful right now, seeing as how there is a lot happening but none of us have any real answers as to *why*. You, especially. Me, more importantly. I will do so how I have to do so, and you will do the same—understood?"

"Got it, boss."

Although Mac wasn't entirely sure he did.

"I do trust you," Luca added after a quiet moment. "Do you?"

"Even if I have to do it from afar for a bit, Mac. You've given me every reason to trust you, and not one reason to distrust you. Keep it that way."

Well, then … what could he say to that?

"It could be related to me," Mac said. "These killings, I mean."

"I have no doubt they are, even if *you're* intended to be a distraction of sorts by whoever it is," Luca agreed. "You work on finding who that is."

"And what will you do, boss?"

Luca sighed. "Apparently, with the way they keep coming closer to the people at my side, I'll try to stay alive and smoke out a rat at the same time. Enjoy your evening with your wife, Mac, I'm sure she'll be happy to see you showed up tonight. I'll be in touch."

Mac's head snapped up and his gaze zoned the street.

Luca knew where he was.

"As I said," Luca murmured, "you haven't given me a reason to distrust you. Don't start now. Have a good evening."

Mac was just hanging up the phone when The Dollhouse's front door opened, and Melina stepped out with keys in her hand. She locked the place up, turned to leave, and froze when she saw Mac.

"You didn't get my note?" she asked, not even saying a word about the Ducati bike.

"I did, doll," he replied. "Just thought you might want

to see me a little earlier, that's all."

Melina's smile bloomed widely.

It was still the best sight.

"Everything okay?' she asked.

Mac nodded. "Yeah, considering."

Or it would be.

CHAPTER THIRTEEN

I'm sticking to you like paper sticks to glue.

Melina couldn't help thinking about the words to the old song because, for once, they actually had some application to her life.

Mac had become closer than her own damn shadow.

On one hand, she could understand it.

Yet another person connected to the Pivetti Cosa Nostra had been killed at yet another event directly related to her and Mac. It damn sure didn't help matters that the man had turned out to be Luca Pivetti's freshly-hired consigliere. The man had just buried his last one for fuck's sake and now this.

So yeah, she could understand Mac's closeness.

He hadn't said anything to her specifically but Melina was no fool. Her husband was worried.

Worried that perhaps they were in more than the usual danger that came along with being connected to Cosa Nostra.

Worried that he was losing the respect and trust he'd fought so hard to gain.

The latter was what made her want to put a bullet in someone's fucking head.

Mac had started off as a foot soldier living in the shadow of a father that was a monumental fuck up, but through working harder than anyone around him he'd moved up the ranks. As a Capo, he was finally reaping the benefits of all his years of labor.

No one deserved to take that away from him.

Not now. Not ever.

Especially if she had anything to say about it.

Mac didn't have a disloyal bone in his body, which made the whispers going around all the more irksome to her.

He may have thought she was unaware, but little got past Melina.

She'd heard the word.

Rat.

It was an insult of the highest order.

Unconsciously, she bit her lip. Mac had no reason to betray his *famiglia*. Despite the less than stellar treatment he'd endured in the past, he was enjoying the benefits now. If anyone had more incentive to make sure that Luca Pivetti stayed in charge, it was her husband. Melina knew how much having his Don's trust meant to Mac. He'd never do anything to jeopardize that.

But someone else was.

They just had to figure out who that person was.

"Are you okay, Melina? You've been quieter than usual today," Victoria said.

Melina offered her sister-in-law a smile. "I'm okay. I just have a lot on my mind."

"Tell me about it. I feel like a crab in a barrel. You have got to get my brother to give us some breathing room. I'm not sure how much more of this I can take."

Victoria's gaze swung to the corner of the salon were Enric Pivetti stood. Though the young man seemed at ease, Melina wasn't fooled. He knew the moment anyone came in or went out of the salon. Every so often his gaze drifted over to them. Melina couldn't help noticing that his gaze seemed to linger on Victoria when he thought no one was looking. She wondered if her husband was aware his new understudy had eyes for his younger sister.

"Ha. This is the first outing I've had not being directly shadowed by your brother. He's not budging."

"How'd you manage to get some breathing room today?"

"Enric is still shadowing you, so there was no reason for the two of them to be here. Besides, I told him if he didn't give me some damn space he wouldn't like the result."

Victoria laughed. "Teach me your ways, great *sensei*."

"If I was such a great teacher, I wouldn't still be being followed. I love your brother to death but all couples need space sometimes."

"I wouldn't know. My going out has been limited with Mr. Smart Ass following me around. You can't exactly go out with a bodyguard throwing death looks at your date all evening."

"Come on. He can't be that bad. At least he's eye candy."

Victoria rolled her eyes. "No. Like not in a million years. I can't stand him."

"Thy doth protest too much. Do I need to remind you how Mac and I were?"

"Completely different situation."

"We'll revisit this in a few months. I'm sure things will have changed."

"Don't waste your breath," Victoria said.

Melina didn't miss the quick dart Victoria's eyes did over to the corner as they gathered up their purses and paid for their services.

Yeah. Something was definitely brewing between those two.

"Ladies. Where are we off to?" Enric asked. He held the door open for them.

"How about Mars?" Victoria said.

"Sure. Just let me juice up my space ship." A smirk curved the corners of Enric's mouth.

Victoria shook her head. "That won't be necessary. If

you don't mind, I'd actually like to go home. I promised Ma I'd help her with some things around the house today."

"Your wish is my command. Mrs. Maccari, is there somewhere I can take you?" Enric asked.

"The Dollhouse. I have some work to do."

"Yes, ma'am. If you'll excuse me for a moment, ladies."

Melina nodded and Victoria rolled her eyes as Enric moved a few steps away to make a call.

"I guess he's letting our handler know our next moves," Victoria surmised.

"He's just doing his job."

"I know, but I wish he wasn't doing it so well."

"Melina, is that you?"

Melina turned at the sound of a woman calling her name. A woman with a black pixie cut was heading her way. The woman had high cheek bones and a warm smile. She wore a pair of blue jeans that hugged her hips and a yellow off-the-shoulder peasant top that showcased her toned shoulders and arms.

No.

It couldn't be, but somehow it was.

"Erika?"

"I know I look a little different, but dang. You act like you just saw a ghost."

Erika came up to where Melina stood and hugged her hard. Melina was so caught off guard it was a minute before she even had the presence of mind to hug her former cellmate back.

"Melina?" Victoria questioned.

The two women parted and Melina turned to her sister-in-law. "Victoria, this is Erika. She was my ..."

"Roommate. Nice to meet you, Victoria." Erika extended her hand.

"Nice to meet you, Erika."

The two women shook hands before Erika turned her warm smile back on Melina.

"Vic, can you give us a minute?" Melina asked.

"Sure. I guess Mr. Smart Aleck can keep me entertained for a few minutes."

Victoria moved away to give the two women some privacy.

"Never thought you would see me again, huh?"

"I must admit, this is a surprise."

"And I know you hate surprises," Erika finished.

Melina laughed. "Yes, but this one I don't mind so much. It's good to see you, Erika. This is a different look than what I'm used to."

"Yeah. I wanted to do something a little different. I figured it was time for a fresh start."

"You made a wise decision. Not every woman can rock a pixie cut so well."

"Thank you. Listen, I don't mean to hold you up. Is there a chance that we could get together sometime soon and talk?"

Melina took out a small notepad, quickly scribbled down an address and handed it to Erika.

"Meet me here tomorrow at noon," Melina said.

Erika looked down at the piece of paper. "Okay. I'll see you then."

With another hug she was gone and heading in the opposite direction. Melina stared at her former cellmate and wondered what other surprises life had in store.

"Do you think that's a good idea having her meet you there?" Mac asked.

Melina finished pulling her hair through the elastic band that held her ponytail in place.

"And what do you mean by that?" She cocked a brow at her husband.

"I'm just saying, maybe it would be better to meet her someplace neutral."

Melina grabbed her keys. "Erika has nothing to do with us and besides I have some work to do. The Dollhouse is my place and I intend to be on top of everything that happens there."

Mac raised his hands in defeat. "I don't want to fight, doll."

"I don't either."

Sighing, she walked closer to her husband and wrapped her arms around him. For a few minutes, they stood there holding each other. It was rare that they had moments like these lately. Between Mac being extra vigilant with not only his business, but keeping an eye on his family as well, quiet moments were few and far between.

"I like holding you like this," Mac finally said.

"I like it when you hold me like this."

Their eyes met and Melina smiled at her husband as she ran a thumb over his brow.

"You're going to have to stop worrying so much. You're going to get forehead wrinkles."

"What's a few wrinkles? You'll still love me anyway."

"True, but that's not the point. Lately, it seems like you have the weight of the world on your shoulders."

"Lately, it has felt that way."

Mac sat down on the bed. Melina joined him.

"Talk to me. I've got time."

He offered her a small smile. "Not much to tell. Perception is everything and right now mine is not so good. It's bad for business."

"People see what they want to see. Only a fool would believe you're responsible for any of this. You have nothing to gain and everything to lose."

"You're right, doll." He raised her hand to his lips and kissed it. "Thanks. You always know just the right words."

Melina shrugged. "What can I say? I'm good at what I do."

"Indeed, you are."

"I hate to rush off, but I don't want to keep Erika waiting. I know you're a little on edge about it, but I need you to trust my judgment. I'd never do anything to put us at risk."

"I know that."

"Good. Now I'm tired of being chauffeured around. I want to drive myself."

Mac shook his head. "One of my guys will follow behind you until you reach the club. Don't deliberately try to lose him."

Melina stood up and poked her husband in the chest. "As if I would do something like that."

Mac laughed. "Doll, you've got mischief written all over your face."

"Well, in that case, I promise to save it for when I get home tonight."

Her husband's eyes darkened as his gaze raked her from head to toe. "Hurry home, doll."

Melina picked up her purse and grabbed her keys. "You know it."

She gave him a quick kiss before she left the bedroom and was on her way to the club.

Melina parked her car in the space reserved for her in front of the building. She was glad that she'd convinced her husband to let her drive, at least. It was a step in the right direction. Still, she wasn't thrilled about being followed the entire way there. Melina had no idea who the man was that had been assigned to be her chaperone, but one thing was for certain … she wouldn't want to meet

him in a dark alley. Tall and built like a Mr. Universe
contestant, the dark-haired man locked the black Chevy
Tahoe he was driving and came over to her as she stepped
onto the sidewalk.

"Mrs. Maccari."

"And you are?" Melina extended her hand.

"Giuseppe, ma'am."

They shook hands. "Nice to meet you, Giuseppe, and
thank you for keeping an eye on me."

The hardened soldier grinned before he quickly
schooled his features. "You're welcome ma'am."

"All right, let's go in."

Before Melina could grab the door handle, Giuseppe
was opening the door for her. She smiled her thanks and
entered The Dollhouse. Because of the nature of her
business, the doors never closed. As a result, there was
someone there at all times, from bouncers to bartenders,
you name it. After all, no one was more invested in her
business than her.

"This is nice, Mrs. Maccari."

"Thank you," she said.

She couldn't keep the pride out of her voice. The
Dollhouse was her baby. A testament that she could be
more than just a mob wife that stayed home and spent her
husband's money. Stopping, Melina took a few minutes to
survey the scenery before her gaze swung to the bar. Her
appointment was already waiting. Erika sat at the bar,
sipping what looked like an apple martini. Melina walked
over and touched her former cell mate's shoulder.

"Hey. You made it."

"Yeah and I'm glad I did. This place is very sexy. It
has a smooth vibe to it."

Melina took a seat on one of the bar stools next to
Erika. "Thank you. A lot of planning and hard work went
into this place. You should've seen it before I got hold of
it. You wouldn't have known it's the same place."

"Now that, I would have a hard time visualizing."

Melina motioned for the current bartender on duty, Emmanuela, to fix her a frozen pear margarita before turning her attention back to Erika.

"That one, you'll just have to trust me on. Now tell me, when did you get out? And how so soon?"

"I've been out for a couple of weeks. They let me out early for good behavior, believe it or not."

The bartender brought over Melina's drink and she took a quick sip before speaking. "About damn time. You should have been out long before this."

"I thought so at first, but I'm firmly convinced everything happens when it's supposed to."

Melina cocked a brow. "Please don't tell me you're about to wax all philosophical on me."

Erika laughed. "No, I'm not. I'm just saying that maybe I needed the time. Those months gave me time to fortify myself."

"Against what?" Melina asked.

"The weakness of my heart."

"Ah. The ex that landed you in the slammer. Is he still in the picture?"

Erika shook her head and Melina noticed the tears in her eyes. "No. He's already moved on."

Melina patted Erika's hand. "I'm sorry that he hurt you, but I'm not sorry he's out of the picture. You deserve better than a piece of shit like him."

The young woman wiped a stray tear from her eye. "You're right without question, but it still hurts that he left me holding the bag and then moved on like I never meant anything to him."

"It's fucked up on all levels, but you are a stronger woman. Nothing and no one is going to break you now. You've been through the worst."

Erika drank the last of her martini. "I sure hope so."

"Life has good and bad. You've already experienced the bad, so you're more than ready for the good to come along now."

"Like you?" Erika asked.

"What do you mean?"

"You're married now and running a business. I heard all about your super wedding while I was still in lock up. Congratulations by the way."

Melina smiled. "Yeah. He put a ring on it."

Erika laughed. "Please. He put a diamond mine on it."

"Whatever. Let's just say he knows the way to a woman's heart, no jewelry required."

"Now that is very sweet, romantic, even. I can't believe Ms. I'm-Not-A-Sappy-Romance-Heroine said that."

"Hey. Maybe marriage has mellowed me out a little bit, that's all," Melina admitted.

"Well, whatever the case is, I'm happy that everything has turned out so wonderful for you, Melina. I know life gave you some lemons, but you definitely made lemonade out of them."

Melina smiled at Erika's reference to the biggest album of the year. "That is one analogy I am happy to take. Now, enough about me. How are things with you?"

"Honestly, it's been a struggle. I had nowhere to go but my mom's and to say she and I are not getting along is an understatement. I've been looking for a job every day and haven't had any luck. It's hard out here."

Melina finished the last of her margarita before she pushed her glass away. Her heart went out to Erika. She knew all too well how hard the job market was these days. It was one of the reasons she'd turned to escorting in the first place, even before her father's medical bills had started to roll in. And Erika was going to have "felon" attached to her name for the rest of her life. That was even shittier.

Unless.

No. *What are you thinking, Melina?* She pushed away the thought and opened her mouth before she could talk herself out of it.

"How would you feel about spending time with some very wealthy gentlemen?"

Erika's eyes widened. "What do you mean?"

"Before I met my husband, I used to go on dates with some well-off gentlemen. If they had an event and they needed a date, I accompanied them. If they just wanted companionship, I provided that, to a certain extent."

"Did you have sex with them?"

"Only if I wanted to and those occasions were far and few in between."

Erika was silent for a moment as she digested what Melina was saying.

"What kind of money are we talking?"

"Let's say ten thousand was the least amount of money I ever made in a month," Melina said.

"You're lying."

Melina shook her head. "Nope."

"Okay, say I was interested, how would I get involved in something like this?"

"Welcome to The Dollhouse."

"I see."

"So, are you interested?" Melina asked.

Erika was quiet and Melina took the moment to check her phone for any missed calls or texts. When she put her phone away, Erika nodded.

"Yes. I'm interested."

"All right. Now, remember, if at any time you decide that this is not a good fit for you, no harm no foul. I won't think any less of you one way or another."

"Thanks. I appreciate your willingness to help me."

Melina smiled. "No thanks needed. Sometimes we all need a little help. Now, I'm going to be here for a little bit, why don't you mingle with a few of the ladies here and I'll catch up with you in a bit?"

"All right. Sounds good."

Melina pointed her friend in the direction of a few of

the girls that had come in earlier before she made a move to go to her own office.

"What a sight for sore eyes."

Melina stopped and turned around to find Anthony standing in front of her. A sly smirk was on his face.

"Anthony, is there something I can do for you?"

"There a great many things, but sadly none are appropriate for the wife of a fellow Capo."

Melina gritted her teeth. This asshole had the nerve to show his face in her club and make sexual innuendos. Clearly the man was looking for trouble and she was more than capable of giving it to him.

"I see it didn't take long for the snake to bare its fangs."

Anthony laughed. "You always have had a way with words, my dear. Glad to see being married hasn't completely domesticized you."

Melina folded her arms. "Is there a reason you decided to come to my establishment and insult me? I'd much prefer you slithered back under the rock you came from."

"I've missed your fire. Since Mac hardly ever lets you out of his sight now, I thought I'd swing by for a few minutes to gaze upon your lovely face."

"I think you've done more than enough gazing, so why don't you make your exit now?"

"Is that the kind of hospitality you extend to a potential customer? That's not good for business."

Melina laughed. "Your business I could do without."

"Mrs. Maccari, is there a problem?"

Giuseppe stepped from the shadows, arms folded across his barrel chest as he gazed at Anthony.

Melina shook her head. "No. No problem here."

Anthony's gaze narrowed briefly before he pasted a smug smile on his face.

"Good to see your husband keeps you well looked after. Now if you'll excuse me. I'll have a look at the delicacies you have to offer before I take my leave."

The older Capo gave her a mock bow before he walked past them and headed in the direction where a few of her girls were gathered talking.

"That guy is a real *cafone.*"

Melina bit back her laughter. "On that we can agree. Thank you for making your presence known."

"You're welcome, ma'am."

Giuseppe returned to his seat at the far corner of the bar. Melina didn't move. She stood watching as Anthony made small talk with the women. Surprisingly, only a couple of them seemed interested in attaining his attention, and even more surprisingly, one of them was Erika. From the way she smiled at him and leaned closer to hear what he was saying, the young woman was expressing definite interest.

And so was Anthony.

She'd always thought perhaps the older Capo had a certain type of woman he preferred, but might not outwardly admit.

Tonight was proving she'd been right.

Anthony's hand slid around Erika's waist, bringing her closer as he whispered in her ear. A moment later, the two of them were heading off toward the back of the club where the private rooms where.

Melina was stunned.

She'd thought it might take Erika a little time to get comfortable with her new job.

Apparently, that was not the case.

She'd watched the woman flirt with one of the slimiest men Melina had ever met and then promptly go with him to a private room. And Melina knew Anthony.

He was not a man looking for long conversation and lingering looks.

Anthony wanted sex.

Plain and simple.

Melina hoped that Erika knew what she was doing.

Glancing at her watch, Melina frowned. It was getting a bit late. She'd promised her husband she wouldn't be gone too long and she had every intention of keeping that promise. Turning, she motioned for Giuseppe.

"Yes, ma'am?"

"I think I'm going to head out now, but I need someone besides my regular guys to be here until Anthony leaves. Can you arrange that?"

"Yes. Give me just a minute, Mrs. Maccari."

Giuseppe stepped away to make his phone call and a minute later he turned his attention back to her.

"Carlito is five minutes away. He said he would be more than happy to stay."

"Thank you."

Melina dug her keys out of her purse and headed toward the door. Giuseppe followed behind her. Anthony's sudden appearance bothered her. She couldn't put her finger on why, though. The man had always been slime and jealous of her husband's success. But there was something different about tonight. Either way, Mac would not be pleased when she told him.

"Do me a favor and drive me home, I've had a couple drinks."

Melina handed over the keys to Giuseppe so that he could unlock her door. As he stepped off the sidewalk and went around to the driver's side, Melina frowned.

The streets around them were quiet.

Too quiet.

The car beeped as Giuseppe unlocked it with the remote. He opened the door and then everything happened at once.

Oil.

Fire.

And burning flesh.

The force of the explosion threw Melina backward so hard she was sent crashing to the ground.

Her head hit the sidewalk with a resounding thud and

the last thing Melina saw before she closed her eyes was a shadowy figure coming her way.

CHAPTER FOURTEEN

"*Fuck.* Jesus, give me the *strength* ..."

"A bad boy who prays, huh?" the nurse asked. "Never would have taken you for that kind of man."

Air hissed hard through teeth in a sucked inhale, and the hospital bed rattled with the force of the man's trembling as another wet, cold cloth was peeled from his skin. And with it came a strip of blackened, burned flesh.

Mac glanced away at the sight of a tear escaping from the corner of Giuseppe's eye.

There was a smell lingering in the hospital room, something that was hard to explain but Mac knew he would never be able to forget. Like dead skin, burnt oil, and antiseptic, all rolled into one. It burned his lungs with every exhale, but Mac said nothing, and he wouldn't. Giuseppe couldn't help the situation he was in, and frankly, the enforcer was lucky to be alive. Beyond that, had positions been reversed, and Giuseppe allowed Melina to drive, Mac knew all too well ...

Jesus.

It could have been his wife in the bed with forty percent of her body burned.

Thankfully, Melina was two floors down in a private suite with a few bumps and bruises, a minor burn on her side, and a concussion. She was also demanding to be let out of the hospital, asking for release the very second she could get it.

Mac wasn't allowing that just yet.

Soon, but not yet.

"Three more and then we'll be able to take a break," the nurse said.

Giuseppe's gaze flicked to Mac, who was standing in the corner with his arms crossed. The two men hadn't been able to talk a great deal with the nurses and doctors coming in and out of his unit, caring for his burns. Giuseppe was hopped up on morphine, which made anybody a little loopy in the head, but it wasn't doing fuck all for the pain. They couldn't give him more without overdosing him, and that was a real concern.

The pain was another thing that could very well kill him.

But he was taking it well.

As the nurse pulled another wet bandage off, this time from the side of Giuseppe's face that had suffered burns, he cursed a blue streak, every muscle in his body protesting as he damn near lifted himself from the bed.

Mac thought the man would have, had he actually had the strength for it.

"That's your three, sweetheart," Giuseppe told the nurse once she had replaced the bandage with a fresh one.

"Mr.—"

Giuseppe barked out a weak laugh, eyeing the pretty, young nurse who was working on his burns. "You're a cute thing—give me a break, huh? Give me five."

The nurse passed Mac a look in the corner, then nodded her head and scurried out with her head down, muttering something about getting more supplies. The room was stocked—she didn't need more, as far as that went. But if the excuse worked to get her out of the room without guilt, Mac didn't blame her.

Being on a burn unit couldn't be an easy job.

"Spit it out," Giuseppe mumbled, turning away from Mac.

Ah.

So that was it.

Giuseppe thought his Capo was angry with him, that perhaps Mac felt as though his man's decisions had been the catalyst to the bomb and Melina being hurt.

Mac had news for the guy. "Thank you."

Giuseppe turned back slowly, blinking though it seemed painful for him to do so. "Pardon, Skip?"

"Quit bugging that nurse for morphine—you're going to overdose."

"The pain is going to give me a fucking heart attack."

"Better your heart stop than to be a made man with 'overdose' stamped on the coroner's report," Mac shot back.

Giuseppe only nodded once, his silent agreement. "You shouldn't thank me. I did my job, and here we are."

"Yes," Mac murmured, "here we are. And this could have been my wife, but it isn't. I think that deserves much more than a thank you, but that will have to do."

"You and I have different ideas of what doing my job means then, Skip."

"Melina's alive. The job is good."

Whether Giuseppe was too exhausted to argue, or he didn't care to, the man said nothing.

"Tell me," Mac started to say, "Did you see anything going on or someone unusual around last night?"

"Everything was good. It was on the up. Melina had a guest or two she wanted an eye kept on, but she was also ready to go. I'd been checking the alley and the lot on and off, plus keeping an eye on her. I don't know when it happened. It shouldn't have happened."

"Maybe it wasn't set in the parking lot," Mac suggested, "or in the alley."

"Where else?" Giuseppe groaned, looking like he was about to throw up as he shifted in the bed, his broken body seeping and bleeding. It was a terrible sight, and Mac could only begin to imagine how the man must feel. "It's not like those bombs are the type to just sit idle."

"Some can, if set right. Do you remember what happened leading up to it?"

"Melina passed me the keys, she'd had a drink or two in the club. She seems like a smart woman, I wouldn't take her to drink and drive. I didn't ask, though, she just gave them to me."

Mac smiled absently. "She wouldn't, no. Then what?"

Giuseppe struggled for a good thirty seconds, rambling about things he couldn't remember and his foggy brain. Finally, he said something that might have been important. "I hit the unlock button on the fob, and then *boom*."

For some, details were unimportant.

For Mac, details were everything.

He was the kind of man that could put a lot together about a person or a situation just by a few choice details.

For now, however, his conversation with Giuseppe was finished, as he could see the young nurse making her way back with arms full of clean towels and a cup of some kind of juice in her hand.

"Stop asking for morphine," Mac reminded Giuseppe. "Because even if it doesn't overdose you, I won't have any guy of mine coming out of the hospital a junkie. I'd put a fucking bullet in your head before I'd let you ruin your name like that."

Giuseppe didn't argue. "Got it, Skip."

Mac found Enric posted outside of Melina's hospital room door. The young man rested in his chair, his gaze focused on the car magazine in his hand. Mac didn't have a lot of men to be passing around and using them for guards when they had other fucking jobs to be doing, too.

Unfortunate as it was, and given how very directed the attacks seemed to be on Mac and his wife, he'd wisely chosen to move Enric from his mother and sister, to his wife for a while.

At least until Melina was out of the hospital and home.

She wasn't going to like it, but Mac was locking her down after this.

Until this shit was figured out—until whoever it was could be put in the ground like the dog they were—his wife was going to be safe, first and foremost.

Mac was still prepping for the battle that was sure to be.

Melina didn't frighten easily.

He figured that was half of her problem, though he loved her for it.

For now, it was one thing at a time.

That would have to wait.

To anyone passing by, Enric probably looked like a family member waiting in the hall for whoever was in the room. He even seemed distracted, given his attention never once left the magazine, even as people passed him by.

That wasn't close to being the case.

Mac was but three feet away and Enric hadn't even passed him a look, but the young man tossed his magazine aside and stood.

"How's Giuseppe?" Enric asked.

Mac frowned. "Managing."

That was the best he could offer. As it was, Giuseppe had asked no one be permitted inside his unit room, even his family. Mac understood why, given the scene it would be over the coming days and weeks and even months as his skin was stripped from his body in an effort to make graphs to help heal the burns.

It was not for the faint of heart.

"And Melina?" Mac asked.

Enric smirked, letting out a chuckle. "Just give it a minute."

Mac's brow furrowed, but sure enough, he heard the snarl of his wife shortly after a nurse had taken in yet another round of medicines and things.

"She's not happy to be in here," Enric noted.

Well, it was what it was.

Mac almost considered running to the coffee shop down the street, just to give his wife a few more minutes to relax. He'd been with her for most of the night and morning, only taking a short break to make a few calls and visit Giuseppe during that time as well.

Still, Melina was not a fun patient to take care of.

He was pretty sure she was every nurse's worst nightmare.

Enric let out a laugh as though he could read Mac's mind. "Don't even try it, Mac. If she asks where you are one more time, I'm going to tell her."

"Pretty sure I'm the one running this show," Mac muttered.

"Pretty sure it's my father."

Mac flipped Enric the middle finger as he began to move past him to enter Melina's hospital room.

Enric's question stopped him. "Did you find out anything?"

Mac hesitated. It wasn't that he didn't trust Enric, because he did, but rather, he didn't know if the information was something he was right on. What Giuseppe had told him was a possible theory, and as of now, nothing more.

Mac would have to ask his wife a few details about her car over the last few days.

"It may have been on a timer," Mac said, "and probably not planted at the club."

As sick as that thought made Mac.

There were very few places Melina went, and one was the club, another was to his mother's place, and finally was their home.

If the bomb wasn't planted at the club, it was very likely that it had been set right under their noses.

That just pissed him off like nothing else.

"Bombs don't just sit idle like that in cars," Enric said, repeating what Giuseppe had noted earlier.

"That's why I said a timer," Mac offered, giving nothing else.

He strolled into the hospital room, leaving Enric behind. The nurse was still in the room, huffing with her arms crossed as Melina glared at the older woman from her perch in the bed.

"It's a *vitamin*," the woman said to his wife. "The doctor wants it added on because it's needed."

"For what?" Melina barked. "To shove more pills down my throat?"

Mac had already heard enough. "Leave the meds, thanks. Please have the doctor stop by as soon as he is able, and I'll handle it from here."

If looks could kill, the nurse would have been dead as she left the room.

Mac turned his sharp eye on his wife, letting every ounce of his displeasure pour into the look. Melina barely even flinched.

"What?" she asked.

"Stop being difficult. Take the medicine."

"They just added random pills to it without explanation!"

Mac sighed, the tremors of an oncoming migraine burning the sides of his temples. He found a seat beside his wife's bed and found her hand with his own, soaking in her warmth and her life.

Because how easily … how close they had been to losing it.

Mac found Melina staring at him, and he could plainly see how unhappy she was in that hospital bed. She probably felt helpless or useless.

Jesus.

He knew the feeling well.

"Tell me about the car, doll," he said.

Melina patted the side of her cheek were a few scrapes were. She'd had glass imbedded in those scrapes, and it had been a very painful two hours watching each little piece be pulled out with tweezers.

"I don't remember," she told him.

She'd said that over and over again.

Mac kept asking because he hoped she could regain *something* he could use.

Anything at all.

The human brain was a funny thing in that way. Any sort of hard whack or trauma and sometimes, the moments in which it happened and the time leading up to the event could be lost. His wife remembered all too well the hospital trip and even up until she lost consciousness. She couldn't remember that night, though.

Mac didn't want to push, but he didn't have a choice.

Melina was the only one with answers.

"Okay, the day before," he said. "What about the car then? Where did you go? Any new stops?"

Melina shrugged. "I picked up dinner for us, but that's not a *new* stop."

"What else?"

"I went to your mom's to get your sister a couple days ago. We went to the salon."

Mac knew about that, too.

His wife hadn't deviated at all from her usual routes, which meant to him that the bomb had probably been planted at one of their familiar haunts.

He needed to be more vigilant, clearly.

Or they were going to die.

"When you left to go to the club, did you unlock the car?" Mac asked quietly.

Melina's brow knitted together. "I don't leave my car unlocked, Mac."

"Sure, but did you unlock it?"

"I …" Melina couldn't come up with a response, and this time, Mac could see it wasn't because she couldn't remember. "I didn't unlock it, I just grabbed the door and opened it."

Mac knew how careful his wife was with her car. She loved it—it was a gift from him, and an expensive one at that. She'd been a little annoyed at first over the purchase, but quickly had gotten over it. Still, she took good care of her vehicle, and leaving it open to get stolen was not one of those things.

Not that he thought anyone would steal the car of a Capo's wife.

That would be fucking stupid.

"I didn't realize until now," Melina said. "Someone messed with my car?"

"They would have had to, in order to set the bomb, doll. But the more important thing to me is the timer it was set on—that says a lot. Any fucking idiot can put together a shitty little pipe bomb and drop it in a garbage can on a timer from a burner phone. It takes some real skill to set up a bomb on a car's unlocking mechanism."

Melina seemed to understand right away. "And how many people do you know that can do that?"

"One, maybe."

But he'd have to go through Luca, first.

It didn't matter.

Mac was going there.

Melina gave her husband a brilliant smile, one of the few she'd managed since entering the hospital. "We'll figure it out."

Well, he would.

He still wasn't ready to tell her about the new rules regarding her and not going very far, though. Not yet. Her mood was better, and Mac wasn't about to ruin that.

Mac smiled back, leaned over the bed, and gave her a quick kiss.

A clearing throat interrupted their moment. Pulling back from his wife with a wink, Mac found the doctor standing in the doorway, his clipboard in hand and his stethoscope slung around his neck. Glancing down at the file, the doctor shook his head.

"Mrs. Maccari, you are giving my nurses some kind of hell, aren't you?" he asked, amusement coloring up his words.

Mac laughed under his breath, even at his wife's scowl.

"I don't *need* to be in here," Melina said firmly. "I'm taking up a bed—"

"Yes, well, until your husband agrees to discharge you, given the price he paid for this room and the tests he asked for, you will remain right where you are."

Fuck.

Fucking *fuck.*

Melina turned those eyes on Mac.

Perhaps he had forgotten to mention that it was him keeping her in here as long as possible. Maybe he had been blaming it on the hospital.

Truth was, he did just want to make sure she was okay.

"And while I am at it," the doctor continued, not giving Melina the slightest *chance* to even argue, "you will take that vitamin the nurse brought in with your other medicine. When you leave, I expect you to make a stop at the drugstore and pick up a bottle of your own for future use. One a day for the rest of the pregnancy."

Mac froze, and so did Melina.

They were both stuck like that, Melina staring at the doctor with her mouth slightly open and her eyes a bit wider than they were.

Mac was just caught staring at her.

Pregnant.

"That's not …" Melina tipped her head to the side like she was trying to comprehend that statement.

"Possible?"

Mac's grin was growing, his hand squeezing tighter around his wife's.

Because hell yes.

"I assure you it is," the doctor replied, turning on his heel to leave. "Congratulations."

The man wasn't gone but two minutes and Melina turned on Mac, a mixture of uncertainty and joy dancing over her pretty features.

"Get me out of this place," she told him.

Mac was already standing before she'd finished her sentence. He leaned down and caught her still-surprised lips with his own, wanting her kiss.

She was going to have a fit, he knew.

She was going to be scared about the changes.

But Melina would be *just fine*.

"Whatever you want, doll."

Mac had a feeling he would be saying that a lot for the next eight or nine months.

Mac peeled out of bed with measured slowness and extra grace, so as not to jostle his wife more than he had to for fear of waking her up. The beeping of his phone had woken him, and the call had been one he was waiting for.

Luca was willing to see him.

Mac checked the clock.

Apparently, the boss would see him at five in the fucking morning.

Quickly, Mac dressed, not bothering with the suit he'd usually wear to see the boss, but opting for a pair of jeans, a button down, and a leather jacket. Just outside the entrance of their apartment building, Mac found Enric leaning against the brick, a cigarette hanging from his lips.

Mac pulled out his own pack and lit one up, ignoring the chill in the air as nicotine burned his lungs.

"Heading out?" Enric asked.

That much was obvious.

Mac didn't grace it with a response. "You never really sleep, do you?"

"Will when I'm dead."

Enric wasn't required to watch the building, the vehicles, or Melina while Mac was around. It was the young man's only off time from the job.

But that wasn't how he worked.

Mac appreciated it, and he sincerely hoped Luca knew the kind of son he had in Enric. The kid was doing this the right way—the whole Cosa Nostra thing, just like Mac had done.

That was something to be proud of, really.

"I'm going to catch a meeting with the boss," Mac said. "I was going to call you and get you over here, but …"

"Figured I already was?"

"I was right."

Enric shrugged. "We don't need another bomb incident."

Point taken.

"Melina is sleeping," Mac said, "so be quiet if you want to go in and get some food or chill."

"I'm good watching the sky, Mac."

Enric was a good kid.

A little strange sometimes.

He had a lot of mouth.

But good.

Without a goodbye, Mac headed into the underground garage to grab his Ducati. He figured it would get him across town to where Luca wanted to meet up a hell of a lot faster than his car, and then it would get him back faster, too.

Traffic wasn't bad, and Mac was just pulling into what

looked to be a rundown, abandoned warehouse less than twenty minutes after he'd gotten the call from the boss. He made good time, if nothing else.

Mac parked around back where his bike wouldn't be seen by the highway, and made his way inside the warehouse. At first, the long hallway seemed quiet, but it wasn't long before a loud snap echoed, like leather whacking hard against skin, and a muffled shout followed the hit.

Mac followed the sound.

He found Luca, and one of his usual enforcers, on the main floor of the warehouse. Mac's shoes crunched on the dirt floor, and it took him a second to distinguish the form hanging from a hook.

A man, it seemed.

Bound, naked, and gagged.

Hanging from his ankles.

Mac's eyes widened at the sight, but he quickly schooled his features.

"That was quick," Luca said, tossing the whip he'd been wielding aside to a table.

The enforcer in the corner, a lever in his hand to control the hook the man was hanging from, never moved and didn't give Mac's arrival any of his attention.

Mac was still staring at the man hanging from his ankles. The room smelled of blood, vomit, dirt, and piss. It was quite a mixture. He didn't recognize the bleeding, bruised, and broken man, but the guy's eyes begged for help.

He didn't have any to offer.

"Amusing, isn't it?" Luca asked, passing his victim a glance over his shoulder.

Even while torturing someone, Luca dressed for his position in a three-piece suit that seemed clean of blood and dirt. Mac had no idea how his boss managed it.

"What is?" Mac asked.

"How quick they are to apologize once they

understand the pain a mistake can cause."

Mac didn't know what to say to that.

Apparently, Luca wasn't looking for a response, but he did wave at the hanging man. "As you can see, I'm still working on my end, Maccari. And this *cafone* is just about the closest I have come to getting anywhere."

"And he is?" Mac dared to ask.

It was hard to say if Luca would answer.

"A decoy," Luca mused, smiling just slightly as he passed the guy another dismissive look. "Planted to distract me, I think. Seems the FBI thought putting a simple cop on the ground in plain clothes with a decent Italian accent would work to get him in one of my Capo's crews. But again—he's a *distraction*."

Mac wasn't getting it. "Sorry, boss?"

"I'm getting nothing from him—they've given him nothing to work with. They want my attention elsewhere, and I need to figure out why."

"Which crew?" Mac asked.

"Audino," Luca said.

Corrado Audino was a Capo Mac tended to stay away from, if only for the fact the man housed his good for nothing bastard of a father. James Sr. worked under that crew for years after his brother's death.

Mac wanted nothing to do with it.

"Seems a little strange that Corrado would have a mole in his bunch and not have even a suspicion about it," Mac said.

Crews were not that big.

If shit like that was happening in *his* crew, Mac would know about it.

Simple as that.

It was part of being a good Capo.

Luca chuckled blandly. "He did know—that's why I am here, and well …" He trailed off, waving at the now-crying man. "So is he, hmm."

Ah.

Now Mac understood.

"You think they made him obvious for a reason, to keep your eye on someone else while they did work elsewhere," Mac said.

Luca waved a finger at Mac. "Sometimes you take too long to figure these things out, you know."

"It's early as hell—give me a break."

"Nonetheless, I assume they believed I would not touch their garbage because he *was* so obvious. I feel like now I need to send them a message." Luca gestured at the man again, adding, "My message will be ready later in the morning, of course."

Nobody could ever say Luca was not good at his job.

Or serious about it, for that matter.

It was a little dangerous—like sticking your hand in the fire—when it came to hurting cops so blatantly. Luca was asking for an arrest of some sort.

Mac decided not to point that out.

"Well, get on with it," Luca said after a moment. "You wanted a meeting—what is it?"

The time was now or never.

Mac forced back the concern he felt over what he was about to ask his boss.

"I need a sit down with Enzo," Mac said, continuing on, before Luca could ask why he was demanding a seat with the family's underboss and the only close friend the boss had left. "The bomb that was put on my wife's car had to have been set up to the car's locking system, and when it was unlocked by the fob, it blew. The car would have locked when Melina got in it to drive to the club— mechanically, of course. Because that's what it does when someone drives off. We know the bomb couldn't have been set at the club, it had to be somewhere else."

Luca was still staring at Mac, silent.

He didn't look pleased.

"Fact is, Enzo is the only man I know in this state with the ability to make a bomb like that with the skill it

BETHANY-KRIS
ERIN ASHLEY TANNER

would take to work the electronics on the car," Mac finished.

It took an entire three minutes before Luca spoke again, and two of those were spent by him whipping his captive until the man passed out.

Mac was grateful Luca's sudden aggression, likely caused by him, had gone elsewhere.

"I know what you're thinking," Luca muttered heavily, "but you're wrong, Mac."

It wasn't often the boss called him by his nickname. It was almost always "Maccari" to Luca.

"I'm not *thinking* anything," Mac replied respectfully.

As respectfully as he could manage, that was.

He was thinking something—that Enzo either had something to do with the bomb, or knew who did. And while Mac was fit to kill, especially any fucker that messed with his wife, he had to go about this the *right* way.

A way that wouldn't get him a bullet and a makeshift grave.

He needed Luca's permission.

"Deny it, boss, but those skills are passed down. If not Enzo, then someone he knows. People don't wake up one day, knowing how to make bombs like this one," Mac argued.

Luca sighed heavily, scrubbing a hand down his face and looking more tired by the second. "Give me some time—I want to look into this."

"You take care of the rat issue—I take care of the other issue. That was our deal, boss."

"Be that as it may, this is …" Luca trailed off, glancing at the enforcer who still wasn't paying them much attention. He still lowered his voice when he added, "This is my friend—my very last friend—and you will give me that respect *before* I allow you a single fucking step toward him. Understood?"

How was Mac supposed to argue with that?

"I'll wait on your call, boss."

As much as it killed him to say those words, Mac knew he didn't have a choice. He would have to check his rage at least until he could do something about it.

Luca dismissed him with a wave.

Mac heard a splash of water and mumbled groans as he was leaving, the sound of whipping starting up once more.

Mac strolled into his living room to find Enric seemingly passed out on the couch and the apartment quiet.

Sleep when he's dead my ass, Mac thought.

He grabbed the tumbler glass full of water on the coffee table, holding it over Enric's head and ready to pour it over the young man.

Enric stopped him with a quiet, "Do that, and you'll owe me a new jacket."

Mac laughed, willing to give the kid his dues. "You've got too smart of a mouth."

"Yeah, you keep telling me that, and it's still working just fine."

Enric pushed off the couch, opening his eyes at the same time.

"Head out," Mac told him. "Today is an *off* day, Enric. I want quiet time, which means I'll be here, with my wife. No one needs to be here. Take a day."

"Sure," Enric said, already heading for the front door.

Mac knew the kid wouldn't listen.

Once the apartment was quiet again, Mac headed for the bedroom, positive Melina wouldn't have even noticed his absence. She was probably still sleeping, given the busy few days they had, and she was supposed to be resting as much as she could.

Surprisingly, his wife wasn't in their bed.

No, Mac found her in the attached bathroom, a large white towel wrapped around her body as she ran a brush through the wet curls of her hair. Mac leaned in the doorway, thoroughly enjoying the view of his wife.

Slick, caramel skin.

The curve of her thighs.

The swell of her ass.

He liked it best when she didn't know he was watching—then he could admire all of her silently, taking her in piece by piece.

What a beautiful life—an amazing soul—she truly was.

Perfect for him.

Mac said nothing as Melina kept on with her routine, setting the brush aside and stepping back from the mirror. She glanced back at her reflection, her gaze darting downward. She undid the towel just enough to peek at her flat midsection in the mirror, almost like she was trying to see if there was any change.

There wasn't.

Not yet.

But Mac felt it … that change of what *would be*.

And it was fucking amazing.

He didn't think his wife had ever looked more beautiful than she did right then, so unknowing of his presence, newly pregnant with their child, and so sweet.

The rushing lust that suddenly climbed up his spine was crazy, almost as if he couldn't help himself. Maybe it was mix of all that had happened, and his lack of ability or knowledge to do something about it when all he really wanted to do was love and protect his wife like he'd promised her on their wedding day.

And maybe it was a little bit more, too.

Like the way she looked.

Even with those scratches and bruises.

She was still so beautiful—crazy sexy.

Mac slipped into the room before he could convince himself not to. Melina didn't even see him coming before he had an arm around her waist and was pulling her back into him. He pressed a lingering kiss to the side of her temple and then he was sweeping her up off the floor, turning her around and sitting her back down on the counter.

When that towel fell from her grip fully, exposing her soft skin and sinful curves to him, all of the stress Mac had been feeling was gone.

He kissed her again, on her mouth that time, taking his time to taste her as she worked at the buttons on his shirt and pushed the article down his arms. He felt her hand tug at his pants, too, working them down around his hips just enough to get his already-hardened cock free.

It was a little fast—maybe rushed.

That was okay, too.

"You weren't with me when I woke up," he heard her whisper in his ear.

Mac kissed the delicate line of her jaw, making her tilt her head back as he spread her thighs wider to get where he wanted. She was wet and hot under the pads of his fingertips, silky fucking smooth and *ready*.

He'd play later—keep her in bed all day with promises of bliss and exhaustion if she wanted.

Right then he just wanted to love—to *fuck*.

"Stuff came up," he said.

Melina didn't ask another thing, but that could be because Mac had shifted his hips and with the base of his cock in his hand, he was right there at the entrance of her pussy. One hard flex of his hips and her heaven was taking him in entirely, fitting him perfectly and swallowing him whole.

For those first few brief seconds, he was gone.

Out of breath.

Tight in stomach.

Hot up his spine.

God, he loved his wife.

Melina's fingernails dug into his sides as she pulled him toward her closer, her heels pressing into the backs of his thighs. "Fuck."

Nothing turned him on more than dirty words in her mouth.

It wasn't unusual for her to swear, as far as that went, but something as pretty as her mouth shouldn't have filthy words on it.

He really didn't mind.

"I'll wake you up tomorrow," he promised as he thrust in once, pulled out, and slammed right back in again.

"The house isn't going to be built in time for the baby," she said.

Mac grabbed her jaw, forcing her to look at him as he fucked her. Those worries of hers would be put to rest as soon as he could make them go. "The house will be ready, doll. Whatever you want, you know that."

Melina's head fell back against the mirror when he let her go, his name falling from her lips as his tempo came a little faster—*harder.*

Her words jumbled together as her bottom lip trembled.

There, Mac, right there and *Jesus* and *Fuck me harder.*

All Mac could feel was a slick heat, tight against his cock and his wife in his hands.

That was really all he needed to feel.

The rest of the world didn't exist then.

Just them.

CHAPTER FIFTEEN

Melina stood in front of the bathroom mirror. She didn't look much different.

Except for the scratches on her face.

Marks that were a stark reminder of what had happened to her and how it could've been so much worse.

At first she'd worried that the scrapes would leave permanent scars, but now it didn't matter. Beauty was only skin deep. There was something so much more precious to worry about. Reflexively her hands touched her abdomen. It was flat and toned, with no evidence that something wonderful brimmed beneath the surface.

She was pregnant.

She didn't know how or why the tiny baby growing inside of her had chosen now to come to life. This wasn't the ideal situation to bring a child into, especially when at any moment she or her child's father could be taking their last breaths. Their child could die before it ever had a chance to really live. Fear touched the back of her throat, like a soft breeze. A gentle reminder that though she was safe at the moment, it could quickly change.

Melina was going to be a mother and though she hadn't said much to Mac, she was struggling. For the first time in her life she had someone to protect, whose very existence depended on her. It was a heavy burden to bear.

"Not a burden. A blessing," she whispered to herself.

Yes. The child she carried was a blessing conceived from the love of she and her husband. She couldn't help remembering the look on Mac's face when the doctor had revealed the news.

Pure, unadulterated joy.

If she hadn't been so shocked, she might've cried.

Mac wanted children, and now she was going to give him a child. Melina had no idea if she carried a boy or a girl and truthfully, to her it didn't matter. As long as their child was healthy, that was her only concern.

"What are you doing, doll?"

Mac came up behind her, wrapping his arms around her. He pressed a kiss to the side of her neck.

"Just thinking."

"About?"

His lips continued to nuzzle her neck. Melina shivered at his touch.

"Our baby."

Slowly, Mac turned her in his arms so that they were facing each other. A small smile tugged at the corner of his mouth as he rubbed her cheek with his thumb.

"Still doesn't seem real, does it?"

Melina shook her head. "No, it doesn't."

"You know I would never let anything happen to either of you, right?"

Mac searched her face, everything in his gaze beseeching her to believe him.

"I know that you will move heaven and hell for me and this baby."

"I sense a 'but' coming."

Melina sighed, unsure of exactly how to put into words the tangle of emotions that were plaguing her.

"You can't protect us from everything."

There.

She'd said it.

She had spoken into existence every secret terror that had newly begun to steal her happiness.

210

GANGSTER MOLL

"I'm trying, Melina."

There was an undercurrent of anger and frustration in his tone. She recognized it instantly and just as swiftly regretted saying anything. "Just forget it."

Melina brushed past him and walked into their bedroom. Mac followed her, standing next to the bed as she curled up in the middle.

"What do you want me to say, Melina? That I fucked up? Fine. I admit it. I fucked up. I let someone get too damn close to you and that shit is eating me up inside."

"I know that and I'm not blaming you. I just ..."

Mac sat down beside her. "Then what is it?"

"I don't want to lose our child."

"I see," Mac said simply.

"Do you? It was one thing to deal with all of this when I only had myself to be concerned with, but now we have a baby that can be caught in the crossfire. I couldn't live with myself if anything happened to our child."

Mac took her hand in his. "Neither could I. Do you know how long I lay awake at night staring at you while you sleep? I'm not much of a praying man, doll, but if showing the man upstairs a little reverence will keep the two of you safer than I can, I have no problem with showing a little humility."

Melina knew how much it took out of Mac to admit that there were some things that were beyond his control. She could see from the tightness of his jaw and the shadows beneath his eyes how their current situation was wreaking havoc on him. The last thing she wanted to do was put anymore burdens on his shoulders.

"Whatever enemies that come against us we can fight, but we have to be able to see them first, Mac."

"I know and I'm doing what I can on my end."

Melina touched his face. "I know you are and I'm not blaming you for any of this. I need you to understand that. I'm just saying we could be better prepared if we knew who we needed to protect ourselves from."

211

"I have a few suspects in mind."

Melina raised a brow. "Anything definitive?"

"Not yet, but something is better than nothing."

"That's one way of looking at things. Have you checked on your mother and Victoria since all of this went down?"

"I've had guards on them around the clock."

Melina gave her husband a half smile. "That isn't the same thing. You need to go and see them. No doubt your mother is feeling abandoned."

"What about you?"

"What about me? I'm going to take a nap. Enric is here."

"Are you sure?"

"Yes. Now go see your family before your mother wants to kick my butt. Besides, I think hearing our news will make her forgive your extensive absence."

Melina pulled Mac close and kissed him softly on the lips before pushing him away.

"Just a taste, doll?"

She laughed. "There'll be more when you get back. Don't I always keep my word?"

"Indeed, you do."

Mac leaned close and kissed her again. Hard. His tongue invaded her mouth and when he moved away from her again she felt bereft.

"You never play fair, Mac."

"All's fair in love and war. You taught me that, doll."

Rising with a final wink, her husband left their bedroom. Feeling as if some of the gloom that had been clouding her mood was slowly lifting away, Melina laid down and held a pillow close to her body.

Yes. Everything would be all right.

Her husband would keep them safe. She'd never met a man more determined than Mac.

Family was everything to him and somewhere along the way it had become everything to her, too.

Melina didn't know how long she'd been asleep.

What she did know was that her stomach was rumbling.

Stretching, Melina rolled out of bed and made her way through the apartment. Stopping in the living room, she found Enric sitting on the couch, sharpening the blade of a knife. She watched for a moment, listening to the rhythmic sound of the knife rubbing up against the stone.

It was soothing somehow.

Order in a chaotic world.

"If you're going to keep watching, you might as well come and sit down."

Melina laughed. "How did you know I was here?"

Enric turned to face her. "You do realize I'm pretty good at my job or your husband wouldn't have trusted me to protect you, right?"

"Yes. I'm well aware of how much Mac trusts you."

"Good." He turned back to sharpening his knife. "I heard you in the bedroom when you rolled over and the minute your feet hit the floor, ma'am."

"Remind me never to try and sneak up on you. Now, I'm going to find something to eat."

"I wouldn't be opposed to a snack either," Enric called out.

"I'll see what I can do."

Walking into the kitchen, Melina went to the refrigerator first. She grabbed the jug of lemonade and poured herself a glass. Then she pulled out the ingredients to make pesto pasta salad with a side of proscuetto and fresh foccata bread. No doubt her husband would love a little something home-cooked when he made it back home. She was certain this pregnancy was going to put her in the Suzy Homemaker mode she had been running from for so long. Absentmindedly, she touched her belly as she reached for one of the large mixing bowls.

A loud crash made her stop what she was doing.

Pop. Pop. Pop.

Gunfire.

Melina held back the scream that threatened to tear from her throat.

Looking around the kitchen, she grabbed a large steak knife. She didn't know what the hell was going on, but she wasn't about to go down without a fight. The sound of gunfire continued and then there was only silence.

And then she heard men's voices.

Melina wanted to run, but she didn't know what she'd be running into. Besides she'd never make it to her bedroom. She held her breath as the sounds of footsteps came closer to the kitchen.

"Hello, cunt."

What the fuck?

James Maccari Sr. was pointing a gun at her.

"What are you doing here, James?" She struggled to keep her voice steady.

"Melina, I always pegged you for a smart girl. Don't be stupid. You don't need me to spell it out for you."

She clutched the knife tighter in her grip. Fear clawed at the back of her throat, but she couldn't give in to it. Not now. She had to survive.

For herself.

For the child that she carried.

Two men appeared in the kitchen behind James.

"What are we waiting on?" one of the men asked.

"I'm just waiting for my daughter-in-law to realize there's no point in fighting and come peacefully."

James' henchmen came around him and toward Melina.

"If you think I'm going to just give up, you have another thing coming."

Melina slashed at the man nearest her. The knife connected with his bicep. He grabbed it as blood started to pour from the wound. The other man moved toward her and Melina struck out again, but he caught her wrist and twisted it, forcing her to drop the knife. She cried out when she heard a loud crunch. Pain shot down her wrist, hot and burning. A hard punch to the face sent her stumbling to the kitchen floor.

"We could've done this the easy way, Melina, but now I don't give a fuck. Take care of her, boys."

Hurriedly she tried to pick herself up, but a kick to her ribs left her panting in pain.

"Fucking bitch."

Melina bit her lip as hot tears cascaded down her face. She wanted to fight back. She wanted to rip their faces off, but her continued resistance could cost her the baby's life. Instead, she allowed the two men to lift her to her feet. Holding her tight by both arms, they marched her out of the kitchen and down the hall. When they came to the living room, she saw Enric lying face down. His blood soaked the carpet. Two bullet holes in his back continued to ooze blood.

She blinked back the tears that threatened to fall.

Enric was young.

So young.

Too young for the brutality of this lifestyle.

It was only when she noticed that three more bodies lay face down in the living room that she felt a small measure of comfort. Enric may have gone down, but he'd taken some of the bastards with him. Melina gasped as a sharp pain stabbed her in the side. Her ribs were bruised and possibly even broken from the force of the kick she'd received. She wouldn't cry. Not now. Not ever. As she was dragged out of her apartment, Melina could only wonder just how deep the betrayal ran and if Mac even had a clue about the shit storm he was about to walk into.

CHAPTER SIXTEEN

"**M**a?" Mac called, stepping further into the house. "Vic?"

"In the kitchen," came the response.

Mac found his mother, and his sister, prepping dough at the island with flour up to their elbows. Both women looked perfectly happy in their element, and especially together. It made him smile.

It wasn't often that he got sentimental, especially where his mother and sister were concerned. But seeing them like this, it reminded him of his younger years when his mother was just teaching them how to cook. Those were some of his fondest memories.

They hadn't had a lot of money. That really hadn't made much of a difference to the life his mother provided to him and his sister. Cynthia had given Mac and Victoria something better in her love, and that was what he remembered the most.

"Something smells good," Mac noted, pulling up a stool to sit on.

Cynthia smiled over at her son, her hands still kneading the heavy dough. "I have a batch in the oven already. You can take some with you when it's done."

"If he stays long enough," Victoria muttered.

"I'll stay," Mac assured.

"Where's Melina?" Cynthia asked.

"At home, getting some rest."

Mac chose his words carefully, knowing damn well his mother wouldn't like the truth of the matter. He'd managed to keep the bomb incident from reaching his mother's ears, and he planned to keep it that way forever, if he could help it. Cynthia wouldn't like knowing how dangerous things were becoming for Mac, never mind Melina.

As it was, his mother didn't approve.

She was *barely* dealing with the enforcers he had trailing her and watching her home.

Barely being the keyword.

"Is she not feeling well?" Cynthia asked, a smile starting to grow.

Mac wondered why on earth his mother would *smile* about Melina not feeling well.

"Something like that," Mac settled on saying, still confused.

Victoria nudged her mother with her elbow, also smiling in a way that said the two were sharing a private secret that Mac was not privy to.

He wasn't sure how much longer he was supposed to let this go on, but he was just about done with it all.

"All right, what am I missing?" he asked.

Cynthia tipped her head to the side, giving Mac a sly smile. "How long have you two been married now?"

"What does that have to do with you two acting strange?"

Victoria sighed, flicking her fingers at her brother and splattering him with dots of flour. He brushed off the spots from his suit as Victoria said, "Is she pregnant or what?"

"Victoria!" Cynthia exclaimed, looking mortified.

His sister acted like their mother hadn't said a thing, never taking her eyes off of Mac. "Listen, Ma won't ask because she's too proper for it—your business, you handle it, okay. But Melina's been shut in for a while. She hasn't called me and she seemed tired the last time we did meet up, and maybe a bit more irritable than normal."

Mac cleared his throat, amused. "And that made you think she's pregnant? Because we all know Melina has her days, Vic."

"That's not an answer."

Cynthia pressed her lips together and then quietly said, "She's right. That wasn't an answer, James."

"You two are far too nosy for your own good."

"I think what you mean is we're very much alike," Victoria replied, grinning.

Mac shrugged. "Same difference."

Cynthia was not paying either of the siblings any mind, she only wanted her answer, Mac learned. "Well, is she? Pregnant, I mean."

"Well …"

His mother stared, still and with excitement palpable. She would be so happy, he knew.

Cynthia would make the best grandmother.

"Yeah, Ma," Mac finally said, "she is. We've got an appointment next week to find out exact dates and all of that."

If the shouts of happiness could have been any louder, Mac's eardrums would have burst. He accepted his mother's congratulations, and his sister's, and then damn near fell off the stool when Cynthia wrapped him in a hug while pressing a kiss to his cheek.

As the two women chatted, lost in their own excitement, Mac slipped out of the kitchen and then out of the house altogether.

While he was visiting his mother to share the news of the pregnancy with her, he also had to chat with the enforcer he had posted outside of her house.

Just to make sure shit was good.

He found the man in his car, doing his job, thankfully. Some enforcers liked to slack a little when they thought they could get away with it. Mac had to keep up on that shit.

His enforcer rolled down the window as Mac approached.

"How's it been?" Mac asked.

The guy had been put on detail after he'd pulled Enric to work on guarding his wife.

"Quiet," the man replied.

"That all?"

The enforcer shrugged his big shoulders. "That fuck up you call a father came around last night, but he didn't stay long after I told him to scram. Although, your mother was already in the process of doing the same thing. That woman is the strangest—"

"Back the fuck up," Mac interrupted.

"Seriously," the enforcer continued, "she brings me out cake and bread, or coffee, and then swears like a goddamn sailor at your father when he comes here drunk in the middle of the night."

Mac's hand slammed hard on the hood of the car. "Back. The. Fuck. Up. My father was here?"

The enforcer blinked up at him. "Yeah, but your mom said it wasn't the first time and not to worry about it."

After Mac had bought his mother her new house, he had been very careful about keeping the information from his father. Not that James Sr. couldn't find where the house was and visit, but it wasn't *for* him, and he knew to stay the hell away.

What was more concerning, was the fact that his mother didn't feel the need to mention her estranged husband was still coming around.

"Next time, don't let the bastard get anywhere near the front door," Mac told the man.

Spinning around and not even waiting to hear the response of the enforcer, Mac jogged back to the house, entering and heading straight for the kitchen where he could hear his mother and sister still talking about baby-related things and family names.

The moment he was standing in the entry way, his mother seemed to know.

"What's wrong?" she asked him.

Mac tried to school his features.

He didn't *want* to be angry with his mother.

She was only doing what she had always done in regards to his father.

"James was here?" Mac asked.

Cynthia waved a flour-dusted hand high as if to wave off his concerns. "It's no—"

"Don't say that it's nothing, Ma."

Victoria frowned, giving Mac a pointed look. "He didn't even get inside, Mac."

"*This* time," Mac argued. "This time he didn't get let in because an enforcer is outside. How many other times has he showed up, forcing his drunk ass into your house and making demands? The old house is one thing, Ma, because his fucking useless name was on the deed. This house is for you—it's yours, not his."

"Watch your mouth," Cynthia said weakly. "No swearing in my kitchen."

"How many times, Ma?" Mac asked, determined to get an answer.

"It's nothing important, really. I let him fumble and stumble around before he passes out, and then he's gone before morning. He rarely makes it past the living room."

"Ma!"

Cynthia's gaze flew up at Mac's shout, meeting his warily. "I—"

"*How many times?*"

"It's just been the last few months," Cynthia admitted quickly. "One night he came with dog bites up his arm, he clearly needed medical attention and …"

Mac wasn't sure when the realization hit him.

At the dog bite statement, maybe.

He distinctly remembered the fact that Luca's dogs had gotten the person who killed Matthew—or at least, bitten them a few good times before the killer got away. At first, it had been assumed the dogs had attacked Matthew, which was why Luca had been so adamant that night that Matthew was on the path and the dogs wouldn't have attacked.

"When was that?" Mac asked.

Cynthia shrugged. "The morning after your wedding. I came home and he was at the old house. His arm looked terrible, but he tried to hide it."

Fuck.

Fuck, fuck … FUCK.

Mac knew what he was missing, now.

It had been his father.

All the issues …

The attacks …

He'd thought his father was too much of a fuck up to really be able to pull something like this off, and he'd totally overlooked the man. Still, the bomb made no sense. James Sr. had no skill of that sort, but maybe he knew someone who did.

Nonetheless, his mistake was James Sr.'s gain.

Mac already had his back turned to his mother, readying to leave.

"Did I do something wrong?" Cynthia asked.

He didn't answer his mother.

He didn't know how to.

Mac was halfway home when his phone buzzed with a call. Hitting the button on the steering wheel to answer, the call went through to Bluetooth and he picked it up.

"Mac here," he said.

"I hear you wanted a sit down, Maccari."

The voice of Enzo only faintly registered to Mac's

ears. He was more concerned about getting home to his wife, and then dealing with his fuck up of a father as soon as possible. Now that he knew for sure that his father had at least one hand in the attacks, he had every single right to do what needed to be done to prevent James Sr. from causing Mac any more problems.

There were benefits to being a made man, after all.

This was one of those.

"Depends on what you're going to tell me," Mac finally said.

Enzo's heavy sigh echoed throughout the speakers of the vehicle. "I've been working on a new project—tinkering, really."

"Bomb timers, you mean?"

"Let's keep the conversation clean, okay."

Mac resisted the urge to hang up on Enzo. "What kind of tinkering?"

"MIT was a breeze for me—that engineering degree was nothing. So tinkering is nothing more than child's play. My son, he's always so interested in what I was doing, and I thought … where's the harm, right?"

Now they were getting somewhere.

"Keep going," Mac said.

Enzo coughed, a sign of his stress about what he was getting ready to say. "I started having issues with my son a few months ago. He's young, seventeen. I thought it was a phase, that maybe I could smack or work it out of him. I had nobody to blame but myself, or that's what my wife kept telling me. Look at everything I'd exposed him to, right? I let him learn the streets and play with guns, so who was really at fault?"

"Is there a point to this?" Mac asked. "Because I would really like to hear you get to it."

Mac was toeing the line of what could be considered disrespectful to a man who held a great deal more power than he did, but he figured given the situation, his attitude was warranted.

"I let him fuck around in the Audino crew, thinking he'd settle down and learn something. Chill out with the drugs, maybe, and earn some money that didn't come from him draining his fucking trust fund."

Jesus Christ.

"That never really happened," Enzo continued sadly. "The night of your wedding was the first time Luca really noticed something was wrong with my boy, that I was letting shit slide. We argued about it and Matthew jumped in."

Mac remembered seeing the scene of that fight, and wondering what it was about.

Now he supposed he knew.

Or partly, anyway.

"So I kept him closer, still letting him do his thing and hoping he was getting his shit straight."

"But he wasn't," Mac assumed.

"No," Enzo admitted. "But he was hanging around me more often, picking up things that I was working on, seeming interested."

"Your son planted that bomb on my wife's car, didn't he?"

"He did it for someone else, because he felt he owed him."

"My father?" Mac guessed.

"How did you know?"

"James is in the Audino crew and he's got a taste for drugs and liquor. I'm not fucking stupid, I can put two and two together."

"My boy is mixed up in a lot of bad things, Mac. Heroin, messing around in the crews, stealing and lying. He's facing charges I didn't even know about with the police, so who knows what the *fuck* he's been telling them."

"And where is your son?" Mac asked, not giving a shit about the other details. He wasn't about to feel the least bit sorry for Enzo's son. He didn't have the time or care for it.

"Safe," Enzo replied. "That's all you need to know. Don't blame me for taking care of my boy, Mac."

The phone call hung up just as Mac pulled into the complex of his apartment.

Immediately, he knew something was wrong.

Ambulances.

Flashing lights.

Crime scene tape.

He *knew* right then.

But it was only when an officer knocked on his window with a flashlight did the weight of it hit Mac.

And it hit like a fucking freight train.

Mac knocked on the glass of the ICU room's door, not wanting to interrupt. Just because the boss had called him into the hospital didn't mean Mac had any right to walk right into the room where Luca currently was.

"Come on in," he heard called out, the voice muffled behind the glass.

The hiss of oxygen was the first thing Mac heard as he opened the glass doors to Enric's ICU room. The second was the loud, beeping monitors—several were scattered about the room, from an IV, to one for his heart function, and another that seemed to be monitoring his brain.

All over again, guilt swamped Mac at the sight of the young man wrapped in bandages, a tube shoved down his throat to keep him breathing, and his body prone with little life.

Luca sat at his son's bedside, a phone to his left, and a cup of to-go coffee in his hand. His gaze never left Enric as Mac entered. The lights were dimmed in the room, and other than the noise of the machines, there wasn't much else to hear.

Mac let the door close quietly behind him, though he didn't think Enric could hear it either way.

"They induced a coma during the surgery," Luca said quietly as he studied his son's lax features. "He was under too much stress—his body wasn't handling it well."

"I'm sorry, boss."

Luca took a minute to reply, and when he did, it wasn't in response to Mac's apology. "The cops have been around asking questions. I know they had you down at the precinct as well."

"The cops are a fucking mess."

One they *really* didn't need.

"Two FBI agents showed up about an hour ago," Luca added.

Mac cringed. "So there is something going on there, too."

"Seems so. Although, I have no idea who is feeding them information. I'm worried—I know something is going to happen, and I'm helpless to stop it because I don't know *who* or *why*. I'm failing. I had one job in *la famiglia*, and I'm failing horribly."

Mac was all too aware that a boss's main job was to protect his men, and his family. It wasn't Luca's fault that things were falling apart at the seams. It wasn't his choices or actions that put all of this into motion.

"We'll figure it out," Mac eventually said.

Luca nodded, finally giving Mac his attention. "Your wife, where is she?"

Mac's throat closed, the reminder that Melina was still in the wind, stuck as a victim of his father's crazy plan. "I don't know, boss."

"Enzo said—"

"Enzo answered a lot that I didn't know," Mac interjected quickly, "and I apologize for thinking he was involved in some way with the attacks."

Luca smiled thinly. "Enzo is a good man. Well, as good as we made men can be, that is."

"I am sorry about Enric. I didn't mean for him to be caught up in all of this like he was. I thought whoever it was wouldn't be stupid enough to attack me again in such a public way."

"Desperate men ..." Luca trailed off, his brow raising as if to allow Mac to finish the sentence.

"My father has been desperate for a long time."

"Seems he found others who are just as desperate to work with him. The better question is *why*, Mac."

Mac nodded, wondering that himself.

Although, if he were honest, he didn't think he had to ponder on it all for very long. From the very moment Mac had gained any kind of traction in *la famiglia*, a feat his father had never managed to do because of his shitty lifestyle and terrible choices, James Sr. had been far too interested in his son's business and where he was going in the mafia. He'd made that clear on more than one occasion.

"I think it was because of me," Mac said.

Luca's attention was back on his son, then. "Continue."

"I think he wanted me to move up in Cosa Nostra, and his way of making me do that, was to force me into it by causing problems like he did. Problems that have, essentially, made rifts and caused trust issues between me and other Capos, and even you, boss. It gives others every reason to come after me, which gives me a good cause to defend myself, opening up seats in the family, we'll say. That's my theory."

Luca sighed. "That's a good theory."

"I should have seen it sooner."

"No one will blame you for overlooking a man whose greatest priority is getting enough money to drink, Mac."

That was true enough.

"I need to find my wife," Mac said. "Right now, that's

my main goal. I think the bomb was meant to kill her, if nothing else, to push me into a situation where I attacked someone—probably Enzo—without really thinking about what I was doing. It's likely that James Sr. might have thought Melina, or even my enforcer, saw him that night outside of the club, and so the desperation came into play, forcing his hand to take my wife."

"You think he'll kill her, rather than keep her for a while," Luca said.

Mac swallowed the lump forming in his throat. "I know he'll kill her."

And his child.

Unknowingly, sure, but it would also kill his child.

"What are you asking then?" Luca asked.

Mac passed Enric a look, knowing this would be the hardest request he ever made of his boss. Here he was, watching a man grieve and pray over his injured son, and he was about to ask that same man to give him permission to force information from another man's son by any means necessary.

"Spit it out," Luca said after a long moment of silence.

"Enzo has his son on lockdown—uh, detox, I suspect, because he thinks he can save the kid. I'm sure you've talked to him, you probably already know where he is. He won't let me near him, I know it."

Luca's head dropped down, his shoulders lowering as well, as though the weight of the world had just come upon him. "You know, when Enric's mother told me she was pregnant, I thought ... no, the child can't possibly be mine. She was a server in one of my restaurants, and we certainly weren't a couple, so to speak. She assured me the baby was mine, and if I was so inclined, I could simply wait until after the birth, and make my choices then.

"And so that was just what I did," Luca continued, smiling softly as he looked over his son. "I waited her pregnancy out—I ended up marrying Neeya during that time, though that came about rather fast, and she had no idea about the baby or the pregnancy. It came before she did, after all, and I was still quite adamant in my own belief that the baby wasn't mine."

"But he was," Mac assumed.

Luca chuckled. "God forgive me ... look at his face, how am I supposed deny him?"

Even Mac had to smile at that.

Enric was the spitting image of his father.

"Neeya was so angry—I loved her, and no matter how many times I tried to tell her that he'd come about *before* her, she wouldn't believe me. It took a while, a lot of begging on my part, a lot of hurt pride and anger, but she heard me eventually. I felt so guilty, too. I'd spent months believing Enric was not my son, and I lost all that time, even if he wasn't in the world yet. I still lost it."

Luca rubbed a hand over his jaw, shaking his head as he continued with, "And so I gave him as much time as I could while he grew up, but he always felt out of place with me and in my family. I could tell. I tried bringing him in more and more, tried giving him more, but he only pushed away."

"Maybe it's that he does better standing on his own," Mac suggested.

"He does, I know." Luca cleared his throat, glancing back at Mac with a blank expression. "Don't feel guilty for what happened to my boy—he'll be fine, Mac. He's a Pivetti, and we always make it out alive. Leave the guilt to me, it's what I do best where he's concerned."

Mac wasn't sure he could do that, but he would try.

"And Enzo's son?" Mac dared to ask.

Luca let out a slow breath. "Find your wife. If it were mine, I would do the same. By whatever means necessary, find her. I'll even call Enzo and get him away from his son, if you think that'll help to grab the fool without unnecessary blood spilling. Enzo let it slip the kid has also been talking to police in an effort to save his ass from charges. That may very well be where part of our rat problem is."

"It could be. Thank you for the call."

"Done."

Mac had his answer.

He left the room before Luca could even dismiss him.

He didn't think his boss would mind.

After all, they were men cut from the same cloth.

Mac fitted the riding gloves on as he strolled across the street to where Enzo's safe-house was located. He was grateful that at least the man was out, thanks to Luca's call, and that the man's wife would not be there to witness Mac taking her son by force.

It was not something a woman should see.

Mac would never want his own wife to witness something of the sort happening to him, or his future children.

Although he knew his wife could and would handle it, being as strong and stubborn as she was. He'd called Melina his Gun Moll once—the girl of a gangster that no one ever expected with a gun hidden under her coat, distracting everyone with the bat of her pretty lashes.

He was sure he'd undervalued her in that respect.

A Gangster Moll would have been more apt to describe her.

She was just as tough him.

Just as fucking capable.

Just as dangerous.

Better yet, Mac hadn't needed to teach his wife how to be or do any of those things. She'd come to him like that—wonderful, difficult, and proficient.

Mac kept repeating that sentiment to himself as he

picked the lock on the front door of the safe-house, needing the comfort it provided. As long as he kept telling himself that Melina was tough enough to handle whatever his father threw at her until Mac found her, then the fear of the unknown and the what ifs wouldn't be able to reach him.

His doll would be fine.

This was just a bump in the road.

A shitty bump, but a bump.

The house was dark and quiet when Mac opened the door. He listened for any sounds, but other than the muffled drone of a television down the hall, he didn't hear anything else. No doubt, given Enzo had said his son was detoxing, the kid was probably stuck in a bathroom somewhere. Enzo had likely put the kid upstairs, locked in somewhere that he couldn't get out.

Mac understood Enzo's desire to protect his only son.

If it were Mac's son, he would probably do the same.

Maybe someday, Enzo would forgive Mac for what he was about to do, though in that moment, he simply didn't care either way. This was a job—the kid was a means to an end.

Mac needed to find Melina.

Enzo's son would get him there.

Mac took the stairs two at a time, and as he came to the very last step, he heard the tell-tale sound that led him down the hall toward the closed door at the very end. A retching, as if someone were violently throwing up.

Quite common with a heroin detox.

He tried the doorknob first, but unsurprisingly, found it locked. Addicts would do whatever they had to for a fix, even if that meant hurting themselves or someone else to get whatever they needed to get their drugs. Mac had suspected that Enzo would lock his son away, if only to assure the kid would stay in place long enough for his father to get a detox and rehab center on the phone that would take him in last minute.

Pulling his foot back, Mac let his boot slam into the door right under the knob. Wood cracked and splintered as the door gave way under the force of the kick, opening wide and slamming hard into the wall.

Mac wasted no time, rushing the room with his gun already out and pointed. He found Tyler, Enzo's son, hunched over the toilet, drool and vomit smeared across his cheeks. The seventeen-year-old barely blinked at Mac when he pulled him away from the toilet, letting the kid fall on his back against the tiled floor.

Tyler stared up at Mac.

Defeat and acceptance stared him straight in the face.

"My dad'll kill you," Tyler mumbled.

It was a half-hearted effort.

Even Mac could tell the kid didn't believe his own words.

"Get up and walk," Mac told Tyler, "we've got business to do tonight, kid."

Tyler blinked rapidly, mumbling something Mac couldn't understand.

What he did hear, however, he didn't like.

"Fuck you, Maccari," the kid said.

"Well, we were going to do this the easy way," Mac replied, shifting his aim ever so slightly before letting a round off. The bullet ripped into Tyler's thigh, and the teenager howled as he grabbed for the new wound. "But the hard way is fine by me."

Whatever it took to get his wife back.

Mac would do it.

CHAPTER SEVENTEEN

A dull throbbing ache radiated from Melina's broken wrist. But it paled in comparison to the sharp stabbing pain in her side. Every breath she took, no matter how small, was a struggle and a reminder of just how dire her situation really was. Melina had no idea where she was, not that it mattered. She had no phone and no way of reaching her husband.

Mac.

By now she was sure he'd returned home and discovered that all hell had broken loose.

What would he think when he found her gone?

Would he even begin to know where to look?

Yes.

He had to.

That's what she just kept telling herself, because the alternative wasn't worth fathoming.

She stretched as much as she could stand in an effort to keep the stiffness at bay that was threatening to take over her body. Her movement was limited though, because besides the injured ribs, her hands and feet were tied together.

She was shackled like a damn animal.

A lamb ready to be slaughtered, unable to fight back.

Melina blinked back tears. Things weren't supposed to be like this. She shouldn't be tied up in a cold, unfinished room waiting to be executed. She should be home enjoying a meal with her husband as they discussed the plans for the new house and their shared fears about becoming parents.

Somehow, someway she had to survive.

She had to give their child a fighting chance and Mac a little more time to find them.

The door to her prison opened and James stepped inside closing the door behind him before he came and stood over her.

"How are you feeling, Melina?"

"How do you think, *cafone*?"

James laughed. "I see my boy has been teaching you some Italian."

"That's not the only thing he taught me."

"I'm sure it isn't, but you know, forget about it. None of that really matters now."

She couldn't help but notice how cleaned up and straight James looked. It was no secret in Mac's life that his father had been a drunk and abused drugs as well as women. But he *did* look clean in that moment.

"Why are you doing this? What could you possibly have to gain by causing all these problems for your son?"

Melina really could give less than two fucks as to why James had chosen to betray the son he claimed to love so much, but she had to keep him talking. It was the only way to save herself and her child.

"You're an outsider. You will never understand how our life works."

"What I understand, James, is that you are a world-class fuck up who made Mac's life a lot harder than it needed to be. What I understand is that he has spent his whole life bearing the burden of being your son. Instead of you disappearing into the ether where you belong, you're here ruining everything Mac has worked so hard for."

James slapped her across the face.

Melina tasted blood, but she smiled at her father-in-law, concealing her hurt. "Struck a nerve, did I?"

"Everything I have done I did for him."

"Delusional much? I'm sure Mac is going to be so grateful to you for trying to blow me up and for kidnapping me. I can just see him falling all over himself to thank you."

James grabbed her face, squeezing her jaw. "That mouth of yours—how does he deal with it? Does he just fuck it quiet? Because that's what I would do. There's plenty of pussy out there that knows their place, but no, Mac had to go for you. A worthless piece of ass, but here you are, being his wife."

"A piece of ass that you can't keep your eyes off apparently."

"You're nice to look at, I'll give you that, but you ruin it every time you open that rosebud mouth of yours."

"Every rose has its thorns."

Melina watched James closely. He was at war with himself, torn between his desire for her and snuffing out her existence at the same time.

"They do. The world won't miss you, Melina. Not the one we live in. In time, my son will understand. Wives are always replaceable."

"You're a fool. Mac will never forgive you for this."

James' fingers trailed down to her neck and he squeezed tight. "What's a woman compared to a boss's seat?"

Power.

James wanted his son in power.

The innocent blood on his hands didn't matter.

The collateral damage, it didn't matter.

All that mattered was that James saw this as his big chance to make up for past mistakes. Now was his chance to give Mac the one thing he'd never been able to have before ... respect. Damn anything and anyone that got in his way. Fuck Cosa Nostra and all it stood for. The only code James Sr. lived by was his own.

"If you weren't such a despicable piece of shit, this might actually be touching. The absentee father rides to the rescue. Too bad this isn't some fairytale."

"Get up. I've had enough of your fucking mouth."

Melina was roughly jerked to her feet and she gasped as the sudden motion made her ribs ache all over again. Her eyes widened when the barrel of a gun was pressed to the side of her head.

"What? Nothing to say now?" James asked.

"Make sure you don't miss."

"Trust me, I won't."

He cocked the hammer of the gun and Melina closed her eyes.

This was it.

No more Mac.

No more sweet kisses, dirty sex and passionate nights.

No *baby*.

She stifled back a scream at the last thought and then gunshots rang out.

Multiple gunshots.

The gun was lowered from her head.

"What in the hell?"

Melina opened her eyes as her father-in-law wrapped his arm around her shoulders, dragging her in front of him like a human shield. The sounds of gunfire hadn't stopped and as James dragged her closer and closer to the door, she started to struggle against him. He wasn't about to use her to save himself.

"Be still, you bitch."

She kept struggling and just when they were about to cross the threshold, salvation appeared in the form of a blood-splattered, gun-toting Mac. He looked like the Angel of Death come to claim his latest victims. Melina's eyes met his, but it was as if he were staring straight past her.

There was nothing behind his gaze.

It was empty.

Melina had seen him cold and callous, but she'd never

seen Mac empty.

Terror clutched her heart in a vice grip.

"Son, what are you doing here?" James asked.

"I think the question you should be asking yourself is why you were stupid enough to leave tracks. If you're going to do something, then at least do it right."

Melina couldn't see James' face but she could feel him stiffening as he held her tight to his body.

"I wanted you to find out."

Mac raised a brow. "Did you? Now that's a lie if I ever heard one."

James slowly backed away from his son, pulling Melina with him. "I wanted you to know everything. Everything I did to put you in the position you deserve."

"You did nothing! All you did was fuck things up, just like you do best. You aren't fit to shine the shoes of the men whose blood you spilled."

"And what makes them so much better than me, huh? I drank. Big fucking deal."

Mac laughed, a cold chilling sound that made the hair on her arms raise.

"If you think that was all you did, then you are more delusional than I thought but at this point I couldn't give less than a fuck. I came for my wife and I'm not leaving here without her."

For the briefest of moments, Mac's gaze slipped to her and she saw a hint of the man she married.

And just like that it was gone.

The man without a soul was back.

"She's not good enough for you, son. You see the way they looked at her—how they've *talked* about her. She's replaceable, and you'll move on."

"What I need is the woman you're holding at gunpoint. Give me my wife—I'm not going to say it one more fucking time."

"I can't do that son. One day you'll understand."

James pressed the gun to Melina's forehead and she

screamed.

Gunfire exploded.

Hot, red blood splattered Melina's face.

Her captor's grip on her loosened and she quickly moved in the direction of her husband. Mac hadn't even looked at her. Melina turned. James Maccari Sr. lay eagle sprawled on the ground. A bullet hole between the eyes oozed blood.

The bastard was dead.

Mac had killed his own father.

Melina faced her husband and found him looking at her.

"Mac?" she said hesitantly.

"I'm sorry I wasn't here sooner, doll. I'm so sorry."

He put his gun into the side of his coat and reached for her. Hands still tied, Melina melted into her husband's embrace and finally gave into the tears she'd been holding back.

"Oh, Mac," she sobbed.

"Shh. It's over."

Melina stopped crying long enough to look up at her husband.

She didn't like what she saw.

"It's not really over, is it? This is just the beginning."

Mac swallowed hard. "Yeah. We're just getting started."

CHAPTER EIGHTEEN

Mac was, once again, sitting at his wife's side as she rested propped up in a hospital bed. He knew this time, there would be no early release for her. The broken rib and wrist was concerning, and would keep her in the bed for at least a few days.

She could use the rest, of course, but Mac wished it wasn't because of this.

Worse, was the detectives standing at the end of his wife's bed, slamming them with question after question. It was unrelenting, and Mac could see that his wife's patience was slipping, though she was doing her best to deflect as much as she could.

Melina had escaped her captor.

She'd made a phone call using a payphone on the corner.

Mac found her.

No, she didn't know who it was.

No, she couldn't lead them back to where she had been taken, it all happened so fast.

Or, that was the story his wife was telling.

The detectives had yet to connect the burning warehouse in lower Brooklyn to the fact his wife had apparently been "picked up" just four blocks away. Mac didn't offer the information, either.

"You're not being very helpful to this investigation,

Mrs. Maccari," one of the detectives said.

Melina looked fucking *exhausted*.

She couldn't take strong painkillers to help with the pain she was experiencing because of the pregnancy. She hadn't been able to sleep because the questioning had been going on for hours. The detectives had a job to do, as far as that went, but so did Mac and Melina. That was only to protect one another, and secondly, Cosa Nostra.

"I think that's about all we've got for you boys today," Mac said, standing from his seat.

The beady-eyed, shorter detective turned his gaze on Mac. "We're not finished—"

"Yes, you are."

"No, we have—"

Mac reached over and hit the red button on the wall that would immediately call through to the hospital security. If he had his way, he'd walk the detectives out of the hospital room with a goddamn gun to their faces as he chewed their asses out for making this fucking night even worse for his wife.

He couldn't do that.

They had too much attention on them as it was.

Melina wouldn't like Mac going to jail.

Those were the things he repeated to himself as he patiently waited for a security guard to make his way down to the room. Once the man did finally show, one of the detectives scoffed at the sight of him.

"We have an active investigation—she's a victim *and* a witness. You can't impede that, Maccari," he told Mac.

Mac just shrugged. "Then come back tomorrow. Give us a date and time to be at the precinct. Shit, my wife is a fucking great cook, we'll have you over for supper once she's back home. But you will *not* ask her one more thing tonight. Get out."

It took another few minutes before the security guard was able to escort the detectives from the room. Mac wasted no time closing the door to the hospital room behind them. Then, he was back at Melina's side and falling into the chair beside her bed.

With her gaze down, locked on her fidgeting hands, Melina seemed overwhelmed.

Mac understood that.

Silently, he found her hand with his own, holding tight and letting their fingers tangle together.

"I'm so tired," Melina murmured.

Mac reached over to cup his wife's bruised cheek, angry because she was hurt, guilty because he'd let it happen, and wishing he could take it all away. "I know, doll."

"They're not going to leave us alone."

The police, she meant.

Mac understood what she didn't say well enough.

"We'll handle them when we need to. Right now, we're going to focus on getting you better, then bringing you home, and always making you happy."

He'd spoil her rotten, or as much as she would let him.

He'd make her happy, just to see her smile every day.

"This is just a bump in the road," Mac told her. "We'll get over it soon."

Melina's gaze drifted to the closed door. "What's going to happen now?"

Mac didn't know, and he had no idea how to answer her.

There were still so many things left hanging up in the air. His actions leading up to finding his wife—like his choice to go after Enzo's son—were just some of the many things he would have to handle over the coming months. The attention of officials was yet another problem that only seemed to be closing in around *la famiglia*, though Mac seriously hoped that would be lessened by the fact at least *one* of the people that had been talking to police was now dead in a ditch.

Tyler, that was.

But how much information could the officials be getting from an unmade kid with an underboss for a father?

"Don't worry about it," Mac found himself saying.

He'd said it only to soothe his wife's worries.

Certainly not because he meant it.

Melina could see right through it. "Are we going to be okay at the end of all this?"

That, Mac *did* have an answer for.

One he was sure was the truth because he would make it happen, no matter what.

"Yeah, doll, we're going to be just fine."

Mac had thought—wrongly so—that his greatest battle in Cosa Nostra would be overcoming the shame his father had left stained on their family's name.

That wasn't the hardest battle at all.

No, the hardest was watching the strong foundation of a Cosa Nostra family, built so firmly upon a base of loyalty, rules, and trust, begin to show its cracks. Because once the cracks began to show themselves, it wouldn't take long for the walls to come down.

Mac watched a month go by, and then another and another. He felt his wife's stomach grow under his palm until he could feel the gentle kicks of a baby that wouldn't quite cooperate during ultrasounds to see the gender. He waited the seasons changing out, wanting warmer weather and less cold.

But what he didn't see, what didn't happen, was *la famiglia* coming back together.

So much distrust and anger had been woven into the strands of the Pivetti crime family. Each and every time another made man in the family was pulled in by FBI, the attention of the family was on that man, accusations flying and suspicions rising.

Why hadn't the officials stopped yet?

Why were they still digging for things no one was offering?

No one seemed to have an answer for that.

Disgruntled Capos left crews hanging and unable to work together. Meetings called by Luca in an effort to straighten out the men usually ended in shouting matches that damn near came to blows every single time.

It was all *bad*.

Mac thought about the last few months as he walked into Luca's office, a late night call that was once again, meant only for the purpose of smoothing out issues between men.

It seemed like *if* one problem was solved, three more popped up.

Luca was struggling with his men.

Mac and Enzo happened to be two of them, unfortunately.

The moment Mac walked into the office, he found the underboss in the corner, a glass of whiskey in his hand and hate coloring up his features.

"Good to see you finally showed up," Enzo said.

Mac refused to rise to the man's bait.

Because that's all it was.

Enzo couldn't retaliate against Mac for the killing of his teenaged son, if only because it was justified in the eyes of Cosa Nostra. Permission had been given by the boss, and Tyler had not been a made man. But that didn't mean Enzo accepted those rules, or for that matter, the very fact that his best friend—Luca—had allowed the killing.

Apparently, Mac's wife could be replaced.

Tyler could not be.

Mac didn't think the two should have been seen as interchangeable souls. Both meant something to the people who loved them, and while he wished things could have been different for Enzo's son, it was what it was.

And Mac would put another bullet between the kid's eyes if he had to.

But that moment was over.

"I'm not late," Mac said, strolling past another Capo to take a seat against the far wall. It left his back protected, and his gaze on the whole room. With the amount of unhappiness in the family, Mac trusted none of these people. Except for maybe the boss. Giving Luca his attention, he said, "Evening, boss."

Luca, sitting on the edge of his desk, nodded at Mac. "You are cutting it close."

"Late night cravings," Mac said to explain away his tardiness.

At the mention of his pregnant wife, Enzo's anger turned to disgust and he looked away. Not in time to hide it, however.

More bait, Mac knew.

He wouldn't rise to it.

Enzo only wanted a reason to come at Mac, to have his retaliation, and nothing more.

Refusing to even give Enzo more of his attention, Mac swept the large office with his gaze, taking in the men that couldn't be bothered to talk to one another, and barely even *looked* at one another.

He was never more aware of how awful an effect the official's attention and the events that led up to it were affecting the men.

Really, it was hurting the whole family.

Luca pushed off his desk, grabbing a folder and opening it up. Flipping through what looked to be photographs, he started calling out names. Mac recognized some, if only because the men's names were members of different crews, some he had worked with when he was just a solider.

All of the names came from crews other than his.

Not one was a man of his.

Every time a new name was called for a different crew, a Capo would stand a little straighter, staring at their boss in both concern and confusion.

When Luca was finally done, he tossed the folder aside, photos of men spilling out across the large desk. "We have a problem."

"Many problems," Enzo added under his breath.

Luca barely passed him a glance. "The men I named—they've all been pulled in by officials over the last *month*. Figure out *why* and if they're a problem we need to fix, or I will do it."

Mac scratched at his jaw, ignoring a couple of gazes that flew to him, realizing he wasn't the only one to pick up that not even one of his men had been in the list. He kept them on a tight leash—it's what a good Capo did.

It wasn't his fault the other Capos were slacking.

"We've got a *rat* problem; I'm about to clean house," Luca continued, his eyes passing from one man to another without pause, "and so help you God, I will start with each of you."

Mac didn't get home until the sun was just starting to peek over the horizon. It would have been a beautiful sight if he cared to stare out the windows and watch the sunrise paint the sky, but he had a *much* more amazing sight to see.

His wife.

Mac found Melina was tucked into the corner of the couch, a cup of ginger tea between her hands, and a smile already on her face. He hadn't woken her up before leaving the night before when he got the call, but she probably wouldn't mind. It seemed like the further into the pregnancy she was getting, and the bigger her stomach swelled, the harder it was for her to get a good night's rest.

When she was able to fall into a deep sleep, Mac let her.

"Morning," Melina said, drawing her cup of tea up to her lips.

Mac strolled across the floor, dropping a kiss to his wife's forehead and soaking in her love and life for those few seconds. "Hey, doll."

"Busy night?"

"Long," he offered.

He could smell the scent of the ginger tea she was drinking, and it wasn't all too appealing. It did help her with the morning sickness that still hadn't waned half way through the pregnancy, so he didn't say a word.

"I got a call this morning," Melina said.

"Oh?"

Mac headed for the kitchen, wanting to make himself a coffee. Just because he was up half of the night didn't mean he would be able to sleep his day away. He still had to work—business didn't end just because bad shit was going down in the family.

God knew he needed to tighten up the leashes on his crew, too, though he wasn't sure just how much tighter he could pull before they broke.

"Yeah," Melina called back, "Neeya, actually."

"I'm listening."

"She wants to have a baby shower for us."

Mac wasn't sure how good an idea that was, if only because it would probably be an open invitation event, if the boss's wife was throwing them a party. Could the men of the family manage to be in the same room together without trying to kill one another?

If last night was any indication, probably not.

Still, Mac didn't want to refuse his wife.

She deserved happy moments and to have her pregnancy celebrated.

"When?" Mac asked, coming back into the living room with his coffee in hand.

"Maybe a month," Melina said. "She really wanted to know the gender, if possible."

Mac smirked, taking a seat beside his wife. "So do we."

Melina put a hand to the top of her small swell, and Mac followed with his own hand, feeling the gentle rolling of the baby under their hands.

"So is that a yes?" Melina asked.

Mac shrugged. "You can't refuse the boss's wife, doll."

Melina smiled, putting her head on his shoulder. "Or me."

"Or you."

CHAPTER NINETEEN

Melina sat next to her husband in the back seat of the limousine.

"Is all this really necessary?" she asked.

"What?"

"This limo, Mac."

"You're five months pregnant and you're on your way to what I know is going to be a magnificent baby shower."

Melina raised a brow. "*Magnificent*, Mac."

Her husband placed his hand over her stomach. At five months it was more than evident that she was pregnant. Their son chose that moment to make his presence known. Melina smiled as the baby moved inside her.

"There's my little man."

At the sound of his father's voice, the baby's movement picked up even more, a particularly sharp kick hitting Melina right under her rib.

"Mac, can you please tell your son to stop kicking me?" Melina asked.

"And why would I want to do that, doll?" He winked at her.

"Because you're not the one having your guts kicked out."

Mac continued to rub her stomach, before he leaned

close and kissed her forehead. Melina couldn't help smiling. Though she'd never admit it, she was basking in the increased attention her husband lavished on her since the beginning of her pregnancy. Back rubs, foot rubs, trips out in the wee hours of the morning to satisfy her pregnancy cravings. Not to mention the constant surprises he was showing up with in preparation for their son's arrival. In all honesty, she couldn't think of a single thing this baby shower could give her that she didn't already have.

"All right, little man, settle down and give your ma a break."

Melina wasn't surprised when their son immediately stopped kicking.

"This is not off to a great start," Melina said.

"What are you talking about?"

"He's already only listening to you and he's not even born yet."

Before Mac could respond, they were pulling up to the Pivetti estate. Men were stationed at the large gates and as the limo slowed down, one of the men ordered all the windows of the car to be let down. The driver complied and Melina watched quietly as the men looked inside the vehicle before they were allowed to pass through the gates.

"Talk about heightened security," Melina said.

"Everyone is on high alert understandably."

"I wish it wasn't like this, especially right now."

"Me, too, doll."

The limo pulled to a stop and Mac opened the door and stepped out before turning to help Melina from the car. Though she'd wanted to wear something much more comfortable, like leggings, she'd opted to dress for the occasion. A white, off-the-shoulder, high-waisted dress that gently cradled her belly and kitten heels was what she'd ultimately settled on. Mac wore a matching white suit and it fit him well. Melina couldn't stop sneaking a glance at her husband as he helped her up the stairs that lead inside the massive mansion.

"You should wear white more often."

"Is that so? This color doing something for you?" Mac asked.

"Let's just say you'll need to tell your son to cover his eyes when we get home," she told him.

Mac's gaze traveled over her and Melina felt the familiar heat that always warmed her blood. What she wouldn't give to head back to their place and fuck for the rest of the day. Instead, they would be spending the next few hours trying to enjoy a baby shower that Melina could have done without. The doors to the mansion were opened by more guards as she and Mac stepped inside. Before they'd even made it down the hallway, Neeya Pivetti was there to greet them.

"Mac. Melina. Wonderful to see you both. Melina, dear, you're glowing."

Melina smiled as their hostess came forward and drew her into a tight hug. Well as tight as her belly between them would allow.

"Thank you for having us, Mrs. Pivetti. Melina and I appreciate everything you've done for the both of us."

Neeya waved her hand. "I'm happy to do it. You both mean a great deal to me."

"And you to us," Melina said.

From the first moment Mac had made it known that she meant something to him, Neeya Pivetti had taken Melina under her wing. The older woman had seen something in Melina that she thought was worth getting to know and for that, Melina would always be grateful.

"I'm glad to hear that. Now, Melina, if you'll come with me. Mac, you'll find Luca and the other men out back."

Mac nodded before kissing Melina on the cheek and heading toward the back of the mansion. Melina watched him go, wishing that she could be with him.

"I have a feeling Mac is going to have a better time

than I am," Melina said.

"I doubt it. These are tense times for all of us, especially the men."

"I know that my husband can speak for himself, but I feel I need to re-emphasize this. Mac has nothing to do with everything that has gone on. He was just as blindsided as everyone else."

"You don't have to convince me of that. I know an honest man when I see one. Now, no more of that talk. Today is about you and the little bundle of love you're carrying inside you."

Melina smiled as Neeya lead her to the ballroom where a throng of women were waiting. At center stage was a large white table filled with gifts. Lining either side of the room were cloth covered tables with navy blue table runners. Each table bore an impressive amount of food and Melina couldn't ignore the rumbling in her belly … or the cool looks being thrown her way.

Yes. This was the part she could do without.

The jealousy.

The distrust.

The phony smiles.

Melina took a deep breath.

"Ladies, the guest of honor has arrived," Neeya said.

A few of the women came toward her and Melina silently reminded herself that she only had a few hours to suffer through this and then she would be home with her husband.

Two hours later, Melina had suffered through more than enough fake congratulations and attempts at small talk. If it weren't for Neeya, and the decent amount of food she'd consumed, Melina was sure that she would have already begged Mac to take her home. While the gifts she'd received were nice—ranging from things as small as pacifiers, all the way up to a giant, pale-blue baby carriage—most of the gifters were less than nice. At this point, Melina was used to it but with pregnancy hormones waging war, her tolerance was at an all-time low.

"Neeya, please excuse me. I'm going to find my husband."

"Of course."

Melina left the ballroom and made her way through the house and outside to where the men were gathered. She'd thought the atmosphere inside was tense. It was nothing to what she felt now. Trying her best to ignore the oppressive atmosphere she felt, Melina searched for Mac. When she saw him, she moved in his direction but soon had her path blocked by Anthony.

"Melina, a pleasure to see you."

"Sorry I can't say the same about you, Anthony."

He smirked. "One day, perhaps you'll see I'm not the villain you make me out to be."

"And then perhaps my wife will see that she was exactly right," Mac said.

He came up to Melina and placed his arm around her waist. The two men stared at each other for a long moment before Anthony cleared his throat.

"Well, as I said earlier, congratulations to you both on the upcoming birth of your son. I wish you both the best."

With a mock bow, Anthony walked away and Melina shook her head.

"He is so full of shit."

Mac laughed. "That's one way of putting it. So how are things inside?"

"Fake. Boring. The usual. I see it isn't much better out here."

"No. It isn't. Everyone is on edge, looking at each other and wondering who can be trusted and who can't."

Screams pierced the air.

Melina watched as police stormed outside with guns raised.

"Everyone, hands in the air."

Mac protectively placed Melina behind him before doing as he was ordered. Melina did the same. She watched as one by one each of the men were handcuffed and arrested, including Mac and Luca.

"What are the charges?" Melina asked.

The police continued to ignore her.

When she attempted to confront the one arresting Mac, her husband shook his head, silently begging her to let it go. She swallowed hard. This wasn't the way things were supposed to be happening. Melina bit her lip as she was forced to watch her husband led away in cuffs … again.

Melina was pissed.

Her husband had been locked up for nearly two weeks.

Two weeks he should've been at home to hold her hand.

Two weeks he should've been there to feel their child kicking inside her.

Instead, he'd been stuck behind bars on phony charges, away from her and their unborn child. The Pivetti crime family had a real fucking problem. Though Mac was scheduled to be released any minute, that didn't stop the feeling of unease that gripped her. She'd thought foolishly that with James dead, the biggest threat to her and her family was out of the way.

She'd been naïve.

So naïve.

It seemed that James wasn't the only threat to their

future.

Shifting uncomfortably in the chair in the lobby, Melina watched and waited for her husband. She was sick of being here. Sick of having her husband harassed by men who weren't worthy of shining his shoes. But most of all, she was sick of the air of uncertainty that continued to hover over their futures. A loud slam drew her attention. She watched one by one as various male members of the Pivetti crime family filed out.

Many of them had shadows under their eyes and terse expressions. A few acknowledged her, including Anthony. Melina gave him a cool nod as she watched for Mac. He finally came through the door and then it was closed behind him. Rising from her seat, Melina opened her arms to her husband. Mac surprised her by taking her face in both hands and kissing her hard.

"I missed you, too," Melina said.

"Obviously. Let's go, doll."

Taking her hand in his, they left the police station and got inside the black town car that was waiting for them. When they were comfortably seated, Melina placed Mac's hand on her belly.

"Your son missed you, too. He's been overly active since you've been gone."

Mac smiled. "See. He's already preparing for his man of the house duties."

Melina rolled her eyes. "Whatever. I'm just glad you're coming home."

"Me, too. I'm one of the lucky ones."

"What do you mean?"

Mac's voice was quiet and measured. "Everyone didn't get to come home, doll."

Melina frowned as she thought back to all the men she'd seen exit the jail. "Luca and Enzo."

"Yes. Them and a few others."

Melina was quiet as Mac's words sank in. The Pivetti boss was still behind bars. "Why haven't they let him out?"

"I'm not certain, but I have an idea."

"Which is?" Melina pressed.

"The kid working with James wasn't the only rat."

"But who else could it be, Mac?"

His hazel eyes held hers. "I don't know, doll, but I mean to find out."

ABOUT THE AUTHORS

Bethany-Kris is a Canadian author, lover of much, and mother to three very young sons, one cat, and two dogs. A small town in Eastern Canada where she was born and raised is where she has always called home. With her boys under her feet, a snuggling cat, barking dogs, and a spouse calling over his shoulder, she is nearly always writing something ... when she can find the time.

Find Bethany-Kris at:
Her website www.bethanykris.com,
or on Facebook at www.facebook.com/bethanykriswrites,
on her blog at www.bethanykris.blogspot.ca,
or on Twitter - @BethanyKris.

Sign up to Bethany-Kris's New Release Newsletter here:
http://eepurl.com/bf9lzD

A proud Alumna of the University of Central Florida and Florida State University, Erin Ashley Tanner writes stories featuring fierce females and the men who love them.

Prior to journeying into the world of contemporary

romance, Erin wrote paranormal romance for Evernight Publishing. Her debut novel, Goddess of Legend released in October 2013, was the first in her Demi-God Daughters paranormal romance series. The follow up, Goddess by Chance was released in November 2014.

Dirty Little Secrets, a sexy contemporary romance was published by Samhain Publishing in July 2015. Her next release with Samhain, Devious Little Lies is scheduled for release in June 2016.

Find Erin at:
Her website: erinashleytanner.wix.com/erinashleytanner, on Facebook: www.facebook.com/ErinAshleyTanner, or her Twitter: https://twitter.com/ErinTheAuthor.